Hadley's Hellions

*Four friends united by power, privilege
and the daring pursuit of passion!*

From being disreputable rogues at Oxford
to becoming masters of the political game,
Giles Hadley, David Tanner Smith,
Christopher Lattimar and Benedict Tawny
live by their own set of *unconventional* rules.

But as the struggle for power heats up so too
do the lives of these daring friends. They
face unexpected challenges to their long-held
beliefs and rigid self-control when they meet
four gorgeous independent women
with defiant streaks of their own…

Read Giles Hadley's story in
Forbidden Nights with the Viscount
Already available

Read David Tanner Smith's story in
Stolen Encounters with the Duchess
Available now

And watch for more **Hadley's Hellions**
stories, coming soon!

Author Note

For both readers and writers, sometimes secondary characters get stuck in our heads. Intrigued by the glimpses we've been given of them, we want to know their whole story. Where did they come from and what will happen to them?

Such was the case with Davie in *From Waif to Gentleman's Wife*. An orphan taken in by an elderly widow, he becomes involved in the lives of Sir Edward Greaves and Joanna Merrill, the penniless governess who ends up on Ned's doorstep. When Davie saves Joanna from danger, a grateful Ned takes him under his wing, impressed by the orphan's courage, ingenuity and intelligence.

By the time I'd finished *Waif* I knew he would grow up to be a Parliamentary leader, instrumental in moving England towards a more egalitarian future with the great Reform Bill. I also knew that he would fall in love with Faith, the youngest Wellingford daughter—sister of Sarah, heroine of *The Wedding Gamble*—a girl far above his station. But how could they find a happy ending?

In *Stolen Encounters with the Duchess* Davie has become that leader, and is still in love with the girl he met when he was just beginning his career. When they meet by chance ten years later he is an influential force, while Faith is a new widow, estranged from her family and Society. Although painfully aware that she is still far beyond his touch, Davie vows to reawaken in her the joy, optimism and self-confidence years of being a scorned, neglected wife have crushed. But love is a force that resists being contained…

I hope you will enjoy Faith and Davie's story.

STOLEN ENCOUNTERS WITH THE DUCHESS

Julia Justiss

First published in Great Britain 2016
By Mills & Boon, an imprint of HarperCollins*Publishers*
1 London Bridge Street, London, SE1 9GF

Large Print edition 2017

© 2016 Janet Justiss

ISBN: 978-0-263-06743-9

Julia Justiss wrote her first ideas for Nancy Drew stories in her third-grade notebook, and has been writing ever since. After publishing poetry in college she turned to novels. Her Regency historical romances have won or been placed in contests by the Romance Writers of America, *RT Book Reviews*, National Readers' Choice and the Daphne du Maurier Award. She lives with her husband in Texas. For news and contests visit juliajustiss.com.

Visit the Author Profile page
at millsandboon.co.uk for more titles.

To Sue Ballard
You light up a room with your smile and
brighten my day with your cheerful optimism.
Thank you for being the inspiration
for my Faith and for me.

Chapter One

Setting off at a pace brisk enough to clear the wine fumes from his head, David Tanner Smith, Member of Parliament for Hazelwick, headed from the Mayfair town house where he'd dined with some Whig colleagues towards his rooms at Albany.

The friends had urged him to stay for a few more rounds, but after a day of enduring the mostly irrelevant objections the opponents of the Reform Bill kept raising to delay bringing it to a vote, he was weary of political talk. He was also, he had to admit, somewhat out of spirits.

His footsteps would echo loudly once he reached the solitary rooms of his chambers. Though he rejoiced that his best friend, Giles Hadley, had found happiness with Lady Margaret, he'd discovered that losing the companion with whom he'd shared rooms since their student days at Oxford had left him lonelier than he'd anticipated.

Since the only woman he'd ever loved was far beyond the touch of a lowly farmer's orphan, he didn't expect he'd ever find wedded bliss himself. Being common-born, but sponsored by a baronet and a marquess, put him in an odd social limbo, not of the gentry, never acceptable to the *haut ton*, but as a rising politician in the Whigs, not a nonentity either.

Rather a conundrum, which spared him attentions from marriage-minded mamas who couldn't quite decide whether he would be a good match for their daughters or not, he thought with a wry grin.

The smile faded as he recalled the stillness of Giles's empty room back in Piccadilly. Who might he marry, if he were ever lonely enough? The daughter of a cit who valued his political aspirations? A politically minded aristocrat who would overlook the lack of birth in exchange for elbow room at the tables of power?

He was rounding the dark corner from North Audley Street towards Oxford Street when the sounds of an altercation reached him. Slowing, he peered through the dimness ahead, where he could just make out the figures of two men and what appeared to be a young woman draped in an evening cloak.

'You will release me at once, or I will call the watch,' she declared.

'Will ye, now?' one of them mocked with a coarse laugh.

The other, grasping the woman's shoulder, said, 'The only thing you'll be doing is handing your necklace over to us—and the bracelet and earbobs, too, if you don't want that pretty face marred. '

'Aye, so pretty that maybe we'll take you to a fancy house after,' the other man added. 'They'd pay a lot for a tender morsel like you, I reckon.'

'Take your hands off me!' the girl shrieked, kicking out and twisting in the first man's grip, as the second pulled on the ties to her cape.

Davie tightened his grip on his walking stick and ran towards them. 'Let the woman go!' he shouted, raising the stick menacingly. 'Now—before *I* call the watch.'

For an instant, seeing his imposing size, the men froze. Then, city blokes obviously having no idea of the damage a strong yeoman could do with a stout stave, they ignored him and resumed trying to subdue the struggling female.

He'd warned them, Davie thought. After having to restrain himself around buffoons all day, the prospect of being able to deliver a few good whacks raised his spirits immensely.

With a roar, he rushed them, catching the first man under his ear with the end of the stick and knocking him away. Rapidly reversing it, he delivered an uppercut to the chin of the second. The sharp crack of fracturing bone sounded before the second man, howling, released his hold. Wrenching free, the lass lifted her skirts and took to her heels.

Davie halted a moment, panting. Much as he'd like to round the two up and deliver them to the nearest constable, he probably ought to follow the girl. Any female alone on the street at this time of night was likely to attract more trouble—at the very least, some other footpad looking for an easy mark, if not far worse.

Decision made, he turned away from the attackers and ran after her. 'Don't worry, I won't hurt you!' he called out. 'It's not safe, walking alone in London at night. Let me escort you home.'

The girl gave a quick glance over her shoulder, but apparently unconvinced, fled on. Hampered by her skirts, she wouldn't have been able to outrun him for long, but before he could catch up to her, she tripped on something and stumbled. With a cry, she fell to her knees.

Reaching her in a few strides, Davie halted at her side and offered a hand to help her to her feet. The girl took it, but then suddenly jerked away with such violence that, when Davie hung on instead of releasing her, the force of the ricochet slammed her back into Davie, chest to chest.

Swearing under his breath, Davie held fast to the lass, who immediately began struggling again. 'Stop it!' he said sharply. 'I told you, I don't mean to hurt you.' Lowering his voice, he continued, 'We'll sort this out, miss, but not on a public street. Let me take you somewhere safer, and you can tell me how to get you home to your family.'

With a deep sigh, the girl ceased trying to pull away from him. 'Please, Davie,' she said softly, 'won't you just let me go?'

The dearly familiar voice shocked him like the sharp edge of a razor slicing skin. 'Faith?' he said incredulously.

To his astonishment, as he turned the woman's face up into the lamplight, Davie recognised that it was, in fact, Faith Wellingford Evers, Duchess of Ashedon, he had trapped against him.

Before he could get his stunned tongue to utter another word, the lady pulled away. 'Yes, it's Faith,' she admitted. 'I was on my way to find a hackney to take me home. Couldn't you pretend you hadn't seen me, and let me go?'

As the reality of her identity sank in, a second wave of shock, sharpened by horror over what might have happened to her, held him speechless for another moment. Then, swallowing a curse, Davie clamped a hand around her wrist and began walking her forward. 'No, Duchess, I can't let you—'

'Faith, Davie. Please, let it be Faith. Can't I escape, at least for a while, being the Duchess?'

It shouldn't have, but it warmed his heart that she would allow such familiarity to someone who'd not been a close friend for years. 'Regardless, I can't let you wander on your own, chasing down a carriage to get you back to Berkeley Square. The streets in Mayfair are better, but nowhere in London is truly safe after dark, for anyone alone. To say nothing of a woman!'

'You were alone,' she pointed out.

'Yes, but I was also armed and able to defend myself,' he retorted. 'I *was* going to take the young lass I'd rescued to a tavern and discover how to help her, but I can't do that with you. Not around here, where we are both known. You'd better let me summon the hackney and escort you safely home.'

She slowed, resisting his forward motion. 'You're sure you can't just let me go?' After his sharp look of a reply, she said softly, 'I didn't set out to be foolish or irresponsible. I *am* sorry to have inadvertently got you involved.'

She swallowed hard, and the tears he saw sparkling at the edge of her lashes hit him like a fist to the chest. *How it still distressed him to see her upset!*

'Well, I'm not. Can you imagine the uproar, if you *had* summoned the watch, and they discovered your identity? Far better for it to be me, whose discretion you can depend upon. If you *don't* want to find out what society would say about a duchess wandering around alone on a Mayfair street, we better return you to Ashedon Place as soon as possible, before someone in a passing carriage recognises you.'

When she still resisted, a most unpalatable thought occurred. 'You…you do trust me not to harm you, don't you, Faith?'

She uttered a long, slow sigh that further tore at his heart. 'Of course, I trust you, Davie. Very well, find us a hackney. And you don't have to hang on to me. I won't bolt again.'

Without another word, she resumed walking beside him. The energy that had fuelled her flight seemed to have drained out of her; head lowered, shoulders slumping, she looked…beaten, and weary.

Good thing he had to be mindful that some *ton* notable might at any minute drive by, else he might not have been able to resist the strong impulse to pick her up and carry her. After a few more minutes of brisk walking, they arrived at a hackney stand where, fortunately, a vehicle waited. Still not entirely believing he was accompanying his Faith—no, the widowed Duchess of Ashedon, he corrected himself, never *his*—he helped her in, guiding her back on to the seat.

After rapping on the panel to signal the driver to start, Davie looked back at the Duchess. 'Are you all right? They didn't hurt you? What about your knees? You took quite a fall.' *If they had harmed her, he'd track them down and take them apart limb from limb.*

'No,' she said in a small voice. 'I was frightened, and furious; my arm got twisted, but I've nothing more than bruises. I think I landed a few good kicks, too.'

'Thank heaven for that! Before we get back to Berkeley Square, can you tell me how you ended up alone on the street at this time of night?'

'Can't you just let me return, and spare the exposition?'

He studied the outline of her profile in the light of the carriage lamps. 'I don't mean to pry. But finding you alone, practically in the middle of the night—well, it's disturbing. Something isn't right. I'd like to help fix it, if I can.'

To his further distress, the remark brought tears back to her eyes. 'Ah, Davie. You've always wanted to make things better, haven't you? Compelled to fix everything—government, Parliament, society. But this can't be fixed.'

She looked so worn and miserable, Davie ached to pull her into his arms. Nothing new about that; he'd ached to hold her since he'd first seen her, more than ten years ago. Sister-in-law of a marquess, she'd been almost as unattainable then as she was now, as the widow of a duke.

Unfortunately, that hadn't kept him from falling in love with her, or loving her all the years since.

'What happened?' he asked quietly. 'What upset you so much, you had to escape into the night?'

She remained silent, her expression not just weary, but almost…despairing. While he hesitated, torn between respecting her privacy and the compulsion to right whatever was wrong in her universe, at last, she shrugged. 'I might as well tell you, I suppose. It wasn't some stupid wager, though, if that's what you're thinking.'

'I'm sure it wasn't. You may have been high-spirited and carefree as a girl, but you were never a brainless ninny, or a daredevil.'

'Was I high-spirited and carefree? Maybe I was, once. It's been so long.'

Her dull voice and lifeless eyes ratcheted his concern up even further. Granted, these two unlikely friends had grown apart in the years since the idyllic summer they'd met, he twenty and serving his first stint as secretary to Sir Edward Greaves, she a golden-haired, sixteen-year-old sprite paying a long visit to her cousin, Sir Edward's wife. But even on the occasions he'd seen her since her marriage, her eyes had still held that warmth and joy for life that had so captured his heart the first time he set eyes on her.

'You *were* carefree,' he affirmed. 'Which makes the fact that I found you alone on the street, seeking transport home, even more troubling. What drove you to it?'

'Ever since Ashedon's death—by the way, thank you for your kind note of condolence—his mother, the Dowager Duchess, has been making noises about how she must support "the poor young Duchess and her darling boys" and see that the "tragic young Duke" receives the guidance necessary for his elevated status in life. A month ago, she made good on her threat and moved herself back into Ashedon Place. She's been wanting to do so for years, but though his mother doted on him, Ashedon knew how interfering she is and wouldn't allow it. It's enough that I must tolerate the sweetly contemptuous comments of other society matrons at all those boring, insipid evenings I've come to hate! Now, I have to live with the Dowager's carping and criticism as well, every day. Then, tonight, when I accompanied her to the party she insisted we attend, I discovered her younger son, my brother-in-law Lord Randall, was there. When he caught me alone in the hallway on my way to the ladies' retiring room and tried to force a kiss on me, I'd had enough. I knew the Dowager wasn't ready to leave, and would never believe anything derogatory about her precious son, so there was no hope of persuading her to summon the carriage. But remaining was intolerable, so I decided to walk towards Oxford Street and look for a hackney.'

She gave a little sigh, the sadness of it piercing his heart. 'Ashedon and his doxies were bad enough, and now this. Sometimes I don't think I can bear it any longer.'

His heart ached for the gentle spirit whose girlish dreams of being loved and cherished had been slowly crushed under the heel of her husband's in-

difference, leaving her trapped, a lonely and neglected wife. As Davie was trapped in his place,
unable to help her.

Except, always, to be a friend.

To his dismay, the tears he'd seen on her lashes
earlier began to silently slip down her cheeks. Putting up a hand to try to mask them, she turned
away.

And then, somehow, she was in his arms, cradled against his chest. She clung to him and he
clutched her tightly, almost ready to bless the ruffians he'd rescued her from, for without that incident, the marvel of holding her would never have
been his. It was a dream come true; oh, far better
than any dream, to feel the softness of her pressed
against him, her lavender scent filling his nostrils,
her silky blonde curls under his chin. He could die
right now, and be content, for he would never get
any closer to heaven.

And if his body burned to possess her fully, he
rebuked it. He'd never expected to have even this
much bliss; he'd not ask for more.

Inevitably and all too soon, she got herself back
under control, and pulled away.

Letting her go, when all he wanted was to hold
her for ever, was the hardest thing he'd ever done.

'Sorry,' she said gruffly. 'Usually I'm not so poor-spirited.'

'Don't be sorry. I'm only glad I was here, to stand your friend.'

'My friend. I have few enough of those. I did try to be careful tonight, I assure you! I suppose...I suppose I was just too tired and preoccupied, because I never noticed the two men who must have followed me. They seemed to appear out of nowhere.'

Davie shook his head with a shudder. 'I'm only glad I happened along. What they might have done to you, I don't even want to contemplate.'

She nodded. 'They threatened to take me to a brothel. Could they drag a woman there against her will, or were they just trying to frighten me?'

'I'm afraid it's quite possible. A little laudanum, and you might have awakened to find yourself locked in a room in some den of vice somewhere,' he answered grimly.

'Except for not seeing my sons again, I'm not sure I'd have cared. I thought of leaving Ashedon, oh, so many times! But I couldn't have taken my boys with me—legally, they belonged to him, of course, and Edward is the heir. Though I saw little enough of them; the Duke didn't think children should be spoiled by having their mother dote on them. Now that he's gone, I've tried to alter that, though I must continually fight against the Dowager and their tutor to do it. As long as I get to be with my boys, one way or another, I will endure it—for now, anyway.'

'Have you talked with your family, your sisters? Do they know how unhappy you are?'

She smiled wryly. 'I…I'm not that close to them any more. The Duke actively discouraged me from seeing my family at the beginning of our marriage. Silly me, I thought it was because he wanted me all to himself. Which he did, in a way. He didn't want anyone around who might interfere with his authority. So over the years, we…drifted further and further apart. As you and I did.'

He nodded. 'I'm sure they regret that as much as I do. Could you not try to re-establish ties?'

'I suppose. But there isn't anything they can do to help me, either. Most of the time I manage better.' She tried to summon a smile for him. 'It's only rarely that I feel as if I'll…burst out of my skin if I don't get away from all of it.'

'As you did tonight.'

'As I did tonight.'

He looked at her, frowning. 'At the moment, I don't have any clever ideas on how to make things better. But will you promise me something?'

'What?' she asked, tilting her head at him with an enquiring look, and instantly, he was catapulted back into the memories.

How many times that summer had she gazed up at him just like that, her eager mind probing further into whatever they were discussing— poetry, politics, agriculture? As if the whole world excited and enthralled her, and she could not learn enough about it.

Fury fired in him again to realise how much of that joy had been squeezed out of her.

Suppressing the anger, he replied, 'The next time you feel you cannot stand it a minute longer, please, don't go wandering around the streets by yourself! Send me a note; I'll meet you somewhere, anywhere, and we can talk. You're not alone, Faith. You'll never be alone, while I still draw breath. Promise me?'

She studied him for a moment. 'You mean that?'

'Of course. I never say anything I don't mean.'

She nodded, the faintest of smiles on her lips. 'Yes, I remember that about you. And how you were always a loyal friend. Very well, I promise.'

'Good,' he said, troubled still, but feeling a bit better about her situation. 'We should be at Berkeley Square shortly, which is fortunate—especially if your mother-in-law noticed you were gone, and rushed home to find you.'

She shrugged. 'She'd probably rejoice to have me gone. Except, she'd no longer have so ready a target for her complaints.'

'You're just weary. Everything will look better in the morning, when you're rested.'

'Will it?' She smiled. 'Maybe for a man who's set out to change the world. I do hear some of what you're accomplishing, by the way, even in the wilderness of the *ton*. Not that anyone talks about it to me directly, of course—politics being too intellectually challenging for a woman. No, we are left to discuss trimming bonnets, managing servants, and perhaps, if we've very bold, speculating about who might make the best lover, or which dancer in the Green Room has become the latest mistress of which nobleman.'

He grimaced. 'There could be so much more than that! As you doubtless know, my friend Giles Hadley, Viscount Lyndlington, recently married Lady Margaret Roberts. She has played political hostess to her father, Lord Witlow, for years; not only does she understand politics, she and her father frequently bring together the best minds in government, science and art to debate all manner of topics at their "discussion evenings".'

'That sounds wonderful—and so much more stimulating that anything I get to experience. Unless...' Her dull eyes brightened. 'Did you really mean what you said, about meeting me? '

'Didn't I already answer that?'

'Then...would you meet me tomorrow afternoon? I usually drive with the Dowager during the Promenade Hour in Hyde Park, but after tonight, I would rather not endure the hour-long lecture she will surely subject me to about my improper behaviour in leaving that wretched party. Would you meet me instead—at Gunter's, perhaps? No one we know should be there at that hour, so we won't be disturbed. I would love to hear more about what you are doing in Parliament. Perhaps I will even understand it.'

He ought to be in committee meetings, but when she looked at him with that appeal in her eyes, he'd have agreed to miss the final vote on the bill. 'Yes, I'll meet you there.'

The carriage slowed, indicating they were about to reach their destination. Davie felt a stab of disappointment; he could have ridden about London, talking with Faith, all night.

Bowing to the inevitable, he hopped out as the vehicle stopped and reached up to hand her down.

'I'll wait until you're safely inside,' he said as she descended.

'Very well.' She took a step towards the front door, then stopped, as if she couldn't quite bring herself to re-enter the Duchess's realm. Turning back to him, she went up on tiptoe and gave him a quick kiss on his jaw.

While his heart stuttered, then raced in his chest, she said, 'Thank you, Davie. For your rescue, and much more. For the first time in a long time, I have a "tomorrow" I can look forward to.'

As did he, he thought as she ran up the steps. The privilege of escorting her about probably wouldn't last long. He intended to relish every second.

Chapter Two

The following afternoon, after dispatching a note to her mother-in-law, a late riser who had not yet left her rooms, informing her a previous engagement would prevent her driving to the Park, Faith let her maid put the finishing touches to her coiffure. 'There, *madame*,' Yvette said, her eyes shining with pride. 'Who could find fault with such an angel?'

'A great many,' Faith muttered. But knowing the soft-hearted girl was only trying to encourage her, she gave her a smile. 'The new arrangement is lovely. Have you a name for it?'

'Trône de la Reine,' the maid replied. 'And *comme ça accord, madame*!'

'Thank you. I shall be the loveliest lady present.' Thankfully, not at the Park, Faith added silently as she descended to the hackney the butler had summoned, her spirits buoyed by knowing she'd not have to grit her teeth while the Dowager recited the long litany of offences she'd committed last night. Instead, anticipation rising at the thought, she would have Davie to talk to.

She'd missed the company of the young man to whom she'd grown even closer than she was to her sisters during the time she'd spent as a guest of her cousin, stretching a visit planned for a month into a summer-long idyll. His calm counsel, his stimulating ideas and his zeal to create a better future had inspired and excited her. Truth to tell, she'd fancied herself a bit in love with him by the time she'd been summoned home to prepare for her upcoming Season.

Only too aware that he was no fitting match for a daughter of one of the oldest families in England, she'd nonetheless hoped she might share with him some of her thoughts and observations of London, but he'd remained at Oxford during her Season. Instead, mesmerised by the Duke's assiduous and flattering attentions, envied by every other unmarried female on the Marriage Mart and their resentful mamas, she'd allowed herself to believe she'd fallen as much in love with her noble suitor as he had with her.

Why had she never noticed how cold and calculating his eyes were, compared to the warmth and compassion in Davie's?

Far too late to regret that now.

With a sigh, Faith let the footman hand her into the carriage. Glancing back towards the shuttered windows of the town house, she felt a pang of foreboding. She was likely to draw enough fire for not attending her mother-in-law's daily ride through the Park; were the woman to learn Faith missed that important event to associate with a man so far beneath her station, she'd be harangued for a month.

Still, it was time to wrench herself out of the influence of her mother-in-law and the misery that evoked. The Dowager had no real control over her; without the dictates of a husband to prevent it, she could involve herself more in the wider world.

Just talking with Davie, she knew, would help her do that. With each street that brought their rendezvous closer, her excitement and anticipation grew.

At last the carriage arrived, Faith so impatient she could hardly wait for the vehicle to stop before climbing down and hurrying into the establishment. She spotted Davie immediately, seated in an alcove on the far side of the room. The appreciation on his face as she approached his table made her glad she'd decided to wear the new grey gown that flattered her figure and showed her complexion to advantage.

'Duchess, what a pleasant surprise,' he said, rising and giving her a bow. 'How lovely you look!'

'How kind you are, Mr Smith,' she replied. 'Though as a mother of three, I'm afraid I've lost the bloom of youth you probably remember.'

'Nonsense, it would take more than a brace of boys to erase that,' he replied, helping her to a seat. 'Tea? Or would you prefer ices?'

'Tea, please.'

After sending the waiter off for refreshments, he looked back to study her.

'You do look rested. Truly fresh as a young girl, and not at all like the venerable mother of three.'

She laughed. 'I'd hoped for more children, but with three boys making the succession secure, Ashedon...lost interest.' *Or had he kept mistresses all along, and she'd just been too stupid to notice?* 'Somehow, growing up with a brother and all those sisters, I expected when I had a family of my own, I'd be surrounded by children. But as their mother, I spend much of the day in my world, and they in the nursery, in theirs.'

Davie chuckled. 'Unlike growing up in a farm

family, where the children are underfoot all day, learning from their mamas or doing chores for their papas. Close even at night, stuffed as they are in the loft just above the main room, like sausage in a casing! Maybe you should have been a simple farmer's wife.'

'Maybe I should have.'

She looked up into his eyes, those kind eyes she remembered so well—and suddenly, saw a flash of heat there, so intense and sudden it shook her.

It shook her even more to feel an answering heat from deep within. Suddenly she was brought back to last night, where despite her fatigue and misery, she'd been intensely aware of being held against his chest.

His broad, solid chest. The tall, rangy youth she'd known had grown into a tall, well-muscled, physically impressive man. Not fitting the wasp-waisted, whip-thin dandy profile now so popular among society's gentlemen, he was instead big, sturdy, and solid, built more like a...a medieval knight, or a boxer. Strong, powerful, and imposing.

For a time, while he held her, she'd felt—safe, and at peace. If she were still the naïve and trusting girl she'd once been, she might even have said 'cherished'.

But that was merely an illusion born of need and wishful thinking.

Still, she hadn't mistaken the desire she'd just seen in his eyes before he masked it, nor the physical response he evoked in her. That unexpected attraction would...complicate a renewal of their friendship, yet at the same time, she was fiercely glad of it. The realisation that he wanted her was a balm to her battered self-esteem, reviving a sense she'd nearly lost of herself as a desirable woman.

She cleared her throat nervously. Welcome as it was, the unexpected sensual tension humming between them was so unexpected, and she had so little experience dealing with it, she felt suddenly awkward. 'Thank you for meeting me,' she said at last. 'I was so relieved not to have to ride in the Park today and feel all those eyes on me, while the Dowager harangued.'

'I suppose that's the price of being a Duchess. You will always be the focus of attention, wherever you go and whatever you do.'

She wrinkled her nose. 'Yes, and it's so distasteful. I don't know why that fact didn't occur to me before I wed a duke, but it didn't. I've never enjoyed the attention.' She sighed. 'Especially as Ashedon and his women provided so much scandal for society to watch my reaction to.'

His jaw tightened and a fierce look came over his face before he burst out, 'Your husband was a fool! Even if I shouldn't say it.'

Gratified, she smiled sadly. 'I didn't mind him being a fool. I just minded that he never loved me. But I didn't come today to whine about poor, neglected little me. I want to hear about something of real importance. Tell me of your work! I always hoped we would maintain our friendship, but after the wedding, and with you at Oxford... I do know that, with Sir Edward and my cousin Nicky's support, you were elected MP from Hazelwick shortly after leaving university. And I seem to remember something about "Hadley's Hellions"? What was that?'

He chuckled. 'Fortunately for a commoner like me, I met Giles Hadley soon after arriving at Oxford. As I imagine you know, although he's Viscount Lyndlington, until very recently he'd been estranged from his father, the earl. After growing up in an isolated cottage, he didn't form friendships with anyone from the *ton*, bonding instead when he was sent to Eton with other outsiders—Ben Tawny, the natural son of Viscount Chilford, and Christopher Lattimar, son of Lord Vraux.

'That name I do know,' she said. 'One of the

"Vraux Miscellany", siblings supposedly all fathered by different men?'

Davie nodded. 'With those backgrounds, you can understand why all of them felt that society and government needed reforming, with the power to change not left in the tight-fisted hands of a few whose only qualification for the job was that their families had always held it.'

'A view of reform you always supported,' she inserted, recalling their spirited discussions of government and politics that long-ago summer.

'I did. When Giles stumbled upon me, reading alone in one of the pubs, he immediately drew me into his circle. First, out of kindness for a commoner whom he knew would never be invited into any of the aristocratic groups. But once we began discussing what we hoped to accomplish once we left university, we soon discovered we aspired to the same goals.'

'And those aspirations, in the eyes of the powerful, were enough for you to be labelled hellions?' she guessed.

'They were bad enough, but we didn't win that label until some of the dons, churchmen all, discovered we aimed to eliminate the clergy's seats in the Lords. An intention, they felt, that could only have been inspired by the devil.'

She tilted her head at him. 'Was it only that? Or was the name partly earned for exploits more scandalous than you care to mention to my innocent ears?'

Had he been a hellion? A little thrill went through her as she studied him from under the cover of her lashes. He was certainly virile enough to excite a woman's desire. Had he cut a swathe through the ladies of Oxford?

She found herself feeling jealous of any female he'd favoured with his amorous attentions.

'Having served with the army in India,' his words recalled her, 'Ben was something of a rabble-rouser, and Christopher was always a favourite with the ladies. Giles and I generally didn't have enough blunt to kick up too many larks, one of the reasons we pooled our resources and began rooming together early on. We helped each other, too, once it came time to campaign. As you may know, your brother-in-law, the Marquess, gave me his generous support when I stood for the seat under Sir Edward's control in Hazelwick, for which I'm grateful.'

'How could Nicky, or anyone else, listen to you explain your views, and not be persuaded? You certainly convinced me that summer! How close are you to accomplishing your aims?'

'A new Parliament convened in June, filled over-whelmingly with supporters of reform. We're very hopeful that by later this autumn, we'll finally get a bill passed.' He gave her a wry grimace. 'There are still recalcitrants who seek to delay us by bringing up an endless series of irrelevant discussions. Sometimes I'd like to knock a few heads together in the committee room, like I did last night on the street!'

'You were certainly effective there!' she declared, shuddering a little as she recalled how close to disaster she'd come. 'So there will be a change in the way the country is governed, for the first time since the medieval era? How exciting!'

'It is exciting, to know you can influence the governance of the nation.'

She gave a wry smile. 'I have enough difficulty exerting influence in the mundane matters of everyday life.'

'As duchess? Surely not!'

She hesitated, tempted to continue, though she really shouldn't confide in him. She'd had to struggle these last miserable years to transform the open, plain-spoken girl she'd once been into a woman who kept her own counsel. But the warmth of his regard, and that inexplicable sense of connection that seemed to have survived the years they'd been apart, pulled at her.

How long had it been since she'd had anyone to talk to, anyone who truly cared about her feelings or her needs?

Compelled by some force she didn't seem able to resist, she explained, 'Ashedon's housekeeper has been there since his mother's day, and is ferociously competent. Since my husband supported her authority, I barely had more to do than arrange flowers and approve menus. Now that my mother-in-law has returned to Ashedon Place, challenging Mrs West's years of unopposed domination, the two are in a constant battle for control, a struggle that frequently traps me in the middle.' She sighed. 'And then, there's the boys.'

'Your sons? Is your mother-in-law trying to take them over, too?' he guessed. 'How difficult that must be for you.' Almost absently, he put his hand over hers, giving her fingers a reassuring squeeze. 'But as their mother, you must make sure your will prevails.'

She ought to remove her hand. But that simple touch evoked such a powerful surge of emotion—gratitude for his compassion, relief at his understanding, and a heady wave of sensual awareness that intensified that sense of connection. She could no more make herself pull away than she could march back home and evict the Dowager.

'I am *trying*,' she said, savouring the titillating, forbidden feel of her hand enclosed in his. 'As I told you before, the Duke didn't consider it proper for his Duchess to hang about the nursery, an impediment to Nurse and the maids going about their duties.' She gave him a wry smile. 'I was reduced to visiting at night, tiptoeing past the sleeping maid to sit at the foot of their beds and study their little faces in the darkness. Since Ashedon's death, I've worked to find ways to spend more time with them, but I've had to fight Carlisle, the tutor Ashedon installed, at every turn. My increased involvement with the boys was the first thing the Dowager criticised when she invaded us. I've held my ground—the first and only time I've defied her—but she reinforces Carlisle as much as she can, making it as difficult as possible.'

'Bravo for resisting her! That can't have been pleasant. Now you just need to figure out better ways to get round the tutor.'

'Yes. And to keep the boys away from their uncle—an even worse example of manhood than my late husband, which is the truth, even if it's not kind of me to say so.' She grimaced, remembering the feel of Lord Randall's hands biting into her shoulders as he tried to force her into that kiss. 'Since his mother has taken up residence, he seems to think he can drop in whenever he wishes, usually to dine, or to borrow money from his mother. One of the few things Ashedon and I agreed on was that his brother is a wastrel who will spend as much of the family fortune as he can get his hands on.'

'Then you definitely need to get the boys away more. There are so many places they might enjoy—the British Museum, riding in the parks, Astley's Amphitheatre—even Parliament.' He lifted a brow at her. 'The young Duke will take his place in the Lords there, some day.'

'Ready to persuade him to join your coalition?' she teased, immeasurably cheered by his sympathetic support.

'It's never too early to start.' Smiling, he raised her hand, as if to kiss it. And only then seemed to realise he'd been holding it.

He sucked in a breath as he looked down at their joined hands, then up to meet her gaze, and his grip tightened. In an instant, a touch meant to offer comfort transformed into something more primal, as heat and light blazed between them, palpable as the flash of lightning, the rumble of thunder before a storm.

In his eyes blazed the same passion she'd glimpsed earlier. The same passion she felt, building in a slow conflagration from her core outward. Struck as motionless as he, she could only cling to his fingers, relishing every atom of that tiny bit of contact between them.

Slowly, as if he found it as difficult to break the connection as she had earlier, his grip eased and he let her go. His ardent expression turned troubled, and for a moment, she was terribly afraid he would apologise.

Which would be beyond enduring, since she wasn't sorry at all.

He opened his lips and hesitated, as if searching for words. Watching his mouth, her mind obsessed by imagining the feel of it against hers, she was incapable of finding any herself.

At last, he cleared his throat. 'Perhaps you could take your sons to call on your sister, Lady Englemere? She's in town with the Marquess for Parliament, I expect. Let the boys become better acquainted with their cousins?'

He looked back down at their now separate hands as he spoke, as if he regretted as much as she did the need to break that link between them.

Forcing her attention back to his words, she replied, 'At the moment, they aren't acquainted at all.

I don't even know if Sarah is in London; she may still be in the country.' Faith grimaced. 'Lucky her. The thing I've hated most about life as a duchess is being trapped in London, far from the "unfashionable" countryside Ashedon despised and I love so much.'

Davie nodded. 'I seem to remember a penchant for riding in breeches and climbing trees.'

That observation brought her a smile. 'Yes. We used to climb that big elm in Cousin Joanna's garden, and I'd read you poetry. There were a few early-morning races on horseback, too, I recall, before Joanna found out and made me ride at a more decorous pace, on side-saddle.' Nostalgia for that carefree past welled up. 'How I miss those days,' she said softly.

'Avoid looking back by building something better to look forward to,' Davie advised quietly.

She glanced back at him, seeing sympathy overlay the passion in his eyes. 'Like you are doing for the nation.'

'Like you can do for yourself. You are free now, Faith. Free to remake the future as *you* choose.'

And what would she choose, if she *were* completely free? Desire resurged, strong and urgent. *What if I said I wanted you, now?*

But of course, she did not say that. 'I may be

freer,' she replied. 'But with the Dowager, and my sons' futures to protect, I'll never truly be free of the shadow of being Duchess. Never truly free to choose *only* what I want.'

She gazed at him, willing him to understand what she could not say. Perhaps he did, for his face shuttered, masking whatever response her answer aroused in him.

'Then, as in Parliament, you must strike the best deal you can get with the opposition, so all can move forward. Speaking of which, I'm afraid I must get back.'

A sharp pang of regret made her want to protest. Suppressing it, she said, 'Of course. You have important work waiting. Which just reinforces how trivial my little problems are. How I wish I could observe you making those real, significant changes!'

'There's nothing more important to the future of the nation than you raising your boys properly! But if you *would* be interested in hearing some conversation about the Reform Bill, Lady Lyndlington still plays hostess for her father. I'm sure she would be delighted to include you in one of their discussion evenings. With it being hosted by a marquess, I don't think the Dowager could ob-

ject to your attending. Shall I ask Lady Lyndlington to send you an invitation?'

Oh, to spend an evening where people talked
about important ideas, where, among statesmen
and diplomats, a mere society female whose opinions were of little value would be ignored. Where
she'd be able to sit quietly and just observe. And
escape, for an evening, all the petty problems that
pricked at her daily.

'It sounds fascinating, but…would you be there,
too? It would be rather intimidating to attend such
a gathering of intellectuals, having only a slight
acquaintance with all those present.'

'I'm sure you'll have met most of them at various
society gatherings. But, yes, if it would make you
feel easier, I could make sure I'm invited as well.'

'Then, I should love it! If you're certain Lady
Lyndlington wouldn't find it impertinent of me to
request an invitation? I've met her, of course, but
could hardly claim to call her a friend.'

'I imagine she would be delighted of your company, but I will ask. Now, we should probably be
getting you back as well. Shall I send you a note
after I've spoken to Lady Lyndlington?'

Glancing over at the clock, Faith noticed to her
surprise that they had been chatting for some time.
'Yes, I should go, too. I'd prefer to already be at

home before my mother-in-law returns from the Park, and the inquisition begins.'

Hating to bring their time together to an end, Faith made herself rise. 'How can I ever thank you enough? Rescuing me not once, but twice, and then offering the promise of a stimulating evening.'

'It would give me the greatest delight to stimulate you.'

Her eyes flew to his face, and though it coloured a little at the blatant *double entendre*, he didn't apologise, nor did he retract the remark. Instead, he simply looked at her, giving her another glimpse of heat before masking his gaze.

Arousal returned in a rush. How easily she could imagine the delight his 'stimulation' would bring her!

She wanted to reply in kind, to make clear she understood and shared his desire. But so inexperienced was she in flirtation, before she could come up with some cleverly suggestive remark, he said, 'I hope you'll enjoy a political evening at Lord Witlow's even half as much as I have enjoyed this conversation. I'll send you a note as soon as I've spoken with Lady Lyndlington.'

She suppressed a sigh, irritated that she'd let the opportunity slip. Accepting his redirection of the conversation back into proper channels, she said,

'Thank you again. I've enjoyed our conversation, too. We mustn't let our friendship lapse again, must we?'

Friendship...and perhaps more? He offered his arm, and she took it, a little surge of energy flashing between them the instant her fingers touched him. As he escorted her out, she was once again intensely aware of his virile presence beside her, the strength, confidence and sense of purpose that seemed to radiate from him.

Ah, yes, her Davie had grown up, and the man he'd become fascinated—and attracted—her. Regardless of the potential danger of that attraction and the possible objections from her mother-in-law about being in his company, she couldn't wait to spend more time with him.

Chapter Three

After seeing the Duchess safely off in a hackney, Davie started walking. He *should* go back to the committee room, but after spending time with Faith, he was too energised, excited—and aroused—to be able to recapture yet the calm and imperturbable mask he wore when doing political work.

And partly, he admitted to himself, he wanted to savour the rare experience of spending time with her. Let himself linger and recall each moment, like a collector taking a precious object out of a treasure box, to admire and examine again and again.

As a girl, she'd glowed with an infectious joy in life that drew people to her, like an inn's beacon attracts travellers on a cold, dark night. He recalled her fixing that warm, intense gaze on him while he spoke, as if he were the most fascinating individual in the universe. To feel like the sole focus of attention of so beautiful and intelligent a girl— small wonder he'd tumbled head over heels.

It hurt his heart to see how sadness had dimmed that glow. But though the fire might have burned low, embers remained. He felt compelled to give her the encouragement and opportunities that would fan those sparks to a blaze again.

Just this one short meeting proved to him it was possible. Offered his understanding and support, and the prospect of an evening away from her usual society duties, she had unconsciously straightened, her expression brighter, her smile warmer, while in her eyes, a guarded enthusiasm grew.

He couldn't wait to see that progress continue, when she actually attended such a gathering.

He shouldn't have made that remark about 'stimulating' her, though the desire coursing through him had been too strong for him to rescind it, inappropriate as it was. She'd been lovely enough, swaddled in her cape in the dimness of lamplight last night; upon seeing her in full daylight, in that grey gown that accented her curves and brought out the brilliance of her blue eyes, he would have to have been made of stone not to have wanted her more than ever. The slender beauty he'd loved for so long had grown into a powerfully alluring woman.

Though she'd not known how to reply to his suggestive remark, she hadn't rebuffed him. Quite the contrary; leaning closer, her lips parting slightly, her gaze heating, he had read in her response that the passion he felt was reciprocated.

Probably not with the same intensity, he conceded. Still, he couldn't help feeling a primal masculine satisfaction upon discovering that the lady he prized above all others found him attractive, both as a friend and as a man. But knowing that she would welcome his touch would also make it harder to hold under control a body already ravenous to taste her.

Because that absolutely could not happen. An affair between two individuals from such radically different levels of society was too delicious a piece of gossip not to eventually become known, no matter how careful they were about meeting. Much as he wanted her, he loved her more. He would not tarnish her honour—or his—with an affair that would make her the target of the malicious, or give her mother-in-law further reason to disparage her or question her fitness to bring up her sons.

Besides, an affair would never be enough for

him. Having all of her for a time and then being forced to give her up would be unendurable.

Better to live with the ache he knew, re-establish their friendship, and use that position to enrich her life as best he could. Even if she would never be his, he wanted her to be happy.

Still not ready to return to the committee room, where he would have to banish Faith's image and the memories of today's meeting, he considered going back to Albany to write Lady Lyndlington a note. But then he'd have to wait upon her reply before he could communicate with Faith, and he didn't want to wait.

Why not call upon his friend's wife now? She would most likely be either at her town house in Upper Brook Street, or her father's home in Cavendish Square.

Energised by the prospect of being able to move forward his scheme, Davie hurried to the hackney stand and engaged a jarvey to take him to Upper Brook Street.

To his relief, Lady Lyndlington was at home, although the butler informed him this wasn't a day when she would normally receive guests. Insisting that he was close enough a friend of the master for that restriction not to apply to him, he persuaded the butler to convey him to the Blue Salon and to enquire whether her ladyship could spare him a few minutes.

Davie paced the parlour, too agitated to sit. He was certain his friend's wife would take the Duchess under her wing, and impatient to learn when they could begin.

'Davie, what a pleasant surprise,' Lady Lyndlington said as she walked in, giving him her hands to kiss. 'That is, everything is all right? Giles hasn't suffered any injury—'

'No, no, Giles is fine! I'm sorry if my sudden appearance worried you, Maggie. It's just, I had a favour to ask, and since I was out, rather than send you a note, I thought I'd try to catch you at home and deliver the request in person.'

Her worried countenance relaxed as she waved him to a seat. 'If it's within my power, I would be happy to grant it. What do you need?'

'I recently ran into—almost literally—an old friend. Faith Wellingford—you would know her as the Duchess of Ashedon.'

'The Duchess? I didn't know you were acquainted!'

'She's a cousin of my sponsor's wife. We developed a friendship many years ago, when I first began working as secretary to Sir Edward, and she was visiting her cousin. We grew to be close, though of course, there was never any question of a warmer relationship between us. I've only seen her a few times since her marriage, and we've grown apart. But upon meeting her again, I was struck by how...unhappy she is.'

'Having been married to Ashedon, I'm not surprised,' Maggie said bluntly.

'She wanted to know what I'd been doing, so I told her a bit about the Reform Bill. We used to have quite spirited discussions of politics. She seemed so intrigued, I asked if she would like to attend one of your political dinners. She was quite enthused by the idea, so I said I would approach you to ask for an invitation.'

'Of course I will include her, if you think she would enjoy it.'

'She has a lively mind, which apparently doesn't get much use during her usual society functions. I do believe she would enjoy the debate.'

'I will send her a card, then. And you, of course.'

'Thank you, Maggie. I'll be very grateful.'

Davie's mind immediately moved to evaluating options for conveying the news to Faith. Should he send a note, asking her to meet him? Or just write, letting her know that an invitation from Maggie would be forthcoming?

Meeting her, of course, would be his preference, but...

'How long have you loved her?' Maggie's quiet voice interrupted his racing thoughts.

Shocked, he jerked his gaze back, to find her regarding him, sympathy in her eyes. He considered for an instant returning a denial, but as she had just granted his rather odd request for help, there seemed little point in dissembling. 'Since the moment I set eyes on her, I suppose,' he admitted. 'Is it so obvious?'

'Probably not, unless one already suspected it.' She smiled. 'Leaving aside the fact that you seemed to be unusually concerned about the well-being of a lady who was merely a friend from long ago, your whole face lights up when you talk about her. There's this intensity in your eyes, and an urgency in your words.'

He sighed. 'I've been avoiding going back to the committee room for that very reason, suspecting I might not be able to hide that I'd seen her again. I'll tell Giles privately, but the last thing I want is for Ben or Christopher to find out. They've harassed me enough over the years about my obsession with the "Unattainable One".'

'They all know about her?'

'At some point, I had to explain why I was always turning Ben and Christopher down when they wanted to go carousing, or when Christopher offered to have his current lady find a friend for me.'

She nodded. 'Better to remain alone, than be disappointed in yourself and your partner, when she can't compare to your lady.'

'Exactly!' he cried, surprised and gratified to discover someone who understood. 'No one else *can* compare. Coming upon her again unexpectedly, the difference was…shocking. As if I'd been living in a grey world under cloudy skies, and suddenly, the sun came out, painting everything with vivid colour. Not that I've found my life dull or purposeless up till now, I assure you. But she just makes things…different. More beautiful.'

'I know. I lived in just such a dull world—before I found Giles to illumine it.'

He gave a rueful sigh. 'Ben and Christopher keep insisting that if I really wanted to, I could forget her and turn my attention to someone more suitable. But just because one knows one can't have something, that doesn't mean one can make oneself stop wanting it.'

'I know. I am sorry.'

'Don't be. Loving her is an old ache, and I've known from the beginning that nothing could ever come from it. A penniless farmer's orphan does not marry the well-dowered daughter of a family whose ancestors came over with the Conquest.'

'And why should the daughter of an ancient family be valued any higher than a commoner who, by his own efforts, has risen to a position of power?'

He smiled at her. 'That sounds like Lord Grey and the Friends of the People. Has Giles been converting you?'

'I should hope I always appreciate individuals for what they themselves accomplish, not for their pedigree. However, you…you do not intend to attempt more than rekindling a friendship, do you?'

He didn't pretend not to understand her. 'No. I wouldn't tarnish her honour—or mine—by attempting an affair. Goodness knows, nothing more is possible.'

She sighed. 'It makes me sound a terrible snob, after just stating how much I value you—and I do, you are worth ten of her wretched Duke!—I have to agree. Hadley's Hellions are doing their best to make the world a more equitable place, but we are nowhere close to being a society that would react to a duchess's remarriage to a commoner with anything but shock and derision. Not so much for you, of course. But for her…I never had any desire to move in the late Duke's circle, but like most of society, I heard enough of his exploits—and the falsely sweet "sympathy" expressed for his "poor little Duchess". She's suffered enough. I'd not be a party to anything that would bring more scorn upon her, or result in her permanent banishment from society.'

'I assure you, all I wish is to offer her is the chance to meet other individuals from her own rank, whose company she may find more interesting and fulfilling than the endless rounds of idle society parties she told me she's come to hate.'

'With all the snide remarks her husband's infidelities must have forced her to endure, I can understand why she detests them. Just promise me you won't complicate her situation. She has already had enough to bear, married to Ashedon all those years.'

'That's an easy promise to give. I want to lighten her burden, not make it heavier.'

'In that case, I shall be delighted to include her in the dinner I'm planning for next Friday. Giles and Papa are assembling some men of less radical views, with the hope of building a moderate coalition that will see the Reform Bill passed more swiftly. I'll send her a card. And one to you as well.'

'Thank you, Maggie. I very much appreciate it. I

think you'll like the Duchess, and I know she will enjoy your gathering.'

'I hope you will as well.' She looked at him, her face troubled. 'You did me a very good turn once, bringing me back to the man I loved. I only wish I could conjure a magic spell, so I might create as favourable a result for you.'

'Helping Faith is the best thing you can do for me.'

'I'll do all I can.' She walked him to the door, halting on the threshold to give him a kiss on the cheek. 'Have a care for yourself, too, Davie. As I know only too well, hearts can break more than once.'

'But only once for the same person,' he replied, and walked out.

He certainly hoped so, anyway.

In the afternoon two days later, having received a note from Davie informing her that Lady Lyndlington would be sending her a card of invitation for a dinner the following Friday, Faith ordered a hackney and went to pay a call on her erstwhile hostess. She'd suffered the expected dressing-down from the Dowager over her dinner-party flight—and her absence from the obligatory drive in the Park the next day—in a silence meek enough not to call down more criticism on her head. She felt safe enough attempting this errand; as Davie had said, even the high-in-the-instep Dowager couldn't fault her calling on the daughter of a marquess.

Knowing how persuasive Davie the politician could be, she wanted to assure herself that Lady Lyndlington truly wished to include her in the gathering...and to discover whether she would feel comfortable enough with her hostess to want to attend.

In the early years of their marriage, Ashedon had done a very effective job in isolating her, distancing her from her family while at the same time actively discouraging her developing friendships with anyone else. At the time, still radiantly in love and certain of his love in return, she'd been too preoccupied trying to learn the duties required of the mistress of numerous properties and a multitude of servants, then waylaid by a succession of pregnancies and the delight of newborns, to fully realise just how alone she'd become.

But as the boys grew and her husband's attentions dwindled, she'd become only too aware that she had virtually no friends of her age and class. The society women in whose company she often found herself all seemed to have already established circles of friendship, which were not interested in admitting any newcomers. And even if they had, most of the members were either indifferent to or contemptuous of the country life and activities that she prized so much more highly than the idle amusements of London.

She could tell that Davie admired Lady Lyndlington, and she valued his opinion. But a man's view of a woman could be very different from one woman's view of another. Would this marquess's daughter, with her superior intellect and expertise in politics, hide beneath polite words the same contemptuous pity for simple little Faith Wellingford that made her association with other sophisticated ladies of the *ton* so unpleasant?

The carriage slowed to a halt, the footman coming over to open the door and hand her down. Heading to the front steps of the Upper Brook Street town house, Faith took a deep breath, suppressing out of long habit a too-often disappointed hope. One way or another, she was about to find out.

The butler showed her into an elegant room done in the Adam style in shades of white and blue. Several bookcases stood against one wall, filled with a variety of volumes. Perusing the shelves to discover several plays and novels she had enjoyed, Faith felt a renewal of the hope she'd tried to squelch.

Perhaps Lady Lyndlington might be someone of similar interests after all.

A moment later, the lady herself entered. 'Duchess, how kind of you to call! I do hope you didn't do so to convey your regrets for the Friday night gathering! I'm very much looking forward to becoming better acquainted. Davie—Mr Smith— is my husband's closest friend, and we both have a very high regard for him—and for anyone of whom he speaks with as much warmth and respect as he did of you.'

'He is very kind.'

'Indeed. Would you take tea?'

'If I wouldn't be imposing, or taking you away from other duties.'

'Not at all. I should like it very much.'

As would I, Faith thought, her cautious optimism increasing as her hostess rang the bell pull and informed the butler to bring refreshments. She'd spoken briefly with Lady Lyndlington at several society balls, among a crush of other attendees, but meeting her here in her own parlour, she was immediately drawn by her warm, open friendliness. She'd already seen enough to decide she could safely accept the dinner invitation. She'd try not to hope for more.

'I understand you've known Mr Smith since you were very young,' her hostess said as she took a seat on the sofa.

'Yes, before I even made my come-out. I was spending the summer with my cousin, and Mr Smith had come to serve as secretary to her husband.' Faith gestured to the bookshelves. 'After dinner one night, we found ourselves both in the library, searching for a book. Which led to a discussion about favourite authors that lasted the rest of the evening. After that, we met in the afternoons when he'd finished his work, and talked or rode. I'd read him poetry; he'd tell me about history and politics and his plans for the future—to become a parliamentarian, and help to change the government of the nation. He was so…intelligent, and caring, and full of conviction! I'd never met anyone like him.'

Lady Lyndlington smiled. 'It sounds as if he hasn't changed very much. He's still intelligent, caring and full of conviction.'

He's changed in one way, Faith thought, conversation lapsing as the butler brought in the tea tray. *The romantic young hero has become a compellingly attractive man.*

'Yes, he seems much the same as I remember,' she continued after Lady Lyndlington handed her a cup. 'Foolishly, I suppose, I expected we would maintain our friendship over the years. But of course, once I married and he began his career we...didn't see each other very often.'

'I expect not. Running such a large household, a duchess must have many duties.'

Declining to correct that erroneous assumption, she said, 'Mr Smith tells me that you've managed your father's household for years, and arrange his political dinners. How fascinating it must be, to literally have a seat at the table of power as matters of national interest are discussed!'

Lady Lyndlington laughed. 'Along with a smattering of gossip and personal anecdotes. But you are right; it *is* stimulating. Not that I did anything special to deserve being so blessed, other than having the good fortune to be born my father's daughter. I do hope you will find the evening enjoyable.'

'I'm sure I shall! I expect to do no more than listen, which I hope will be acceptable. What's the old saying—'Better to be silent and be thought foolish, than to speak and remove all doubt'? I shall refrain from displaying my ignorance!'

'Listening to the discussions, you will soon have a fairly accurate picture of what's transpiring. Please, feel free to ask questions! Coming into the debates with no preconceived ideas, you will have a fresh perspective that could be most helpful.'

'Well, I don't know about that, but I shall certainly listen most carefully.'

'The discussions often become quite lively—and I hope they will be, for there's no cards, or singing, or other entertainment. I would hate to bore you on your very first evening with us.'

'I don't care at all for gaming, and I shall be quite content to listen to intelligent discussion of issues that matter, rather than the snide, biting comments that so often form much of the conversation.' She shrugged. 'Perhaps because I have been so often the subject of them.'

Lady Lyndlington frowned. 'Surely people are not disrespectful to a duchess!'

'Oh, no, they are obsequious—to my face.' Perhaps it was the ready sympathy she read in the other woman's expression, but once she'd started, Faith couldn't seem to keep herself from adding bitterly, 'But I often "overhear" comments made, I'm sure, deliberately just within my hearing. About what a poor little dab of a thing I am, how it's no wonder, after getting his heirs on me, my husband looked elsewhere. And now that my mother-in-law has moved back in, I am treated daily to a recital of all the ways in which I fall short of being worthy of the high position I occupy.'

'I feel so fortunate in my family, who have supported me through the worst of times!' Lady Lyndlington shook her head. 'I'm so sorry you haven't experienced that, and I wish I could protest that most in society are kind. But as I know only too well, many are not.'

Faith grimaced. 'They seem to assume I don't have the wit, or the courage, to toss back some biting response. I *could* answer in kind. I just don't want to. Isn't there enough heartache and cruelty in the world, without deliberately adding to it?'

Impulsively, her hostess seized her hand. 'I so agree! And I understand more than you know. Before I met Giles, after being a widow for several years, I began to think about remarrying. I'd been acting as Papa's hostess for some time, and had a number of interested suitors. Sadly, having married my childhood best friend, I was completely naïve, never questioning that the admiration a man expressed might be due more to my wealth and family connections than to the charms of my person.'

'Now that, I cannot believe!' Faith protested.

'Believe it,' Lady Lyndlington said with surprising bitterness. 'One particularly ardent suitor, who had political aspirations my father's support could assist, convinced me of his love, and I persuaded myself I returned his regard. Just before we were to wed, I discovered that he maintained a little love-nest where he continued to entertain *chère-amies*. Apparently I was the only one in London who didn't know about it. I broke the engagement, but you can imagine the titters behind fans and malicious comments I "overheard". But you may know this already; it was quite the *on dit.*'

Hardly believing so lovely, confident, and intelligent a lady could have been subject to such treatment, Faith said, 'I didn't know. So you truly do understand.'

'Yes. By the way, I did, quite inadvertently, discover a way to respond to the malicious that did not require descending to the same level as the speaker. Soon after the...incident, I overhead a comment that so infuriated me, I couldn't utter a word. I simply turned and stared at the perpetrator, as if she were a worm I'd discovered on one of my prize roses and intended to crush. She ended up looking away first, and never bothered me again. The technique worked so well, I used it on several other occasions during that awful time, to good effect.' She patted Faith's hand. 'I recommend the tactic.'

Faith had to smile. 'As a marquess's daughter, you were probably born to it, but I doubt I could manage the "look". Papa lost all our money when I was still so young, I grew up with no expectations of making a grand match, more comfortable climbing trees and riding in my brother's old breeches than mastering curtsies and clever drawing-room conversation. But thank you. I'm sure I'll have occasions I could try out the technique, whether or not I can carry it off.'

Lady Lyndlington nodded. 'Practise it in front of your glass. I did.'

At the idea of this elegant lady practising set-down looks in a mirror, Faith had to laugh out loud. 'No! I don't believe it!'

'Oh, it's true. I'd remember the remark that so incensed me, and look into the mirror until I perfected an expression that should have made the glass shatter and vaporise into dust. You must try it.'

Subsiding with a giggle, Faith set aside her cup. 'Perhaps I will. But now, I've taken up enough of your time.'

She rose, and her hostess rose with her. 'You will come to dinner on Friday?'

'Yes. I shall be looking forward to it.'

'Excellent. I think we should be friends. After all, we principled ladies must stick together.'

Drinking in the warmth and encouragement like a wilted plant responds to water, Faith could almost feel her withered optimism and trampled hope begin to stir. 'That would please me very much.'

'Until Friday, then.'

After an exchange of curtsies, the ladies parted, Faith returning to her carriage with more anticipation for the future than she'd felt in years

Bless Davie! Not only had he given her a stimulating evening to look forward to, he might have steered her towards something she hadn't had since she'd been distanced from her sisters.

A close female friend.

If only she could keep them both.

Chapter Four

On Friday night, Davie arrived early at Lord Witlow's town house, already so energised at the idea of seeing Faith again, he'd been more or less worthless in committee that afternoon. Once or twice he'd seen Giles send an appraising look in his direction, from which he'd turned away without acknowledgement. But, arriving as far in advance of the appointed hour, he knew that sooner or later his hostess's husband was going to take him to task.

Lord Witlow's butler showed him to the Blue Drawing Room, remarking with a touch of reproach as he directed him to the wine decanter on the sideboard, that, it being so far in advance of the hour for dinner, the host and hostess had not yet come down. Chuckling at that veiled set-down about his poor manners, Davie began pacing the handsome chamber, trying to dispel some of his nervous excitement and anticipation.

As luck would have it, the first to join him in the drawing room was Giles. The look of enquiry on his friend's face told him that he was about to be taken to task for his renewed interest in 'the Unattainable'.

Considering that he'd volunteered a few judicious words of caution to his mostly unappreciative friend when Giles was first pursuing Maggie, he figured it was only fair that he suffer Giles's comments with good grace. Particularly as he knew whatever Giles might say would stem from a genuine concern for his welfare.

'So, Maggie tells me that you asked her to invite the Duchess of Ashedon to our little gathering?' Giles asked, confirming Davie's expectations.

'Yes. I ran into her unexpectedly a week or so ago. She still…hasn't found her feet since the death of her husband, and seemed very low. Years ago, when we first met, she had a lively interest in politics. I thought attending this evening would help draw her out of grief, and let her focus on something other than her own cares for an evening.'

'From what Maggie tells me about the character of the late Duke, I doubt the Duchess is experiencing very much grief.'

'More like regret for what might have been, probably,' Davie admitted, advancing to the wine decanter on the sideboard. 'I understand the Duke… frequently availed himself of the company of other women, particularly after the Duchess had borne him several sons to secure the succession.' Choosing two glasses, he poured them each some wine.

'Now that I've reconciled with my father and been more or less forced to attend *ton* gatherings, I've had to listen to a lot of gossipy rubbish,' Giles said, accepting the glass from Davie. 'One bit, from that fribble Darrow, said the late Duke met his demise while attempting to…copulate with his current doxy while racing his high-perch phaeton. A drunken wager, apparently.'

Shocked, Davie froze, the wine glass halfway to his lips. 'The devil he did!' he exclaimed a moment later. Faith told him she'd never enjoyed the attention paid to a duchess. *Especially as Ashedon and his women provided so much scandal for society to watch my reaction to.* How embarrassing and degrading it must have been to face down that bit of salacious gossip! 'I hadn't heard. Poor F—poor Duchess.'

'Not much to lament about the passing of such a man,' Giles said acerbically.

'I don't believe he ever truly cared for her,' Davie said, trying to mask the anger that fact always aroused in him. To have been able to claim the beauty and innocence and joy that was Faith, and not appreciate it, was stupidity of such colossal proportions he could never forgive it.

Why couldn't that gift have been tendered to a man who would have treasured it? Not him, of course—it could never have been him—but surely there was *some* man of suitable birth and station who could have loved her and made her happy.

At least now she was free of the husband who hadn't. He squelched the little flare of excitement that resonated through him. *Free, maybe, but not for you.*

Ah, but a man could dream, couldn't he?

He surfaced from that thought to find Giles frowning at him. 'Maggie told me two days ago that you'd asked her to invite the Duchess tonight, so I made sure Ben and Christopher were occupied elsewhere. You ought to tell them, before they find out from some other source, that you're...involving yourself in her life again. I'll make sure they don't harass you about it. But...be careful, Davie. Don't let yourself hope too much from this.'

'I'm not!' he assured Giles—and maybe himself? 'If I can help her break free from the unhappiness of her life with Ashedon that will be enough.'

'Will it?' Giles asked, giving him a penetrating

glance. 'I'm not sure how much she can "free" herself from that life. Don't forget, Davie, she's a rich widow, her oldest son now the Duke, her minor children protected by a trust. Her family may well have further plans for her.'

A fierce protectiveness rose in him as the austere, disapproving face of the Dowager surfaced in his mind. 'As long as she has a say in making those plans, rather than have them imposed on her.'

'As long as you remember it's not your place to determine that.'

'I just want to stand her friend. She has few enough of them.'

'Well, here comes one who should be.'

Davie looked over as a tall, well-dressed gentleman entered the parlour. 'Englemere,' Giles said, walking over to shake the Marquess's hand. 'Good to see you. Perhaps tonight we can make some progress on hammering out that coalition.'

'I hope so,' the Marquess replied. 'If your lovely wife has anything to do with it, there will certainly be a lively discussion. Good evening, Mr Smith. You'll add your voice of reason to that debate, I'm sure.'

'Always,' Davie answered, reaching out to shake the hand the Marquess offered. He owed a great deal to Englemere, the best friend of his sponsor,

Sir Edward Greaves, and one of his backers for his Parliamentary seat, and respected him even more. Did the Marquess know his sister-in-law was going to be present this evening? he wondered.

Almost before he'd completed the thought, the lady in question appeared at the doorway as the butler intoned, 'The Duchess of Ashedon.'

For a moment, everything in Davie's world halted while he took in the loveliness that was Faith. Her gown, a lavender confection of lace and silk, hugged her tiny waist and moulded itself over her rounded bosom in a way his hands itched to trace. Her golden hair, pinned up in an elaborate arrangement of curls, made him yearn to rake his fingers through it, freeing the heavy mass to cascade around her shoulders, as it had when she was a girl. She wore only simple diamond drops in her ears, the soft expanse of bared skin and shoulders rising above the bodice of her gown her only other adornment.

She married the look of the angel she'd always been with the allure of a siren. Davie wasn't sure which was more powerful—the ache of his love for her, or the burn of desire.

While he simply watched her, spellbound, Englemere answered his question as he paced forward to take her hand. 'Faith! What a delightful surprise!

I didn't know you would be here tonight. How are you? It's been far too long.'

He took her hands, and Faith leaned up to give him a kiss on the cheek. 'Lady Lyndlington was kind enough to invite me. I didn't know you'd be here either, Nicky. How lovely to see you! How is Sarah?'

'Still carefully nursing Elizabeth, our youngest, who was very ill with a congestion of the lungs last winter. Gave me quite a scare, I have to admit. With Lizzie so slow to regain her strength, I wanted her out of the noise and smoke of the city, so I've taken a house near Highgate Village, with a large garden for her to walk in and fresh country air to breathe. If you have time, I know Sarah would love to have you call.'

'Fresh country air? How Sarah must love that, and…and I would, too. I will try to visit her, Nicky.' She raised her chin, almost defiantly, Davie thought. 'We've grown apart, and I'd like to rectify that.'

'As would we,' Englemere said, giving her hands a squeeze before releasing them. 'But I mustn't monopolise you. You know Lyndlington? And Mr Smith, of course.'

'My lord,' she said, making a curtsy first to Giles, then to him.

'Duchess,' he said, taking the hand she offered. Savouring the contact, he retained her fingers for as long as he could without exciting comment before forcing himself to release them. To his delight, she gave his hand a brief squeeze as he let hers go.

'Who else can I expect to see tonight, my lord?' she asked Giles.

'Elder statesman and your host's political sponsor, Lord Coopley, whom I'm sure you know. Lord Howlett, another member of Witlow's Tory coalition in the Lords. Two of my Reform MP colleagues, Richard Rowleton and John Percy.'

'I'm acquainted with all of them,' she said, her apprehensive smile steadying. 'Particularly Lord Coopley. He used to take Ashedon to task about his behaviour, which annoyed my husband exceedingly.'

Bravo for the baron, Davie thought. Counting on his age, lineage and position to protect him from retribution for criticising a gentleman of higher rank? Or too principled and courageous to care?

Laughing, Englemere said, 'I'm sure it did, though I wager Ashedon didn't choose to respond. Coopley has never shrunk from calling a spade a spade, and he's too intelligent—and belligerent— for most men to willingly argue with him.'

'As I've experienced on several occasions, when

promoting ideas he does not favour,' Giles inserted wryly. 'But you mustn't worry, Duchess. Lady Lyndlington has you seated beside her father, and near Mr Smith, so you'll have a dinner partner you know well to chat with.'

'And to assist me, I hope!' Faith replied, darting a look at Davie, to which he returned an encouraging nod.

'I doubt you'll need any assistance, but Mr Smith will certainly provide it, if necessary,' Giles said. Then his eyes lighting, he said, 'Here's my wife and her father! Excuse me, please.'

Davie watched Faith, who was watching the alacrity with which Giles hurried to meet his wife, giving her a kiss on the cheek and murmuring a few words that made her blush. Sadness washed over her face, and he saw the shimmer of tears in her eyes.

'They look very close,' she said. 'How wonderful for them.'

'They're all April and May, like two young lovers. Ben, Christopher and I heckle Giles all the time about it.'

Just then, the butler announced the arrival of the other guests Giles had mentioned. Spotting her, Lord Coopley walked over to Faith.

'How kind of you, Maggie, to invite another

beauty for an old man to talk with!' he exclaimed, making Faith a courtly bow.

'You are very kind, my lord,' Faith replied. 'But I intend to do more listening than talking.'

'Nonsense, say whatever you like—I know it will be clever!' As Giles and Davie exchanged startled looks—both well aware how merciless the baron often was to inexperienced souls who dared venture opinions about the political topics that obsessed him—the old gentleman added, 'Always enjoyed chatting with you, my girl. Talked about books and horses and hunting. Right fancied you for my eldest, before Ashedon swept you away. Would have made you happier.'

As a blush of embarrassment tinted Faith's cheeks at that too-frank assessment, Lady Lyndlington inserted smoothly, 'Since we all know each other so well, we can dispense with formal introductions. Shall we proceed to table? Lord Coopley, will you escort me in, before I succumb to jealousy over your attentions to the Duchess?'

Chuckling, the older man clasped the arm she extended. 'Of course, Maggie! You know you'll always be first in my heart. The daughter I never had, much as both your papa and I might have wished you'd been a son who could have carried on our work in the Lords.'

'Oh, but I provided you a magnificent husband to take that place,' she teased.

Since as the leader of Reform, Giles was the man to whom the baron was most often opposed, her remark earned a laugh from the entire assembly.

'Minx,' Coopley reproved, wagging a finger at her. 'If I thought he could be seduced into it, I'd send *him* off in a horse cart with a doxy.'

'No chance of that,' Lady Lyndlington flashed back. 'If I thought he could be seduced into it, I'd murder him first.'

Davie watched Faith anxiously, but rather than causing her additional distress, the light-hearted remarks touching on her late husband's ignominious demise drew the group's attention away from her, giving her a chance to recover her composure. Before he could add a quick word of encouragement, Lord Witlow walked over to claim her arm.

'I'm so pleased you joined us this evening, Duchess,' he said with a warm smile. 'My daughter tells me you are quite interested in the work we're now doing in Parliament, so I trust we won't bore you this evening.'

'Oh, no, my lord! I'm sure I will be informed and—' she shot Davie a mischievous glance '—stimulated.'

At her words, the arousal he'd been trying to ignore hardened further. Devil's teeth, but he needed to master the always simmering, ever-increasing desire her nearness evoked! *Concentrate on making sure she feels comfortable and included*, he instructed himself.

'I hope so,' the Marquess said as he led Faith into the dining room. 'My Maggie lives and breathes politics, but she's never had a female friend who shared that passion. She's thrilled to find that you have an interest. You must come visit us more often—even if, as I expect, your association with Mr Smith would have you favouring the Reform agenda. With my daughter now married to a reformer, I shall be beset on all sides!'

'Mr Smith and I used to debate politics, but that was many years ago. As you know, the late Duke was not politically inclined, so I know much too little about the bill under consideration to "beset" anyone with my opinions,' Faith said as her host seated her.

'You've come to the right dinner party, then,' Lord Coopley remarked from his end of the table. 'With these rum customers present—' he gestured to Giles and the Reform MPs '—you'll hear every point of view, worthless as some may be.'

'I trust, my lord,' Giles said, taking a seat adjacent to Coopley, 'we shall eventually hammer out a compromise even you can agree with.'

'Are they always at loggerheads?' Faith murmured over her shoulder to Davie, who had followed her in protectively and halted beside her chair.

'Always, though now that Giles has married his friend Witlow's daughter, Coopley isn't quite so brutal,' Davie replied softly. 'Giles used to feel lucky to return to our rooms with his skin intact.'

'I know so little about the discussion tonight,' she said, once again sounding apprehensive. Impulsively, she reached out to touch his hand. 'You will help me, so I don't make a complete fool of myself?'

Davie's toes curled in his shoes as he resisted the to desire to link his fingers with hers. 'You could never do that. But if you get confused, send me a look. I'll insert some explanation. Don't worry—you'll be fine.'

She gave him a tremulous smile. 'Thank you, Davie. You're always so kind.'

Though, as the highest-ranking woman present, Faith was seated as was proper beside their host, Davie was surprised to find their hostess had indeed fudged protocol by placing a commoner adjacent to her, rather than further down the table. As he looked at Maggie with a lift of his brows, she smiled and said, 'As a Member of Parliament, you should rank with the others. And besides, isn't the ranking of men based on their talents, not their birth, a tenet of your beliefs?'

'Humph.' Coopley sniffed. 'An excuse to give any upstart with a glib tongue the power to agitate the rabble! Though in fairness, I must grudgingly agree that Mr Smith possesses considerable talent.'

'Far more than some men of exalted rank,' Giles observed.

Coopley gave a bark of laughter. 'Far more than the one we mentioned earlier tonight, that's for certain! No matter, we'll tend you now, girl,' he said, turning to Faith. 'Only sorry I don't have any unmarried sons to send courting.'

Much as he'd wanted her to have a husband who appreciated her, Davie felt an immediate stab of protest at the idea of Faith marrying again. *Please Heaven, not yet. Not until...*what future could he possibly envision?

'I don't need that sort of "tending",' Faith was replying, the blush returning to her cheek. 'I'm not even out of mourning yet.'

'Not much to mourn for,' the irrepressible baron declared. 'Ah, here's the first course. Always know there will be fine food on your table, my dear!' he said to his hostess. 'Need to fortify myself before the hard bargaining starts.'

For a time, as the various courses came and went, conversation was general. Davie ate little and talked less, his attention focused on Faith. Urged on by their skilful host, she was induced to talk about her sons, a topic about which she soon became animated, describing them and asking the Marquess's advice about their upbringing.

'I would certainly recommend getting them into the country more,' Lord Witlow replied to her question. 'Never too young for the little Duke to start learning about his land and tenants. Though I regret he never developed an interest in politics, I'm proud of the work my son Esterbrook has done on our estate, which he began running when he was still a boy. Besides his duty to Parliament, there's nothing more important than a landlord's care of his land.'

'I would like to get Edward to Ashedon Court more often, but now that the Dowager has moved back with us, it's no easier than when her son was living. Both much prefer staying in town.'

'Take them on your own, then,' the Marquess advised. 'They no longer have a father whose permission you must secure, and I imagine the trustees will approve any decisions you make about their care that seem reasonable.'

'I really may?' Faith asked, her eyes lighting. 'I

would love that! Although we visited so seldom, I know almost as little about Ashedon Court as my sons.'

'Time to learn more,' Witlow said.

'Might have a care, though,' Coopley added from his end of the table. 'It's a hotbed of radicals, from Liverpool and Manchester, out into Derbyshire and Nottinghamshire.'

'Is that a problem?' Faith asked.

'Those are the cities and the areas that currently have no, or limited, representation in Parliament,' Davie explained. 'Over the years, there have been demonstrations and protests.'

'Riots and destruction of property, more like,' Coopley countered. 'Depending on how close Ashedon Court is to the disturbances, I could see why your late husband might not have wanted to install his family there. Though proximity to his London doxies rather than his family's safety is more likely the reason for his remaining in town,' he added, mirroring thoughts Davie wouldn't have been tactless enough to voice.

Apparently armoured now against the baron's bluntness, Faith barely blushed. 'Mr Smith told me the new industrial cities of the north, having not existed when Parliamentary districts were drawn up in medieval times, were among those most vocal in calling for revamping the way Members are chosen. There were also towns and districts from that old assessment who now have very little population, yet retain their representatives, aren't there?'

'Exactly,' Rowleton, one of the Reform MPs, said. 'For instance, Dunwich has thirty-two voters, Camelford twenty-five, Gatton seven, yet each of these send two representatives to Parliament. While Liverpool and Manchester, with thousands of souls, send none! It's a travesty we must address, and the Reform Bill does.'

'Perhaps, but you would take away votes from some districts that have always had them,' the Tory, Lord Howlett, said. 'That's not just, either.'

Normally, Davie would have launched into the discussion himself, but tonight, he was much more interested in watching Faith, her eyes sparkling, her lips curving into a smile as she followed the banter and debating points being scored up and down the table.

All too soon for his liking, the meal ended, brandy was brought in, and Lady Lyndlington rose. 'Before anyone comes to fisticuffs, we ladies shall leave you gentlemen to sort out the details. Duchess?'

'A fascinating discussion, which I am so pleased

you allowed me to witness,' Faith said. 'I can now claim to be much more knowledgeable about the great work going forward.'

'Yes, and you can warn those drawing-room idlers like your late husband that they need to get their lazy arses to the Lords,' Coopley added. 'Find out what is going on, with the most important decisions to be made in four hundred years about to voted on! A crusty old curmudgeon like me couldn't persuade them half so easily as a lovely and eloquent lass.'

'I appreciate your confidence, my lord,' Faith said. 'I shall certainly do my possible to encourage every peer to attend.'

At Lord Coopley's endorsement, Davie could almost see Faith's self-confidence grow. More appreciative of the crotchety old gentleman than he'd ever been previously, Davie felt as proud as an anxious tutor whose student has just passed a difficult exam. How right he'd been to encourage Faith to attend this gathering!

How sad he was that the ladies were about to withdraw, ending this special evening with her. But there was no way he could leave now and escort her home without arousing a great deal of unwanted speculation.

'Will you stay for tea, Duchess?' their hostess was asking as Faith walked over to meet her.

'No, I should return to my boys.'

'Then I shall retire as well. Shall I have Rains summon your carriage?'

'He could have a footman find me a hackney. The Dowager was using the carriage tonight.'

'Ah, I see. I'll have him get your wrap. Mr Smith, would you be kind enough to keep the Duchess company until her hackney arrives? I'm sure these gentlemen could spare you for a few minutes.'

Davie's gaze shot to his hostess, who gave him a quick wink. 'I'd be honoured. Duchess?' He offered Faith his arm, stifling the sigh of delight that nearly hissed through his teeth when she laid her hand on it.

As he led Faith out behind their hostess, Giles gave him a concerned look, Coopley a questioning one. After the courtesy of farewells, however, the other gentlemen ignored them, becoming consumed once again by their debate.

'Thank you, Maggie,' he whispered to his hostess a short time later, while the butler was assisting Faith into her evening cloak. 'For dinner, and this.'

She nodded, but her look was speculating and

her eyes were sad. 'Just remember your promise. Friendship only.'

'Friendship,' he repeated, even as his traitorous body stirred and hardened. Memories of holding her flashed through his head—the softness of her body against his, her golden hair under his cheek—and sent desire spiralling.

The butler exited to order the hackney, Faith walked back to them, and their hostess turned to her. 'I'm so pleased you enjoyed the evening, Duchess. I hope you will join us for many more—and call here often. There is work we can do together!'

'I would like that very much. But you must call me Faith, then.'

'I would be honoured! And you must call me Maggie, as Mr Smith, does.'

'I, too, would be honoured by your friendship.'

Maggie nodded. 'That's settled. I'll bid you both goodnight—and count on seeing you both again soon!'

With that, bows and curtsies were exchanged, and Maggie ascended the staircase, leaving him alone with her.

How to best use these precious few minutes?

A radiant smile on her face, Faith stepped nearer. It took every bit of self-control he could muster not to close the distance between them and take her in his arms. Or at least, take her hands in his. Somehow, he made himself stop. The mere inches of air separating them vibrated with sensual tension, making his heart pound so hard in his chest, he thought surely she could hear it.

Slowly, while he gritted his teeth with the effort to remain motionless, she reached out a hand and gently stroked his cheek. 'Thank you for tonight, my sweet Davie,' she murmured. 'I haven't felt so…energised, and appreciated, and alive, since…'

Since I held you in my arms a week ago, he thought, consumed with the need to take her again. But he'd promised…something.

'Well—for a long time,' she finished. She went up on tiptoe, and for an instant, he had the wild hope that she would kiss him again, as she had when he'd escorted her home that night. Then, as if realising how inadvisable that was, she returned to her feet.

For long, endless moments, they stood frozen, staring at each other from a hand's breadth apart. He devoured with his gaze every curve and angle of her sweet face, every plump contour of the lips he hungered so much to taste, the desire pulsing through him stronger than he'd ever experienced.

And then, with a little sigh, she angled her head

up, offering her lips, her eyes drifting closed, as if she were as helpless to resist the force between them as he was.

Heaven knew what idiocy he might have committed, had the butler not chosen that moment to stomp back in, announcing the arrival of her hackney.

The man's voice sent a shock through him, and they both stepped back. 'Your hackney, Duchess,' he repeated inanely, seized by a looming sense of loss.

'When will I see you again?' she whispered, voicing the thought that consumed him.

'Perhaps...perhaps,' he replied, thinking rapidly, 'I could escort you to visit your sister, in Highgate. Englemere doesn't come to town every day, I imagine. I could...bring him some committee reports.'

'Yes!' she said, her eyes lighting with enthusiasm. 'I would like that.'

'Bring your boys, too. They could become acquainted with their cousins.'

'Witlow said I should be able to take them where I like, now that I don't need their father's permission. When shall we go?'

'Arrange what is convenient for you, and send me a note.'

She nodded eagerly. 'I will. Tonight was wonderful! Thank you again.' With a glance towards the waiting butler at the open front door, she said, 'Goodbye, Davie. I'm so glad I'll be seeing you again.'

'Make it soon.'

'I will.' She turned to leave, hesitated, then gave his hand a squeeze before hurrying over to the door.

As she disappeared into the night, Davie raised his hand, inhaling her faint scent of lavender. The skin she'd touched still sparked and tingled, the aftermath of a desire so powerful he'd almost done something foolish and irreparable.

It shook him to realise how swiftly being with her, alone, had unravelled his control.

Maybe it wasn't wise to see her again, lest his hold over himself crumble altogether, leading him to commit some irreversible act that would tarnish his honour and hers and sever for good this tenuous revival of their friendship.

And yet... With her sons along to play chaperone, they wouldn't be alone on the road to Highgate. After they arrived, she'd most likely be closeted with her sister, while he could discuss the latest compromise position with Englemere, focusing his mind on business and away from her enchanting face. With her within the protective embrace of her family, there would be no opportunity for passion to get out of hand; he'd be able to enjoy the delight of her company without fearing for his sanity or his honour.

Besides, he knew in the depths of his soul that he could never stop himself from seeing her unless she herself forbade it.

Chapter Five

Faith's euphoria buoyed her through the short hackney ride back home. She hadn't felt so energised, challenged, and *alive* since the early days of her marriage—before she discovered what a tragic farce her dreams of being loved and cherished had become. To attend a society function and meet encouragement and appreciation, rather than smug or pitying glances, made it seem as if she'd suddenly emerged from the dark room of isolation and sadness in which she'd been trapped for so long into a glorious dawn of new possibilities.

And then there was that thrilling, titillating connection with Davie. How could so strong a bond re-establish itself so quickly with a man she'd seen only half a dozen times over the last ten years?

She couldn't thank him enough for this evening, where he'd stood beside her, encouraging with a glance, assisting with a helpful comment, supporting her with his silent presence. And always, simmering underneath—until it had nearly erupted into action in Witlow's front hall—was the powerful physical link that seemed to strengthen each time they were together.

How could she find words to thank him for the sense he gave her of being attractive, desirable, and wanted, nurturing her crushed and battered spirit to a renewed confidence? His obvious desire unleashed an unprecedented, heady sense of feminine power—and an urge to use that power to satisfy the increasing demands of desire.

Ah, yes, *desire*. Having endured so many years of unhappiness made her a little reckless. She'd never be permitted to marry a man like Davie—if marriage were in fact on his mind, which it probably wasn't. Lust certainly was, as it was on hers.

Dare she yield to it? Would he let her?

She didn't know. Continuing to associate with him would lead her into a maze full of risks and dangerous choices—but also to the possibility of fulfilment, even joy. She wasn't prepared yet to decide whether to proceed down that path. For the present, she'd seize every opportunity to be with him, and just enjoy.

Make it soon.

She'd write a note to Sarah this very night, seeking a convenient time for a visit.

Still aglow with energy and optimism, she sprang down from the hackney and waltzed up the front steps. Not until the butler admitted her, informing her that the Dowager had returned from her entertainment and would enjoy a glass of wine with her in the Blue Salon, did her soaring spirits make an abrupt descent.

She was home again, and back to being the much-maligned Duchess.

But not any longer, she told herself. Not that she would be rude to her mother-in-law, but she did not intend to meekly endure her criticism. Though she wasn't sure Lady Lyndlington's 'stare' would work to silence so overbearing and self-important a woman, she would certainly excuse herself, if her husband's mother decided that a 'chat over wine' meant a litany of reproof for her behaviour today.

Bracing herself, she entered the Blue Salon. 'Did you enjoy the opera?' she asked, seating herself and accepting a glass from the footman the Dowager waved to serve her.

'It was tolerable. Although it had to be more entertaining than a dull political evening at Lord Witlow's. I can't imagine why you accepted that invitation.'

'I didn't find it dull at all. Conversation about the new Reform Bill was fascinating, and Lady Lyndlington is a very gracious hostess.'

'Lyndlington? Ah, yes—Witlow's daughter, Lady Margaret, married that jumped-up by-blow of the Earl of Telbridge—who is to inherit, despite the fact that the earl divorced his harlot of a mother! Quite the scandal!'

Just like the Dowager, to have some bit of disparaging gossip to divulge about every person one could mention. Avoiding any response that would allow her to elaborate, Faith said instead, 'My brother-in-law, Lord Englemere, was also present, and asked me to call; his youngest child has been ill. I shall send my sister a note directly to see when is convenient. You mustn't be alarmed,' she added quickly, when the Dowager held up a hand in protest. 'I know what a dread you have of illness, so there is no need for you to accompany me.'

'Very well, if you feel you must, although I think it is very *inconsiderate* of your relations to ask you to visit a sick house, especially as you are a mother with three children of your own to protect!'

'I believe the child is recovering, and most of my visit will be spent with my sister.'

'I still think it encroaching. But I didn't ask you to stop by to discuss some dull political gathering—I have exciting news that will certainly raise your spirits! Which have, quite properly, been downcast since the demise of our dear Edward—' The Dowager paused, her voice wobbling as she wiped her eyes with a bit of muslin. 'Well, no longer must we suffer being a household of women. My dear Randall has consented to live here with us! Now we shall have a gentleman's escort to any entertainments we find proper to attend!'

The memory of her brother-in-law's leering face, drunken smile and hard, grasping hands swept over her, followed by a wave of revulsion. Faith set down a glass that suddenly wobbled in her hand.

'How...useful,' she said at last.

'I would have expected you to exhibit a bit more enthusiasm,' the Dowager said tartly.

'I'm tired, and the news is...shocking.'

'Shocking? What is so unusual about a son coming to care for his mother?'

Faith bit down hard on her lip to stifle the replies that immediately sprang to mind. That the arrangement was probably more about the estate taking care of Lord Randall's needs, than him caring for his mother. That he was highly unlikely to escort them to a gathering unless he wished to attend, and since he preferred spending most of his evenings at gambling hells, bordellos, and other establishments of dubious repute, they would be as often without masculine escort as they were currently.

The appalling news settled in, setting other thoughts careening back and forth in her head like a shuttlecock in a lively game. She'd never be able to convince the Dowager that her younger son was an unreliable, dissolute wastrel—or that he'd made advances towards Faith. Was there any way to prevent Lord Randall from installing himself, a leech upon the estate? Did she have the power to eject him, or would, upon her appeal, the trustees do so?

Gulping down the last swallow of wine, she said, 'I know you will be much comforted by his presence.'

'But you're not?' the Dowager said with a frown. 'Heavens, you're always the most ungrateful child! All excited about running off to visit your sister's sick brat, and no enthusiasm at all about having your dear departed husband's precious brother coming to bear us up in our hour of grief!'

She would not stay here and be harangued. 'Grief does exhaust me, and it's late,' she said sharply. 'I'll bid you goodnight.' Nodding to the Dowager, she rose and paced out of the room, blocking out whatever response the Dowager might have made.

A sick hollow in the pit of her stomach, she took the stairs up to her chamber. Having to tolerate her mother-in-law was bad enough—but Lord Randall's presence was much worse.

Had his amorous attentions been inspired by the drunken boredom of an idle evening—or would she now have to watch her back, every minute, in her own home?

A shiver went through her as she reached the dark hallway outside her chamber. Sighing, she stood surveying the stout oak door. Could she obtain a key to double-lock it? One that he could not duplicate?

She was about to unlatch the door when the all-too-familiar smell of strong spirits alerted her to his presence an instant before she recognised Lord Randall's voice, approaching out of the dimness.

'Well, well, if it isn't my sweet little sister-in-law.' Reaching her, he leaned a hand against the doorframe and peered down into her face. 'Looking surprisingly energised after an evening of political discussion. Or is it some politician you're lusting after, now that Edward isn't here to keep your depths well plumbed?'

Outraged by his crudeness, she remained silent, staring at his hand on her doorframe. After a moment, he removed it.

'What are *you* doing outside my room?' she said at last.

'Didn't our esteemed mother tell you? I live here now. When I confessed my current...pecuniary difficulties, dear Mama insisted I should become your houseguest, for as long as needful.' He laughed. 'And with Mama footing the bills that should be a long time indeed.'

'The estate footing the bills, you mean. Edward would never have permitted it!'

'True, but he's not here, is he? Might be a little dab of a thing, but you were never a hypocrite, so you'll not convince me you're sorry about that. Still, I shouldn't object to our giving each other a little comfort in our bereavement.'

He leaned towards her, the liquor fumes threatening to make her gag. 'Life with two widows should be far too dull for your taste,' she said, stepping back. 'Why not move in with one of your doxies?'

He rubbed thumb and fingers together. 'Takes the ready to support those doxies, m'dear sis. Which I'm alarming short of at the moment.'

'More gaming losses?' she said derisively.

'Lady Luck's as unfriendly as you are at the moment. Maybe you should give me a kiss, to console me for my losses.'

'Have you no sense of decency at all? Speaking like this to your own brother's widow?'

He shrugged. 'Never any love lost between us. Had the same inclinations, so why must he be the heir, and the one with the deep pockets to fund them? Besides, I know he wasn't giving you as much of it as a lusty young woman needs. While I wait for something better to happen along, I'm happy to fill the empty well.'

'You disgust me!'

He merely laughed. 'Maybe. But I could also pleasure you. Suckle those sweet little breasts, taste that—'

Revolted, she slapped his face as hard as she could. 'Get out of my sight!'

He stumbled from the force of the blow before righting himself, rubbing the cheek she'd struck. 'My, what a little wildcat you are. Didn't know you had it in you! But that will make taming you all the sweeter. Maybe not tonight. But soon. And afterwards, you might find yourself begging me for more.'

'You might remember that I have a pistol, and know how to use it,' she retorted. Pushing past him, she went into her room and closed the door. To her infinite relief, he did not try to follow her.

This time.

With trembling hands, she turned the latch. At the sound of the lock clicking into place, Lord Randall laughed. 'Sleep well, sweet sister,' he called through the thick wooden panel.

Faith leaned against it, her heart pounding, furious—but worried. Would he try something, or was he just playing with her, the tomcat toying with the defenceless mouse? What if he were able to get into her chamber in the middle of the night, while she was sleeping and unaware?

She would shoot him in a minute with no regrets. But if he chose to, could he force himself on her before she could defend herself?

Why this, just when life finally seemed to be offering her alluring new possibilities? Tears threatened, and angrily she brushed them away.

She'd have to think of something. She was done being the pawn of some idle aristocrat who thought his position entitled him to take whatever he wanted.

And she'd rather shoot *herself* than let that slimy ferret have his way with her.

Chapter Six

In the morning three days later, having overruled the protests of the boys' tutor about his charges missing their lessons, Faith went up to the schoolroom to fetch her sons for the journey to visit her sister. The carriage was ready; Davie was walking his horse in the mews, waiting on them, and the boys were almost as excited as she was to be meeting their cousins for the first time since the birth of five-year-old Colin, her youngest.

For today, at least, she could put out of mind the unpleasant fact that her brother-in-law was now in residence, a worry that seldom was far from her mind. Though, as yet, Lord Randall had provided no reinforcement for her fears. As far as she could tell, he'd been absent from the house since she'd encountered him that first night.

She suspected that his mama had provided him with funds, which he was happily occupied in spending on women, spirits, and games of chance. Since in that case, he'd probably not return to Berkeley Square until he ran out of blunt, she sincerely hoped his luck would hold.

'Will there be a pond, and horses?' seven-year-old Matthew asked when she entered the schoolroom.

'Dogs? Trees?' Colin piped up, pulling away from the nursery maid who'd helped him into his jacket, and running over to her.

'I don't know about a pond,' she said, ruffling his blond curls, 'but there will certainly be trees, horses and dogs. Probably ponies, too, which the grooms might help you ride while I visit with your aunt Sarah. The older boys will probably be with their tutor, but your younger cousins will be able to show you about.'

'I should not like to be helped by a common groom,' eight-year-old Edward said, standing with his arms crossed.

'One should never refuse the help of an expert, even if he is a commoner,' Faith replied. 'If we'd spent more time in the country, Edward, you would already be a proficient rider, with your own pony. I hope soon, we will go to Ashedon Court, and you may begin lessons.'

'I want to climb a tree!' Colin announced.

'Mama's climbed lots of trees. I want to be up in the branches, taller than everyone!'

'Looby, Mama is a duchess,' Edward said with an exasperated look. 'She doesn't climb trees.'

'I don't know—I might still be able to manage it,' she replied, a bit disconcerted by her eldest's pronouncements. 'I certainly climbed any number while I was growing up. We shall see about that later today, Colin. Now, into the carriage, boys. Mary, bring their extra things.'

Excitement rising higher, Faith helped the nursery maid usher the boys from the room. Though she was disappointed to learn from his note that Davie planned to ride escort, she could understand why he'd not want to be confined for several hours in a carriage with three active boys. He'd keep pace at her window, his missive said; they would be able to chat.

But not touch, her frustrated senses knew. Although she was thrilled to be taking her sons to meet the family they hadn't seen in so long, having them with her meant that she would have no time alone with Davie.

Which might be a good thing, she acknowledged as she descended the stairs behind her sons, the younger two whooping as they chased each other. She was still undecided on what to do about this…

passionate connection between them. It would be a good deal safer to content herself merely with a revival of the camaraderie they'd shared long ago.

In truth, Davie's unfailing good humour, intelligent conversation, and supportive concern were so many miles beyond what she'd experienced in these last meagre years of isolation, despite the frustration of her senses, she felt blessed enough to have that.

'Mary, take Colin's hand and help him avoid the puddles,' Faith instructed as they caught up with the boys and exited the back stairs into the garden. Reaching over to snag Matthew's, she added, 'I'd at least like to begin the journey with the boys not all-over mud.'

But puddles and mud and boisterous boys fled from her mind as they walked out the gate to the mews where the carriage waited—and she saw Davie, dismounted beside his horse.

He was dressed for riding in breeches, jacket and boots, a simple neckcloth knotted at his throat and a modest-sized beaver hat on his head. The coat sat easily across his broad shoulders, the breeches loose-fitting enough that they suggested, rather than outlined, his powerful thighs. Neither garment was fashionably tight enough to have required the efforts of a valet to force him into them, and for a naughty instant, she regretted his body was not encased in garments that would have more closely outlined his form.

Then he was bowing before her, smiling. Her hands itched to brush the dark hair off his forehead as he straightened, and for a moment she allowed herself to focus on nothing but the steady warmth of those blue, blue eyes.

'Even the weather smiled on you today, Duchess,' he said. 'I was afraid we might have to journey in the pouring rain, which would have made conversation impossible.'

'Then I am glad, too, for the fair weather. But let me make you known to my boys. Mr Smith, may I present Colin Evers, Matthew Evers, and my eldest, Edward, now Duke of Ashedon. Boys, this is Mr Smith, a Member of Parliament for Hazelwick. He graciously agreed to escort us today since he has matters of government business to discuss with your Uncle Nicholas.'

After the men large and small made their bows and exchanged greetings, Edward said, 'You have no title, Mr Smith?'

'No, Your Grace,' Davie replied.

Edward looked over to his mother. 'Carlisle says that a duke and duchess should travel with outriders. Not a simple "mister".'

Faith frowned, not pleased with the pattern of her eldest's comments this morning. She suspected that his tutor, almost as toplofty in his opinions as the Dowager, must have stepped up his efforts to instil in the boy a sense of the consequence due his position, now that he was the Duke. Quite prematurely, in her opinion.

'Perhaps, during Tudor times, when the whole court went on progress, there were outriders and equerries,' she replied. 'But not for a simple visit to your uncle's house, a short drive out of London.'

'Can we go now, Mama?' Matthew said. 'I want to see the horses and dogs and ponies.

'Up with you, lads,' Davie said, helping Matt and Colin to clamber into the carriage, his good humour seeming not at all affected by Edward's slighting remark. Her annoyance with her son, his tutor, and her intentions to challenge the man faded as Davie stepped over to assist her.

Pushing all problems aside, she let herself savour the pleasure of his one hand on her arm, the other pressed against her back to steady her as she mounted the steps. She had a sudden notion to lose her balance, so he might catch her in his arms.

She was seated, regretting the loss of his touch, before her mind wrenched control back from her senses. *Behave yourself,* it reproved. *You're a mother of three, not a silly, swooning girl—or a doxy on the stage.*

Her cheeks burning as she acknowledged the truth of that assessment, she nonetheless couldn't keep her gaze from veering back to Davie, as, with an easy grace, he threw himself up into the saddle. Then the coachman snapped his whip, and they set off.

The narrow streets and congestion of the city prevented Davie's riding beside her window until they'd reached more open country. While her boys crowded the windows, pelting him with questions, Davie pointed out pastures, woods, grazing cows, inn signs and, once, the excitement of a mail coach passing with a blare from its horn. Even Edward relaxed his demeanour, becoming once again an eight-year-old excited by an excursion into the country, rather than a peer preparing to don his ducal coronet.

Fortunately, before Davie tired of their barrage, the carriage turned off the main road and headed down a drive that led to a red-brick manor house set at a distance in a pretty park. The drive threaded around old trees and crossed a rushing brook before passing a stable block and approaching a handsome porticoed entrance.

'Would you ask the coachman to stop here?'

Faith called to Davie. 'I'd like the boys to stretch their legs before trooping into the house, and I could do with a short walk myself.'

Davie passing on her request, the coach halted. 'Can we visit the stables, Mama?'

'Will the dogs be out?'

'Can our cousins take us to fish?' the three boys' questions overlapped as they jumped down.

'To the house, first, boys,' she replied. 'You must greet your aunt properly before you go haring off across the property.'

With a collective sigh, the boys fell in line, Colin skipping as he followed his older brothers. Faith slowed to relish the feel of her hand in Davie's as he helped her down, then began walking beside him. 'I'm sorry about Edward's impertinence,' she murmured.

Davie waved a disparaging hand. 'He's just a boy, and mimicking what he hears, I suspect.'

'Yes, I believe it's his tutor's influence. Carlisle has a starched-up sense of consequence which my late husband appreciated, and I don't. I would wish my poor son the freedom to be a boy before he has to shoulder all the responsibilities of a duke. Which I would like him to shoulder responsibly, without the toplofty sense of superiority his father and uncle possess.'

'If you don't like the tutor, dismiss him.'

Faith halted, surprised. 'Can I do that? Would the trustees allow it?'

'Find a respectable replacement and notify them. If they do object, you can always apologise and promise not to exceed your authority in future.' He grinned. 'Ask forgiveness, rather than permission; that's always been my motto. In the meantime, you'll be rid of an employee who doesn't please you.'

'Perhaps I shall,' she said, cheered by the idea of dispensing with the impediment Carlisle had become. 'But I don't have any idea how to find a replacement.'

'Ask Englemere, or your sister. Surely they've engaged several tutors for their sons over the years.'

By then, they'd reached the entry steps, the butler holding open the front door to admit them. Before Faith finished handing over her wrap to the butler, her sister Sarah came hurrying out.

'Faith! My darling Faith! I'm so delighted to see you! And your sons—my, how they've grown. Come give your Aunt Sarah a hug, boys!'

As she knelt down, her smile warm and her arms open, the boys scampered over like eager puppies, even Edward unbending to accept her embrace.

She rose, leaving her arms loosely around the

shoulders of the two youngest. 'Mr Smith, how kind of you to escort my family here safely. And to bring out those committee reports, sparing my husband one day's ride in and out of London. We both very much appreciate it.'

'It was my privilege. Your princess is doing better, I hope?' Davie said.

'Yes, Lizzie seems much improved this last week. With it being so sunny today, I may even let her go outside with her cousins—I've given them all a holiday from their lessons, in honour of your visit. Cook made some special jam tarts, too. Once you boys have had some tea in the nursery, you can go outside.'

'To see the horses?' Matthew asked.

'Horses, ponies, dogs. I think we have some hoops and sticks in the stables, too. A pond with frogs, or you might drop a line in it.'

'Fishing?' Edward said, his eyes brightening.

'Whatever you wish,' Sarah replied. 'It's not often that my nephews visit. Now that you know the way, I hope you'll come back.'

'Me, too,' Colin said. 'I love tarts!'

'We will come back, won't we, Mama?' Matthew asked.

'Yes. Yes, we will,' Faith replied, meeting her sister's questioning regard, a wave of warmth and affection sweeping over her. This was *her* family, the older sister who'd been more mother than sister to her, whose children she barely knew. Freed from the shadow of her disapproving husband, she intended to rectify that error.

'I'll leave you to your family party,' Davie said. 'Though I will regret missing those jam tarts! Is Englemere in the library?'

'Yes, I'll have Wendover show you the way. And don't worry, I'll have some of those tarts sent in for your tea, too.'

'Thank heavens! You're an angel, Lady Englemere. Duchess.' Giving Faith a nod and a little wink, Davie walked down the hallway after the butler.

Faith stared after him as he disappeared. The pang at the loss of his company was eased by a growing sense of warmth and well-being—the feeling of coming home again, she realised with a little shock.

She looked back to see her sister watching her watching Davie. Colouring a little, she turned to her sons. 'Shall we go up to the nursery and meet your cousins?'

'Yes, yes,' the boys chorused as, laughing, Sarah took each of the younger ones by the hand. 'Follow me, then.'

'You must tell me how they are doing,' Faith said as they climbed the stairs. 'Aubrey, Charles and Nicholas will be studying with their tutor, since you chose not to send any of the boys to Eton. And Elizabeth is still with Nurse, recovering?'

'Yes, I've kept Elizabeth away from her brothers, so she's not tempted to exert herself too much yet, though as I told Mr Smith, she is much better. Charles and Nicholas are very much anticipating taking a holiday from study today with your boys, but Aubrey isn't with us; he left for Oxford earlier this year.'

'Oxford?' Faith exclaimed in shock. 'Impossible! He can't be old enough yet!'

'He's turned seventeen,' Sarah said, a mingling of pride and sadness on her face. 'A young man now, off preparing himself to enter a man's world. I miss him dreadfully. Charles is fifteen, and even little Nicholas is now seven. My babies are growing up!'

Faith shuddered. 'I'm happy my eldest is only eight!'

The party reached the schoolroom, where Sarah's sons bounded out to meet them. As the sisters reintroduced the cousins to each other, Edward gravitated towards the oldest of his counterparts. 'Do you have a tutor?' he asked Charles.

'I do, although Mama and Papa read with us, too,' the boy replied, then halted, dismay on his face. 'I'm so sorry—Mama told me you lost your papa this year. You must miss him awfully.'

Edward shrugged. 'I never saw him much.'

Charles's eyes widened. 'Did you not? How unlucky! I get to see mine every day, unless he must stay overnight in London for a meeting. I suppose your papa travelled a lot.'

'I guess,' Edward answered vaguely.

Regret, anger and anguish stirred in Faith's gut. How long would she be able to shield Edward before he discovered just what sort of 'travelling' had led to his father's premature demise?

After a concerned glance at Faith's face, Sarah said quickly, 'Boys, I've sent for your tea to be brought up—'

'With jam tarts, Mama?' Nicholas interrupted.

'Yes, with jam tarts.' While he and his brother Charles cheered, she continued, 'After tea, you must take your cousins to the fishing pond and the stable. I think all the boys would like to take a turn on your ponies.'

'That would be beyond everything wonderful, Aunt Sarah!' Matthew cried.

'I would like to see that fishing pond,' Edward admitted.

'You boys enjoy yourselves, while your mama and I have a comfortable coze.' Sarah leaned over to give her two sons a kiss. 'Don't let them break anything important, like an arm or a leg.'

'Nothing bigger than a finger, Mama,' Charles promised with a grin.

Leaving the boys in the schoolroom with the nursery maids, Sarah led Faith to her private sitting room. 'We'll have our tea here, and catch up.'

'Oh, Sarah, it is so good to see you and the children again! I am sorry I stayed away so long.'

'So am I. I did call on you several times in those early years, when Nicholas was in London for Parliament. I was always told you were "unavailable". Which I know was on Ashedon's instructions, not yours.'

'"Unavailable"?' Faith cried. 'You truly came to the house, and were turned away? That's—that's incredible!' She seized her sister's hand. 'I'm so sorry! And, no, it was certainly not on my instructions. I would never have been too busy to see you!'

Sarah squeezed her hand before releasing it. 'I thought as much. I wasn't angry, just sad, and worried about Ashedon exerting so much control over your life—just as I'd feared he would.'

'He'd certainly discouraged me from contacting

any of my family. How like him to make sure that dictate was enforced, by forbidding the staff to let me know you'd called,' Faith said bitterly. 'And how gracious you are, not reminding me that you'd strongly advised me not to marry him.'

Sarah gave her a sympathetic look. 'It's hard to dissuade a girl as much in love as you were.'

'A girl too stupid to recognise the truth when her sister told it to her.'

Sarah waved a disparaging hand. 'Not stupid at all! Even I, who was suspicious of his intentions, had to admit his display of affection was convincing. For your sake, I'd hoped it was genuine. But from what I knew of his character, I suspected it was not.'

'He got exactly what he wanted—a girl so bedazzled she tried to anticipate his every desire, a girl too meek and obliging to resist him even long after she realised he'd only married her to get a well-bred brood mare to produce his children, one spineless enough not to create scenes or tax him about his affairs.'

Sarah gave her a hug. 'You are too hard on yourself. You offered him the love and warmth and sense of joy you radiate to everyone around you. It was his loss that he did not appreciate such a gift.'

'Well, enough about the sorry past. We're seeing

each other again, and I intend that we shall continue to. Bad enough I didn't begin until it was too late for my boys to know Aubrey; I want to make sure the rest of the cousins can become as close as we siblings were, growing up.'

'I should love that, too! So, what do you intend to do with yourself, now that you no longer have to please a husband? You...haven't given a thought to remarriage yet, have you?'

Recognising that as a subtle enquiry about her relationship with Davie, Faith felt her face flush. 'Having just got out of one highly unsatisfactory marriage, I'm not sure I ever want to risk the institution again. I doubt that my powers of discernment are much better now than they were at seventeen. How could I trust that a man valued me for myself, and not for my wealth and position? And even if I could trust his affection—' in her mind's eye, she saw Davie's face '—how could I trust that it would endure, once he spent as much time with me as a husband would?' She shook her head. 'I think I would do better to content myself with mothering my boys.'

And what of passion? her senses demanded. She pushed the question away, not ready to make a decision about that yet.

'Nicholas told me that you'd attended a dinner

at Lord Witlow's,' Sarah's voice recalled her. 'And seemed to enjoy discussing politics. Don't I remember you used to discuss that, and all manner of things, with Mr Smith?' She laughed. 'For six months after the summer you spent with Cousin Joanna, I heard nothing but "Mr Smith thinks this" and "Mr Smith said that".' She pinned Faith with her frankly assessing gaze. 'You seem to have resumed your friendship.'

'Yes,' Faith replied. 'But don't give me that *look*. I've already said I have no interest in remarriage; even if I did, I know that Mr Smith, despite his rise in politics, wouldn't be considered suitable. But surely now I am free to choose whatever *friends* I like! And friendship is all I'm interested in.'

And maybe something warmer than friendship? the sharp voice of honesty added.

'You can't fault me for wishing, after all the unhappy years you spent, that you might find the same happiness I have with Nicholas,' Sarah protested. 'But as long as you are getting out, mingling with friends and engaging in activities you enjoy, I shall be content.'

'As long as I can do that, and spend time with the dear family I have been estranged from for too long, I shall be content, too,' Faith replied.

'Speaking of family, shall we go see what the boys are up to?'

Comforted and encouraged by their talk, Faith rose. 'Yes, let's join the children.' Arm in arm, they descended from Sarah's salon to the terrace and down the gravel path to the tree-bordered garden.

They encountered the boys, a pack of dogs running and barking around them, as soon as they turned the corner at the edge of the walled kitchen garden—all except Colin. A spurt of alarm zipping through her, before she could ask Charles what had become of her youngest, she spotted him, proudly perched on the first branch of a nearby oak tree. 'Mama, look!' he called. 'I can do it! Charles only had to help me a little. I'm taller than everyone!'

'So you are. Bravo!' she replied, smiling with fond affection at her fearless, adventuresome son.

'Can you climb up, too, Mama? There's room.' He patted a place on the limb beside him.

'Since this is a day for finding my roots again,' she said, grinning at Sarah, 'maybe I should.'

'Oh, Mama, don't be silly,' Edward said.

Irritated at his dismissive tone, she turned to him. The look of distaste on his face, the disparagement of his tone, made him seem the image of his late father—who'd been so unappreciative of who she was, who'd tried in every way to squelch the freeness of spirit she was finally rediscovering, or smother it by forcing her always into company with those just as disapproving.

Sudden fury filled her. Before she knew what she intended, she'd marched to the base of the tree, kicked off her slippers, and reached up to grasp the lowest branch. After examining the trunk to find the best toe-holds, she steadied her grip, swung herself up and dug her feet into the furrowed trunk.

While the boys whooped and clapped, Colin laughed in glee and Edward looked on, astonished, as she managed to pull, push and shimmy herself several feet up the trunk, where she eased to a resting position on the branch beside her son. A beaming Colin scooted over to give her a fierce hug. 'You're the bestest mama ever!'

'It appears I still have the knack!' she announced, hugging him back.

'So it does.'

Shocked at the sound of Davie's voice, Faith twisted, nearly losing her balance. She felt her cheeks flush as she watched him and Englemere stroll into the garden, suddenly aware of the dirt on her hands, what would doubtless prove to be stains on her skirts—and the fact that her climb had ruched up those skirts so she was now displaying a very indecorous amount of ankle and leg.

'Well and truly caught, my dear sister-in-law,' Nicky said, coming over to wrap an arm around his wife.

'You do climb as well as you did as a girl,' Sarah said, laughing.

'Not quite,' she replied, still embarrassed. But as she saw Davie's gaze trace her leg from the stockinged toes to the curve of her calf, heat of a different sort washed through her. Suddenly breathless, she said, 'It—it was much easier to climb in breeches. I'm not sure how I shall get down without creating a spectacle.'

'Let me help.' Davie walked over to the tree and stationed himself below her. Raising his arms, he said, 'Lean down a little, and give me your hands. I'll have you safely on the ground in a trice.'

Looking down, she was surprised to realise he was indeed tall enough that she needed to stretch down only a small distance to reach his extended hands.

'Slide forward off the branch,' he coached. 'I won't let you come to any harm.'

'I know you won't.' She leaned forward and placed her hands in his.

'I have you now. You can push off.'

And he did have her. She couldn't take her eyes from the face, confident, slightly smiling, that gazed up at her encouragingly. He tightened his grip, pulled, and then she was falling, falling into the void—and into his arms.

He cushioned her descent, letting her slide down his strong, solid body until her feet touched the ground, and then steadied her, his eyes never leaving her face.

She stared up at him, suddenly unable to draw a breath, the memories racing back. He'd rescued her once before, when in the gathering darkness of a summer evening long ago, she'd misjudged her descent from the tree in cousin Joanna's back garden where she'd been reading to him, and slipped. Waiting below, he'd caught her and eased her to the ground, bracing her until she found her footing.

And then, as a spangle of stars sparkled over them, he'd leaned down and kissed her.

From the sudden tightness of his grip, the blaze of heat in his eyes, she knew he was remembering it, too. The babble of the children's voices, the gambolling dogs, the presence of her sister and brother-in-law watching them—all of it faded, until she could feel only the energy pulsing between them, see only his rapt gaze focused on her face, her lips.

With every fibre of her being she yearned for

him to kiss her again. Even though she knew it was impossible.

He must have concluded that, too, for he stepped back and pushed her away, breaking the spell. 'Safe on the ground again,' he said gruffly.

On the ground again, perhaps, she thought. But not at all safe.

'How about you, young lad?' Davie called up to Colin. 'Are you ready to hop down?'

'Will you catch me, like you did Mama?'

'Of course.'

'Here I come!' With that, Colin launched himself from the branch.

Davie caught him easily, then swung the boy round and round while he shrieked with glee, before setting him on his feet again.

'I love climbing trees! Will you bring us again tomorrow?'

Oh, how I would love that! Faith thought. 'I'm afraid Mr Smith has to work, Colin.'

'Climbing trees would be heaps more fun,' the boy coaxed.

Davie laughed. 'You must know the committee members I have to deal with.'

'All right, boys, back to the house,' Sarah ordered. At the sighs and protests of dismay, she added, 'Did I mention that Cook might have an additional treat waiting in the nursery?'

'More jam tarts?' Matthew exclaimed. 'Bet I beat you there, Nicholas!' With that, he took off running, the other boys pelting behind him.

'Did your discussions go well?' Sarah asked, turning to the gentlemen.

'I think we're getting ever closer to a compromise Englemere will be able to persuade his colleagues to accept,' Davie said.

'That's excellent news!' Sarah exclaimed.

'We'll take up the work again when I ride in tomorrow,' Englemere said. 'Thank you again for bringing out the latest documents, so I might be prepared, Mr Smith.'

'It was my pleasure.'

'And mine,' Faith said. 'Let me add my thanks, for allowing us to accompany you. It was so wonderful to spend time with my family again!'

'You must visit them often,' Davie advised.

Every day, if I could claim your escort, Faith thought.

'Shall we join the children back at the house?' Englemere said. 'Much as I hate to break up the party, it's probably time to call for your carriage, if you are to return to London for the boys' supper.'

'I should do some additional work on those documents before tomorrow, too,' Davie said.

Realising with regret that their interlude together was nearly at an end, Faith recalled Davie's earlier advice. 'Nicky, Sarah, could I ask your help?' she said, taking her sister's arm. 'I've never got on well with the tutor Ashedon engaged for the boys. Then, since Ashedon's death, he seems to be trying to instil in Edward an excessive concern for his own consequence. Though I am sure the Dowager encourages him, I cannot like it.'

'You must have someone who agrees with your ideas for the boys' education,' Englemere said. 'Edward has plenty of time to develop a sense of what is owed to him as a duke. Shall I make enquiries and send you some recommendations?'

'That would be wonderful! I'd like to give the current tutor his notice immediately.'

'Then do so,' Englemere said. 'Edward's only eight; he'll not suffer any permanent damage from missing a few lessons while you look for someone who will suit you better.'

'Thank you!' *And you, too, Davie, for encouraging me*, she thought, giving him a grateful nod.

All too soon, they had collected the boys, who begged to be allowed to walk down to the stables to meet the coach before being confined again for the journey back to London. Bidding her sister's family goodbye with vows to visit again soon, Faith and Davie set off behind the boys for the short stroll to the stables.

'You have a fine horse, Mr Smith,' Matthew said as they walked. 'Did a groom teach you to ride?'

Davie laughed. 'No, I grew up on a farm, my first mount a gentle old plough-horse.'

'A farm?' Colin said. 'With trees and horses and dogs?'

'And fields and chickens and goats and ducks and pigs, too.'

'You could ride and fish every day?' Matthew said, awe in his voice. 'That must have been wonderful!'

'There was a lot of ploughing and weeding and milking and feeding stock, too, along with the riding and fishing,' Davie told him. 'But it *was* wonderful—for a time. When I was still young, there were bad harvests, and my family lost the farm. My parents went into the city to work in a factory, and were killed in an accident.'

'How awful for you!' exclaimed Faith. Though she knew Davie had been orphaned, he'd never before mentioned the circumstances.

'The tragedy did allow me to get back to the

country. An older widow took me in to help her with her cottage and the farm work.'

'Where Mr Smith later encountered Sir Edward, who was so impressed by his abilities that he sponsored him at Oxford and, with your Uncle Nicholas, supported him to become a Member of Parliament. He now has a very important role in the governing of England,' Faith told the boys.

'Do you not have any land?' Edward asked, frowning. 'My tutor said every gentleman must own land.'

Before Faith, once again annoyed at Carlisle's officious teaching, could rebuke her son for his implied criticism, Davie said, 'I didn't for many years, Ashedon. But I was recently able to buy back from Sir Edward the farm my parents used to own.'

'So you have a farm, too?' Matthew said. 'Can we visit it?'

'Some day, if you like,' Davie replied, giving Faith a wink to forestall her objections. 'It's rather far away, though.'

'Do you have horses and trees and dogs?' Colin asked.

'Yes. In fact, the horse I'm riding today was bred there. A tenant manages the land for me, since I spend most of the year in London, working on government business.'

'I'm sorry you don't have a title,' Edward said. 'But I s'pose it's all right, if you own some land.'

They'd reached the stables by then, the boys running off to have one last look at the horses before being corralled into the carriage for the journey home. Turning to Faith, Davie said with a smile, 'I think I've just been accorded the ducal approval.'

'Please, don't encourage him!' Faith said with a groan. 'I'm going to give Carlisle his notice tonight! I shall do everything I can to make sure Edward doesn't grow up to be a replica of his father.' Looking up into Davie's strong, kind, handsome face, she added softly, 'I shall try to help him grow up to be like you. Compassionate towards his fellow man—those of his own rank, and those who are not. Diligent in his duties to his land and its tenants. Responsibly involved in the governing of his country.'

Davie reddened under her scrutiny. 'I appreciate the compliment, but I certainly don't deserve it. I'm no paragon, Faith. I have just as many flaws and faults as any man.'

'Don't disillusion me by pointing them out,' she said with a smile.

'Carlisle might turn…unpleasant when you dismiss him. Are you sure you want to tackle that now? You could wait until Englemere finds you a replacement.'

'It won't be any easier then. I'm not always a meek little mushroom! I can be hard, even top-lofty, if the reason to be so is compelling enough. No matter how unpleasant the interview, knowing Carlisle will be gone at the end of it will make the experience worth it!'

'How fierce you are,' he teased.

'Fiercer than you might expect,' she tossed back. 'Now, before the boys return and the groom brings out your horse, let me thank you one last time for escorting us today.'

'You seem to thrive, back with your family, here in the countryside you've always loved. You certainly haven't lost your talent for climbing trees!'

'I do sometimes have difficulty climbing down, though.'

'Ah, that's the part I like best. The climbing down.' He stepped closer, close enough for her to feel the heat radiating from his body.

The coachman and grooms were still in the stable with her boys. For this moment, blocked from view by the coach, they were almost…alone.

'I liked the "getting down", too,' Faith said, her throat suddenly so constricted that the words came out in a whisper. The passion that had been simmering beneath the surface all day flared up to envelop her in heat and need. Helpless against his appeal, she closed the distance between them and angled her head up.

For a moment, he hesitated. 'This is madness,' he muttered. But even as she whimpered with frustration and urgency, he cupped her face with his hands and leaned down to kiss her.

His touch was gentle, tender, his lips tracing hers almost with reverence, the contact so sweet, she felt the burn of tears. But then, as she clutched at his coat, he coaxed her lips to part and delved inside.

She gasped as his tongue found hers, laved and stroked at first lightly, then with increasing force. Desire flaming hotter, she brought her hands up to clasp his neck, urging the kiss harder, deeper.

He tasted like tea, with a sweet echo of jam. She couldn't get enough of the strength of his body against hers, the tender hold of his fingers on her face such a contrast to the fierceness with which he was devouring her mouth. She wanted more, closer—

And then he was stepping back, thrusting her away, keeping her at arm's length when she would have closed the distance between them again. Only then, her senses swirling in a vortex of desire, did she hear it—the gruff tones of the grooms in counterpoint to the soprano of her sons' voices, the whinny of the team being led to the traces.

Davie cleared his throat. 'Shall I assist you into the coach, Duchess?' he said loudly, his voice a little ragged. Not meeting her glance, he thrust out his arm for her to take and led her to the door, which one of the grooms trotted over to open.

Still beyond speech, she could only look back mutely at him as the groom took her hand from Davie and helped her up the steps. Then, before she could recover, he turned to accept his horse's reins from another groom, and swung himself into the saddle.

'I'll ride ahead for a while,' he told her over the giggles and chatter of her sons as they climbed up, agile as monkeys. 'I feel the need of a good gallop.' Giving her a nod, he put spurs to his mount and set off.

Her heartbeat only now beginning to slow, Faith watched him ride away. How she, too, would have appreciated the freedom of breeches and the possibility of a hard gallop, with a sharp wind to cool passion's fire and clear the fog of lust from her brain!

She hoped he wouldn't regret the kiss, for she certainly did not.

No, it had not been prudent; had they been caught, explaining it away would have been difficult, and she would place no reliance at all on the willingness of Ashedon's servants, whose master had for years provided them with so much delicious fodder for gossip, to refrain from whispering about it.

But all she could think about was how wonderful it had been. And how, in a more discreet place and time, she could induce him to repeat it.

Chapter Seven

Idiot, idiot, idiot. The words echoed in Davie's head with the cadence of hoofbeats as he pressed his mount hard.

Fiercely as he repeated to himself all the reasons why his rash act in kissing Faith was regrettable, he couldn't make himself feel sorry.

Not being sorry didn't mean he didn't recognise that he absolutely could not repeat such recklessness. He'd been given a trust in escorting her, offering his guarantee in turn to care for her and keep her safe. And then, he'd risked that very safety and reputation because, with opportunity and, admittedly, her encouragement, he hadn't been able to control himself.

He'd told her he had the same failings as any man. He was only human, and a man could stand only so much temptation. But was he a man of honour, or a cad, to indulge himself in brief carnal satisfaction at the cost of her good name?

It was more than lust, his heart rebuked. How could he have resisted, when the girl he'd loved for so many years turned her angelic face up, inviting his kiss? He could no more have refused that invitation than he could stop himself from breathing.

So he'd better learn to hold his breath. Or not see her again.

Everything within him revolted in furious denial at that alternative. He would be better, his senses coaxed his implacable sense of honour.

For Giles was right. The family of so rich and high-ranking a widow, still so young and beautiful—and perhaps the lady herself—would be formulating plans for her future, once a decent period of mourning was over. Plans that sooner rather than later would sweep her out of his orbit again.

He had one brief, precious chance to enjoy her company. He wanted to soak up every minute before it was no longer possible.

Could he trust himself?

He would have to do better. Because he had to see her. He wouldn't squander this only-once-more-in-this-lifetime opportunity to be with her.

Freshly resolved, he rode back to the coach.

With no real possibility of private chat, any awkwardness between them soon dissipated. Daylight was fast fading, allowing him to point out to the boys scenes they'd observed on the drive out, but in a different aspect. Torches burned outside inn entrances, casting their flickering light on the roads; the carts of merchants unloading the day's remains of goods impeded travel, while other business owners were closing and latching the shutters on their shops. Boisterous voices rang out from the taverns they passed, townspeople and farmers stopping at the end of the day for a convivial round of ale before travelling home.

All too soon, their little caravan reached the mews behind Berkeley Square.

While he dismounted, one of the grooms ran in to summon the nursery maid, who hurried out to lift the sleeping Colin off his mother's lap.

Matthew bounded over to shake his hand. 'Thank you ever so much, Mr Smith, for taking us to Aunt Sarah's! You will take us again soon, won't you? And maybe to visit your farm?'

'That will depend on your mama, but I will if I can,' he said, smiling at the eager boy.

Edward also lingered, waiting his turn to shake Davie's hand. 'Thank you, Mr Smith. And I'm sorry for what I said earlier. You were a very good escort, and so I shall tell Carlisle.'

'A handsome admission, Ashedon,' Davie said, his lips twitching as he masked his amusement at the boy's serious manner. The child certainly did need a tutor who could encourage a bit more liveliness in him.

And then Faith stood before him, looking up at him gravely. Staring into her beautiful blue eyes, words failed, and everything within him turned to yearning.

He gritted his teeth to stifle it, sternly reminding himself of his pledge.

'A marvellous day at Sarah's,' she said. 'And an even more marvellous ending to it.'

'The ending was marvellous,' he replied, glad she was addressing the matter so openly. 'But it can't happen again. You know that, Faith! It's much too dangerous. How can I pledge to protect you, and then put you at risk of falling victim to the worst sort of gossip and conjecture? Haven't you suffered enough of that at Ashedon's hands?'

She shuddered, and he knew his words had struck home. 'Yes, but it wasn't like that, Davie! Not like his...amusements.'

'Maybe not. But society wouldn't see it any differently.'

'That's so unfair,' she said softly.

'That he might "amuse" himself as he chose, but you must be circumspect? Unfair, certainly, but the way of the world. And remember, even Ashedon, for all his high rank, ended up forfeiting his reputation for his actions.'

'I suppose you're right,' she agreed with obvious regret before her eyes widened, her expression turning alarmed. 'You aren't going to tell me that you won't see me again, are you?'

'I probably ought to…but I can't,' he admitted. 'I will tell you that I intend to do much better. I couldn't live with myself if, through my own weakness, I endangered your reputation, or generated the slightest bit of gossip about you. Perhaps it would be best if we met only at Lady Lyndlington's.'

'Or in the company of my sons? They all like you so much, even Edward! I know they would enjoy it immensely if you could accompany us to the park, or on an outing—I intend there to be many, once I get rid of Carlisle! Of course, I know you are busy, so it's presumptuous of me to assume—'

'No, I enjoyed spending time with them, too, and would like to spend more.'

'Family time. That will be…safe, won't it, Davie? Now that we have met again, it would be very hard for me to give up a friendship that, despite our... indiscretion, our outing today showed how much I've missed.'

'Family time,' he repeated. 'Friendship. Yes, I can agree to that.'

She gave him that beautiful Faith smile, the one that seemed lit from within and warmed him to his toes, as if he stood before a blazing hearth.

'Good. So...I'll see you at Lady Lyndlington's? I got a note today, inviting me to another dinner later this week. You will be there?'

'Thursday? Then, yes,' he said when she nodded.

With a moue of distaste, she said, 'Unfortunately, I must go in. Thank you again, Davie. For taking me back where I belong, to what I should never have left. After today, I can just begin to see my way back to my family. To who I truly am.'

How he wished there might be a place for him in that life! 'In the country, climbing trees,' he teased to ease the ache in his heart.

'Especially climbing trees. Maybe we can even get my far-too-pompous Edward up in one.'

'He's still so young. Take away the pompous tutor, and you'll likely see a change.'

'I hope so. Well—again, thank you, and goodbye.'

'Goodbye, Duchess.'

Holding the reins of his horse, Davie lingered, watching her until she was lost from sight beyond the wall into the garden. Then, sighing, he remounted his gelding and nudged him to a trot.

Could they remain friends this time, as they had failed to do when she married Ashedon?

Probably not. When she wed again, which she surely would—much as it stabbed his heart like a dagger to think of it—he imagined her husband would frown on her friendship with another man.

Unless she married a political figure.

Which was possible. She was certainly lovely and intelligent enough to make an excellent wife for a man with a government or diplomatic post.

Could he stand remaining just a friend, knowing that some other man could taste the lips he'd tasted tonight, bind against him the softness of her bosom, that delectable warm round of bottom... possess her completely? His arousal, which the gallop had barely dissipated, hardened again.

Unthinkable to turn away from her, and torture to imagine her with another.

But if she were to wed a politician, why not you? an insidious little voice whispered.

Impossible, he answered it. A duchess does not wed a commoner. A man, as her son succinctly put it, without a title or a grand estate.

Maybe not now… He'd already been awarded some profitable government sinecures, whose income had allowed him to purchase back his family's farm and provided a steady source of funds greater than he'd ever expected to earn. If the Reform party swept the next few Parliaments, he might well rise to a Cabinet post, even the Prime Ministership.

Where commoners were often knighted.

A widowed duchess might be able to marry such a man.

Except a young, beautiful widowed duchess wouldn't remain unmarried long enough for him to become a man worthy of her hand.

Uttering an expletive that made his horse shy, Davie set his jaw and headed for the livery. Enough anguishing over impossible alternatives. He'd put it all from his mind, concentrate on going through the dossiers he must discuss tomorrow, and think no more of Faith.

At least, not until next Thursday.

Buoyed by her time with her family and heartened by Englemere's and Davie's support, Faith marched back into the Berkeley Square town house ready to do battle.

She had her first opportunity at dinner. When

the Dowager began to complain again about her visit to the country, Faith interrupted with a reminder that, as her brother-in-law was a marquess, the Dowager surely would not wish her to insult such a high-ranking peer by failing to respond to his invitation. As the Dowager sat, mouth gaping in surprise at being cut off in mid-sentence, with a great deal of satisfaction, Faith added, 'Besides, now that the boys are older, it's time they became better acquainted with their cousins. I intend to visit my sister at Brookhollow Lodge quite frequently.' Then, after calmly sipping her soup, she enquired in a pleasant tone what her mother-in-law had done with herself over the course of the day.

The heady sense of accomplishment she felt after sparring with her husband's mother made her positively relish the interview with Carlisle. Summoning the tutor after dinner, she told him in the same pleasant but firm voice that, much as she appreciated his efforts on behalf of her sons' education, she now wished it to go in a different direction. She would see he was paid the rest of his quarter's salary and be happy to write him a character, but she would very much appreciate it if he could vacate Ashedon House by the end of the following day, as her cousin, the Marquess of Englemere, was sending her a replacement and she wished to have his quarters made ready. Before the stunned and hapless man could stutter out a reply, she nodded graciously, said, 'That will be all,' and waved the footman to usher him out.

The alacrity with which the servant complied told her the tutor hadn't been a favourite with the rest of the staff, either. Probably always puffing off his superior position as an intimate of the new Duke.

Not any longer, she thought. As soon as the sound of their footsteps faded down the hallway, she bounded out of her chair, hugged herself and did a little dance around the room. If she hadn't been afraid she might be overheard, she would have given a whoop of triumph that would have done her sons proud.

After that interview, she capped off the pleasure of the evening by waltzing into the Dowager's sitting room to inform her that, as the country air had made her sleepy, she would not be joining her for tea and cards, but would repair to the library to do some reading. While her husband's mother stared at her as if she had grown two heads, probably wondering if some actress off the stage was impersonating her normally meek and obedient daughter-in-law, she danced to the library to choose a book, startling the butler by ordering a most out-of-the-ordinary celebratory glass of wine.

Now, if she could just master as well the conundrum of what to do about her fascination with Davie...

That being as yet beyond her ability, she settled in with a sigh to enjoy the wine and the novel. Not until she'd read long enough to truly become sleepy did it occur to her that, with Carlisle on his way out, there was no one to countermand her reading a story to her boys.

Energised by the thought, she sprang up, her step only slowing when, at the bong of the mantel clock, she realised it was rather late. Her sons were probably long abed.

At the least, she could look in on them. Picking up a volume of stories, she took the stairs up to the nursery.

Once there, she discovered, as she'd suspected, that the boys were already asleep. As she tiptoed through the room, her spirits soared at the realisation that her days of having to sneak into the nursery were over. She would now direct her sons' education. She would now be fully involved in their lives.

Where would she take them for their first excursion? she wondered as she halted by each bed, smoothing a curl off Matthew's forehead, straightening the covers Colin had tossed aside. To see the antiquities at the British Museum...the menagerie at the Tower?

So many possibilities, and they were still young enough that she would have years to spend with them before she was confronted by the necessity, as Sarah had just been, to send Edward off to Oxford. She intended to savour every moment, reviving those old dreams that, despite her husband's discouragement, she'd never relinquished of having them grow up a close and loving family like her own.

Thinking the day could hardly have been more perfect, she closed the nursery door softly behind her and descended the stairs to her chamber. Humming to herself, she was walking down the hallway towards her own door when the voice emerged from the dimness behind her.

'If you're ready for a cicisbeo, you needn't resort to some low-bred politician. I'm quite ready to accommodate you.'

A shiver of shock, anger, and unease rippled through her as she turned to face Lord Randall. 'Vastly obliging of you, but that so-called "low-bred politician" is a friend of long standing. Which you are not. Goodnight, sir.'

She resumed her walk, but moving with cat-like speed, he slipped in front of her and crowded her up against the wall, one arm raised to prevent her passing him. 'Not now, maybe. But I could be. I could be a very...intimate friend. Show you some things that farmer's whelp could never imagine.'

'Learned in the most expensive brothels in London?' She looked down at his arm blocking her progress. *Never show weakness, never show fear.* 'I believe this conversation is over. You'll remove your arm, please.'

'Of course. After I've had a little taste of this.' Trapping her against the wall, he forced her chin up and kissed her.

Furious, she resisted the tongue pushing at her lips, trying to part them. Though she twisted and turned, she wasn't able to wriggle out of his hold.

Struggling only increased the tightness of the grip that was bruising her arm, so she changed tactics, letting herself go limp instead. He gave a mutter of satisfaction as she raised a hand, as if to stroke him through his trousers, and eased his hold, moving back a fraction to give her access.

It was just enough. With all the strength she could muster, she brought her knee up and slammed it into his groin.

With a howl, he released her and backed away,

clutching himself. 'You little bitch! You're hardly better bred than he is! Daughter of a bankrupt gamester, the only reason you caught a duke was the extravagant dowry Englemere furnished you.'

'I may not be better bred than he is,' she retorted, 'but I'm better bred than you—who would try to seduce your own sister-in-law! I expect you'll remember for some time how I am good with a knee. Don't give me reason to show you how much better I am with a pistol.'

Turning her back on him, she walked into her chamber and slammed the door behind her.

She turned the latch and leaned against it, shaking, but this time Lord Randall stomped off without whispering any further provocations through her door. She hoped his private parts pained him for a week.

How had he known that Davie had escorted them to Sarah's? she wondered—before she recalled the room his mama had assigned him looked out over the back garden, towards the mews. He must have seen them return this afternoon.

She shivered a little, remembering the strength of his grip. After all the experience she had arm-wrestling with her brother Colton growing up, he an adventuresome boy just a year older, she a pest of a tomboy always tagging at his heels, she'd thought she'd be able to break free of dandified Lord Randall.

As her anger faded, the concern engendered by their previous confrontation intensified. It appeared he did not intend to leave her alone. She was still confident of her ability to wing him with a pistol in whatever part of his anatomy she aimed at—assuming she had enough notice of his intent, and her weapon at hand.

She rubbed her fingers over the lock of the latch. Would it be sturdy enough to keep him out—or loud enough, if he forced it, to give her time to react?

He was a bully, and like most bullies, only picked on those he thought weaker than himself. Tonight she'd showed him she wasn't easy prey. Would he slink away and leave her alone now? Or would he, with his overweening sense of masculine superiority, still believe she was easy *enough*? Had her getting back some of her own only angered him and strengthened his resolve to have his way with her?

There wasn't any point complaining about him to his mother. She'd immediately assume Faith had tried to entice her son; if she even bothered to ask him about it, Lord Randall would certainly claim the same.

Maybe she should take the boys and go stay with

Sarah until she could figure out a way to evict Lord Randall. But she'd hardly begun to re-establish her ties with her family. Sarah would think it extremely odd if she were to suddenly appear on her doorstep with her children in tow. Faith wasn't a very good liar, and the idea of confessing what had happened to her was so shameful and mortifying, she knew she couldn't do it. Just thinking about Lord Randall having his hands on her, trying to force his tongue into her mouth, made her feel *soiled.*

There wasn't anywhere else she could go.

She'd not leave Berkeley Square—not yet. Not unless things progressed to the point where she no longer had any confidence that she could protect herself.

Suddenly she was conscious of her stinging lips. Licking them, she tasted the metallic edge of blood, and a noxious mix of tobacco and strong spirits that could only be Lord Randall. Revolted, she rushed to the washbowl on her dressing table, poured in water, dipped a rag in it and gently scrubbed her mouth and lips.

How much different Davie's kiss had been! Tender, gentle, his passion controlled, taking the kiss deeper and harder, but at the pace she invited. His caress made her feel cherished, rather than defiled.

Tears stung her eyes, and angrily she brushed them away. She would not let Lord Randall make her feel like a victim. This was her house, not his. And he would be the one who must leave it.

Even if, as yet, she had no idea how she was going to make that happen.

Chapter Eight

The following Thursday night, Davie stood in front of his glass, knotting his cravat in preparation for walking to dinner at the Lyndlingtons'. He smiled at his image, recalling the scornful predictions of his fellow Hellions that, now that he had income and a position, he would get himself a proper valet and turn into a veritable Macaroni.

'No, my friends,' he'd answered. 'At heart, I will always be a simple farm boy.'

As Faith would always be a duchess.

And there they were.

Sighing, he completed the knot and shrugged into his coat. Those unalterable facts might not have changed, but neither had his resolve to seek out—in a more restricted environment—and enjoy her company for as long as he could.

Which would make the inevitable parting even more wrenching, the voice of prudence warned.

So be it, he answered. *You don't refuse to hang a borrowed Rembrandt in your study just because you can't keep it for ever.*

Catching up his hat and walking stick, he set off. A stroll through the cool night air would calm him, let him distance himself from the complex and tedious business of managing the reform legislation and concentrate instead on the anticipation of spending time with Faith.

Giles was in the drawing room to greet him when he arrived, once again unfashionably early. Handing him a glass of wine, he said, 'Did I mention this was to be mostly a family party? Maggie's father, Lord Witlow, and her great-aunt, the Dowager Countess of Sayleford, are coming—and also Ben and Christopher.'

Davie stifled a groan. 'The very friends who have most strenuously urged me to forget "the Unattainable". Do they know I've been seeing her again?'

'Not unless you've told them. That's your business, and I try not to meddle. Though I did recommend you let them know before they found out some other way.'

Davie shrugged. 'Then they'll find out tonight. I only hope they will behave themselves.'

'I don't think you need to fear any embarrassing disclosures at table. But when we meet for our usual conference tomorrow morning at the Quill and Gavel—I can't predict their response, but if I were you, I'd be prepared with answers to some hard questions.'

Davie smiled wryly. 'I only wish I had some.'

Giles hesitated, then took a sip of his wine before saying, 'Are you sure seeing the Duchess is wise?'

'I'm sure it is not,' Davie replied. 'But, having unexpectedly been handed the opportunity to do so, I'm also sure there is no way I could have refused it. And I do think I can help her.'

'As long as you emerge from it with a whole skin.'

'I gave her my heart long ago. There's nothing more I can lose.'

'I only hope you're right,' Giles said cryptically before the butler announced the arrival of the next guests, Benedict Tawny and Christopher Lattimer.

Having been forewarned, Davie wasn't unsettled by the appearance of their fellow Hellions. In fact, in the few minutes between learning of their impending appearance and their actual arrival, he'd decided to take Giles's advice and tell them about Faith straight away, before the rest of the party made its entrance.

'Just a convivial dinner tonight—we'll save the politics for another time,' Giles said as he handed each a glass of wine.

'No politics?' Ben rejoined. 'What, you would have us miss an opportunity to continue pressing—very politely, of course—Lord Witlow on moving forward with the Reform compromise?'

'I would. I want my father-in-law to relax and enjoy the company. There will be other females present besides Maggie, so the two of you start thinking of something that could be considered acceptable conversation for a lady's dinner table.'

'One lady attending is someone you won't be expecting,' Davie said. 'The Duchess of Ashedon.'

Both Ben and Christopher turned to stare at him. '"The Unattainable"?' Ben asked. 'But how—why?'

Quickly Davie summarised the events that had brought them together, and his intentions for the immediate future. 'She should be arriving any moment. I didn't want her presence to take you by surprise—'

'Leading us to make some…inappropriate remark,' Ben inserted.

'Like calling her "the Unattainable" to her face,' Christopher added.

'Yes, that,' Davie said, having a hard time not

snapping back, though he knew his friends were trying to goad him. 'Or tasking her about her intentions, now that Ashedon is dead, or referring in any way to the...unfortunate circumstances of his passing.'

'Were they unfortunate?' Ben asked, raising his eyebrows. 'How so?'

'Later,' Davie ground out.

'Actually, she's not so "Unattainable" now,' Ben remarked.

'A widowed duchess?' Christopher said. 'Of course she is, halfwit.'

'Only if Davie has *marriage* on his mind,' Ben said, giving Davie a sly look. 'Whereas, after worshipping her from afar for so many years, the Saint might just be ready for something a little more car—'

'Pray do not transfer your lustful ambitions to me,' Davie said, holding on to his temper with an effort made more difficult by knowing there was more truth than he'd like in Ben's assessment. 'Unlike you, I don't feel compelled to seduce every woman I meet.'

'Be a sight more affable if you did,' Ben shot back, unrepentant.

At that moment, the butler announced the arrival of the rest of the party. Giles's wife walked in on her father's arm, following by her great-aunt, Lady Sayleford, who was chatting with the Duchess.

'Can't wait to meet your paragon,' Ben murmured as Giles walked over to take his wife's arm, then turned to make the introductions.

'Just make sure you behave yourself,' Davie muttered.

'Oh, around ladies, I always do.' Ben flashed him a smile.

Knowing what his friend always did around ladies, Davie stifled a curse. Ben loved females, and they returned the favour, responding to his practised charm and tall, lithe, handsome form with universal gratification and approval.

Whereas Davie, who confined most of his conversation to politics, had never developed the art of strictly social conversation. On the few such occasions he had joined his friends, Ben's flattering attentiveness and clever wit with the female guests made him feel like a large, backward, doltish farm boy.

The idea that Ben might try to captivate Faith made Davie want to wrap his hands around his friend's throat and throttle him. Surprised at the intensity of that reaction, he made himself take a deep breath. Ridiculous that he should be jealous of his friend.

Fortunately, Ben was only barely more suitable a match for a widowed duchess than he was.

Then Faith stepped out from behind the Dowager Countess, and smiled at him, and every other concern slipped out of mind while his whole being responded to her. She looked glorious, as always, gowned tonight in dark grey overlaid with a silver net that seemed to twinkle and glow as she moved in the candlelight. Small diamond drops winked at her ears, and something equally sparkly was threaded through the curls pinned atop her head. She looked like a chef's iced confection, good enough to eat.

He wasn't aware of walking towards her, but suddenly he was at her side. To his annoyance, so too was Ben. 'Duchess,' his friend drawled, 'I'm so delighted to make your acquaintance at last. Davie has sung your praises on innumerable occasions over the years.'

Faith smiled at his friend. 'Mr Smith has told me about you, too, Mr Tawny. You served in India, did you not?'

To Davie's relief, before Ben could launch into one of the amusing army stories that always delighted female listeners, the Dowager Countess said, 'Shall we go in at once, Witlow? I'm fam-

ished, and it's not good to keep an old lady waiting. Might faint dead away.'

Lord Witlow laughed. 'If you like. Although I'd
wager you possess as much vigour as all of us put
together. Duchess, if you're ready?'

'Certainly, Lord Witlow. I'm sure we will talk
more later, Mr Tawny,' Faith said, before going
over to take her host's arm. Giles led in the Dowager Countess, Maggie took Davie's arm with a
smile, and they all followed, arranging themselves
as directed. To his delight, Davie was once again
seated adjacent to Faith, while Ben and Christopher flanked Maggie at her end of the table.

'Duchess, I'm pleased to see you looking so
well,' Lady Sayleford said to Faith. 'My niece tells
me you have an active interest in politics, which
the late Duke did not share. How fortunate that
you can now attend events that may provide more
stimulation than the usual society party. I must
warn you, though, politics is somewhat of an obsession with Maggie and my nephew. Given the
least encouragement, she will have you riding to
the hustings with them.'

'I can't think of anything more vital to the well-
being of our country,' Faith replied. 'Lord Coopley urged that more society ladies encourage their

relations and acquaintances to take an active part, and I shall certainly do that. If I could be of any use on the hustings, I'd be happy to assist.'

'I'm making a note of that offer,' Maggie warned from her end of the table. 'I shall certainly call on you when the time comes!'

'You're in for it now,' the Dowager Countess said with a chuckle. 'Maggie is a force as powerful as one of those new steam locomotives when some political business needs to be done. But don't I recall that you began debating politics with Mr Smith some years ago, when he was secretary to your cousin, Sir Edward Greaves?'

'Why, yes—but that was quite long ago, before I made my come-out,' Faith said.

Maggie laughed. 'Aunt Lilly knows everything about everyone—or soon finds out. So, gentlemen...' she looked over to Ben and Christopher '...if you have any secrets, beware.'

Faith blushed a little, and Davie wondered if she were remembering that forbidden kiss. A timely reminder that nothing in society ever remained secret, providing helpful reinforcement of his intention to be more prudent in future.

Conversation became more general, a smattering of politics interspersed with some of the sto-

ries Ben was induced to tell about his army days in
India, which led to a lively discussion of the relative merits and peculiarities of society in England
and the subcontinent. Davie was content mostly to
watch Faith, but as the evening went on, that en-
joyment became tempered with concern.

To Davie, it seemed that she was somewhat...
withdrawn, for though she smiled, and answered
any questions put to her, she made no attempt to
initiate conversation. When the conversation was
centred elsewhere, her smile faded and a quiet,
almost troubled look took over her countenance.

What could be causing her unease? Surely not
some gossip about their lapse at her sister's earlier this week—something that scandalous would
be so volatile, Giles would have heard of it and
warned him.

Some confrontation at her home?

'You seem preoccupied tonight,' he said quietly,
under cover of the larger conversation. 'Is Carlisle
giving you trouble?'

To his relief, she brightened. 'Oh, no! As I was
planning to tell you, that interview went off very
well. I was firm, and purposeful, and didn't let
him get in a word of response. Very duchess-like!
Even better, he vacated the house yesterday. Until

I finish reviewing the dossiers Englemere sent and choose someone to replace him, I'll have the boys all to myself.'

'That's wonderful! Where do you mean to take them?'

'We went to Green Park today, watched the milk-maids with their cows and bought some fresh milk. Tomorrow, if the weather is fair, I may take them to the Tower of London.'

'They should enjoy that! Especially if you embellish the visit with stories of the famous inmates, mentioning scaffolds and beheadings.'

She laughed. 'Yes, the more bloodthirsty the story, the better.'

Dinner concluding, Maggie stood. 'This being a family party, we'll not leave you gentlemen to port and cigars, but all go in to tea directly.' Waving them to the salon, she took her husband's arm. Lord Witlow walked with his aunt, allowing Davie to claim Faith.

After cups had been filled and emptied, Lord Witlow said, 'We don't have any formal entertainment planned, but Maggie did promise to play for me. Normally after dinners in company, I'm stuck with a bunch of loquacious old politicians fighting some old election or arguing for a new.' He gave

Giles and the other Hellions an amused glance. 'Listening to music is a treat I get too rarely.'

'Yes, I did promise,' Maggie said. 'But though my fond papa enjoys my piano, I'm competent merely. If you gentlemen would rather seek more skilled entertainment, there's still time to make the theatre or the opera—or your favourite gaming house.'

'Or house of another sort,' Lady Sayleford said with a pointed look at Ben.

'Aunt Lilly!' Maggie said with reproof. 'In any event, we very much enjoyed having all of you to dinner, but you mustn't feel obligated to remain.'

'Not that I don't appreciate your playing, my dear, but these old bones are longing for their sofa,' Lady Sayleford said.

'Ben and I arranged to meet some associates later. *Political* associates,' Christopher emphasised, with a smile for the Dowager Countess.

'Is that what they're calling them now?' she responded with a twinkle.

'Off with all of you, before you put me to the blush,' Maggie said.

'If it won't seem to be intruding, I should like to stay and listen,' Faith said. 'I'm no good at all, but my sisters used to play for us in the evening.

It's one of the things I missed so much after leaving my family,' she concluded, her voice wistful.

'We should be delighted to have you stay,' Maggie said. 'And Davie, if you like.'

'You know how much I enjoy hearing you play.' Although he'd stay for a caterwauling soprano, if Faith remained.

With expressions of thanks for the fine dinner and congenial company, Ben, Christopher, and the Dowager Countess took their leave. Lord Witlow, Maggie, Giles, Davie and Faith moved into Maggie's private parlour, where a piano stood near the window. Lord Witlow chose a wing chair near the hearth, while, declining to sit beside Faith on the sofa, Davie angled a straight chair next to it. That put him close enough to feel her nearness, but saved him the torture of sitting next to her, knowing with one subtle movement in the candlelit dimness, he could slide his leg over to touch hers.

'I'll start with your favourite, Papa,' Maggie said, and launched into Beethoven's *First Piano Concerto*. With a little gasp, Faith leaned forward.

Before Davie could enquire what the matter was, she turned to him to whisper, 'Lady Lyndlington was far too modest. How wonderfully she plays!'

'She is very good, isn't she?' Davie agreed, delighted that the company he'd introduced her to was providing another unexpected treat.

For the next hour, while Lord Witlow tapped his toe in time to the music before eventually nodding off, Maggie played and Giles sat beside her on the bench, turning the pages for her. From time to time, Maggie looked over at her husband and they shared a smile; once, as she paused between one passage and the next, he whispered a 'bravo' and kissed her cheek.

As Faith became more immersed in the music, the tension Davie had noticed in her at dinner seemed to ease. Though he was relieved that the music's magic had driven from her mind whatever was disturbing her, he still fretted over the cause. He would have to try again to get her to tell him.

With the tutor gone, was she having more problems with the Dowager, who didn't approve her sending Carlisle away or spending so much time with her sons? As he speculated about what the problem might be, he heard the echo of Giles's voice warning that Davie couldn't solve Faith's problems, that she and her family would direct her future.

Despite Giles's well-meant advice, he didn't seem able to keep himself from wanting to make everything smooth in her world. It might not be his responsibility or his privilege, but during the short time they had together, he would do what he could.

At that moment, Maggie paused again, the piano falling silent before she began the next movement. She looked over at Giles, who returned a glance so tender, Davie felt a stab of envy and longing. He gripped the arms of his chair to keep his hand from reaching out for Faith's.

Just before the music began again, Faith sighed. To his infinite delight, in the dimness of the candlelight, while their host and hostess remained absorbed in the music and each other, and Maggie's father dozed, she moved her hand from the arm of the couch and reached for his. Both of them still watching at the musicians, conscious of sharing a guilty pleasure, he let his hand slip from the chair's arm and reached over to link his fingers with hers.

'They look so happy,' she whispered.

'They are,' he murmured. 'Well suited, and perfectly attuned to one another.'

'It must be wonderful, to be in a marriage like that.'

'They are certainly a good advertisement for the wedded state.'

She nodded. 'My sister and Englemere as well.'

'Maybe you will find that one day. No one deserves it more.'

She looked back at him then, her melancholy gaze sharpening, her eyes sparking with some more powerful, physical reaction.

'Maybe I want something else just as much. Something more…immediate.'

He felt it, too, the pulse of desire that seemed to vibrate around them, in the music, with the music, urging them together. They were like Beethoven's sonorous chords, he thought, distinct and separate notes that could blend into a harmonious whole, something new, more powerful and more beautiful than the single note alone.

'I want that, too,' he whispered, tightening his grip. 'But we dare not have it.'

'I know.' She sighed again and detached her fingers from his as the movement ended with a final triumphant chord.

They both clapped, the sound waking Lord Witlow, who added his applause. Much as Davie enjoyed the music, he felt more like protesting its conclusion than applauding its performance.

The end of the piece meant the end of his time with Faith. Though, unlike at the political dinner, he might leave when she did, even offer to see her safely home without anyone present thinking his behaviour suspicious, he knew he didn't dare subject himself to the temptation of riding alone in the coach with her.

After the music ended, Giles would take his wife up to their bedchamber and make sweet, slow love to her. The spell of the music having only intensified the connection of mind and attraction of body he already felt to Faith, Davie couldn't keep himself from envisioning doing the same.

Seeing her sitting there, the candlelight sparkling off the spangled silk of her gown, he could imagine leaning over to worship the bare skin of her neck and shoulders with his lips. Wrapping her in his arms, angling her head up for another mesmerising kiss...

Sweat breaking out on his brow, he wrenched his mind from the images. Maggie belonged to Giles in a way Faith would never belong to him, he told himself angrily. Could he not keep that one simple thought in his head?

Faith rose, and he followed her lead, bludgeoning his disobedient mind into performing the normal rituals of politeness, complimenting Maggie on her playing, thanking her for a fine dinner and a lovely evening. After giving her hostess an impulsive hug, she turned to Davie. 'I suppose I must have my carriage summoned and go home.'

'I don't want the evening to end either,' he admitted. A sudden thought occurred, and he frowned. 'Are you worried that you'll have to endure another of the Dowager's harangues?'

'No. That's actually better, too, now that I've stopped meekly following all her commands. Every time she begins to criticise, I either interrupt her or leave the room. I don't think she's yet figured out exactly what to do about it. It's lovely, to finally feel I have some power within my own house.' Her bright smile faded. 'Though not enough, I fear.'

Before he could question her about that, Lord Witlow finished his conversation with his daughter, and looping her arm in Giles's, Maggie walked over to them. 'We've sent for your carriage, Faith. Papa is so fatigued, he's decided to spend the night with us. Davie will wait with you until it arrives. Would you like him to escort you home, too?'

'No, that won't be necessary. John Coachman and the grooms will see me safely to Berkeley Square.'

'I'll bid you goodnight, then, and see my father to his room. You will call again soon, won't you? I already have some ideas about some political work we could do together.'

'I should be delighted to help in whatever way I can.'

'Good.' Maggie reached out to give Faith a hug. 'I knew we would make great allies!'

Each footfall as they descended the stairs seemed like the bong of a clock sounding the hour marking the end of their time together. Unwilling to part without knowing when he might see her again, Davie said, 'With the special election and Parliament reconvening last June, many members with agricultural interests haven't been home to see to their tenants and crops. We'll soon be taking a brief recess so they can check on the upcoming harvest before the vote is called later this month. If you'd like, I could take you and your sons for a walk around Hyde Park. In the morning, of course, when we're less likely to get trampled by horsemen and carriages.'

She turned to smile at him. 'That would be lovely! I know the boys would enjoy it.'

'Shall I meet you at Hyde Park, or call for you in Berkeley Square? Maybe I could help you review the dossiers of tutors Englemere sent you before we go out.'

To his surprise, that offer brought the anxious look back to her face again. 'I don't really need to review them. Englemere has already ensured all those he recommended possess the proper credentials. I only need to interview the candidates to see which one seems the best fit. Perhaps it would be best if we meet you in the Park.'

Taken aback, Davie couldn't help feeling a little hurt. Obviously, Faith didn't want him appearing at her front door. Was she embarrassed that some other society caller might discover she had received him?

Immediately, he rejected the thought. He knew Faith cared little for the opinions of society. But the Dowager would certainly not approve of her associating with someone so far beneath her station. Most likely, she was reluctant to invite him into her mother-in-law's domain, thereby almost goading the Dowager to give her a lecture on the proper behaviour of a duchess.

'Very well, the Park it shall be. Hyde Park Corner, day after tomorrow at ten o'clock, shall we say?'

'At ten, yes.' She smiled, her look of anxiety fading, confirming to him that he had correctly interpreted the reason for her disquiet. 'How can I thank you enough? Taking me to see Sarah, bringing me into a circle of congenial friends, and then, tonight, reminding me of a joy I'd almost forgotten. I only wish I could provide something so special for you.'

You do—just by letting me be near you. But that

sounded too hopelessly besotted, so he said instead, 'Being a friend is special enough.'

Her smile grew tender. 'It is indeed.'

Then the butler walked over, announcing the arrival of her carriage, and helped her into her evening cloak. 'Goodnight, Davie. I shall be looking forward to the Park!'

'I'm determined to get a laugh out of Ashedon, if I have to play hopscotch through the mud with him. He needs to learn to act like a boy again.'

'A dignified Member of Parliament, hopping through the mud?' she laughed. 'Now that, I truly must see.'

The butler was holding open the door for her. Giving him one last smile, she walked out, leaving him staring after her. Leaving him bereft, with only his lonely room and lonely bed to return to.

But he had the park to look forward to, the day after tomorrow. Which would give him time to make the outing something truly memorable.

Chapter Nine

In the middle of the morning two days later, Faith sat at the desk in the small salon adjoining her bedchamber, making notes on the dossiers of prospective tutors Englemere had forwarded her. It was rather difficult to imagine, from sterile lists of academic backgrounds and previous references, which candidate might be most amenable to the freer, more egalitarian system of education she wanted for her sons, particularly Edward. She would have appreciated Davie's help in narrowing the field of those to summon for interviews.

Before he'd quickly masked the expression, he'd seemed—offended, that she'd turn down his offer. Another iniquity to lay at the feet of her worthless brother-in-law, she thought, scowling. Since she never knew when or whether Lord Randall would appear, she didn't dare invite Davie to call. The very idea that he might meet Randall, and what Randall might say to him if they did, made her feel queasy.

She made a final note and assembled the dossiers into a neat stack, then wearily dusted off her hands. She'd barely slept lately, worried that she'd hear his footstep in the hallway, the rattle of the door she kept securely locked, with a chair pushed up against it for extra measure.

As far as she could tell, however, her unpredictable brother-in-law had once again taken an extended leave from the house. Though the Dowager had complained last night that he'd not shown up to escort them to the rout given by one of her closest friends, an event she'd most particularly informed Randall she'd wanted him to attend with them, Faith was relieved by his absence and could only hope it would continue.

As the mantel clock bonged the hour, her spirits rose. Finally it was time to collect her sons for their trip to the Park…where she would see Davie again. Impressed by her old friend during their trip to visit her sister, her boys were almost as excited to have his company again as she was.

After a quick stop to gather up her pelisse and gloves, Faith went to the nursery, to find the boys eager and ready. They trooped to the waiting carriage in an excited cascade of voices, and as soon as the vehicle started on its way, began assaulting her with a volley of questions.

'One at a time!' she protested, laughing.

'Mr Smith said he would take us riding again. Is he bringing ponies, Mama?' Edward asked.

'No, we're to walk today.' As his eager expression faded, she added quickly, 'There will be a pond, with ducks. Cook made me a packet of bread-crumbs to feed them.'

'Will there be cows, too, Mama?' Matthew asked.

'No cows—and no fresh milk. Although I imagine we might find some meat pasties somewhere, before we venture home again,' she added, chuckling at his whoop of enthusiasm anticipating that treat.

'There are trees in the park, aren't there?' Colin asked. 'Can we climb some?'

Anger and sadness coursed through her, that though her children had been in London for years, apparently their tutor had not been moved to take them beyond their own back garden.

'Yes, there are trees, but no climbing today. There are also long gravel paths, and you may have a footrace. We're passing Green Park now; we'll be entering the park gates soon.'

At that, the boys crowded the window, eager to inspect this new playground. As the carriage passed under the arches at Hyde Park Corner to enter the grounds themselves, Faith scanned the paths for Davie.

The vehicle slowed, beginning a circuit down the carriage row, then stopped altogether. Leaning out over her sons' heads, Faith spied Davie, who'd waved down the carriage, and her heart leapt.

Fatigue, the burden of responsibility she felt to make the right choices about her sons' tutor and education, her worries over the Dowager's interference, and the looming danger posed by Lord Randall—all faded away, washed from her mind by a rush of joy and anticipation at being able to spend the morning with the men who brought light and happiness into her life—her sons, and Davie.

What a blessing it would be, to have Davie's kind, clever and alluring company every day, the wistful thought occurred. Sighing, she banished it; she would treasure today and not repine that she would not be able to experience such treats more often. All too soon, Davie's responsibilities—and probably boredom with the company of a matron of no particular talents and her three rambunctious sons—would put an end to such adventures.

She intended to suck every iota of joy out of the ones she managed to grab.

As he approached, the footman handed her down

and the boys tumbled out of the coach and ran to meet him. With affection and pride, she watched Edward hold up a hand to halt his brothers before they reached Davie, make him a proper bow, and wave his brothers to copy that behaviour.

Not to be restrained any longer, Matthew tugged at Davie's sleeve. 'Mama said we would only walk today, but might there be ponies later?'

'We are going to the Serpentine to feed the ducks,' Faith inserted, not wanting her children, who had no idea of the cost involved in renting ponies or hiring grooms, to wheedle Davie for expensive treats.

'An excellent idea, Duchess,' Davie said, making her a bow. 'How nice to see all of you again.'

'And you, Mr Smith.' As he straightened, their eyes met, and for a moment, Faith let her tremulous smile and the intensity of her gaze convey all the longing and delight she dare not put into words.

He seemed to understand, for he stared back just as intensely, and for a moment, Faith thought he might take her hand.

Instead, he gave her a tiny nod and turned to Matthew, who was once again tugging at his coat sleeve. 'Shall we go see those ducks, young man? As for ponies, I thought afterward, we might go to Astley's Amphitheatre.'

Edward's eyes widened and he gave a gasp. 'Where the riders do tricks on horseback? That would be splendid!'

'How kind of you to offer such a treat, Mr Smith, that's not necessary; the tickets must be rather dear, I should think.'

Being led forward, as Matthew tugged at one hand and Colin the other, he looked back over his shoulder. 'I'm not a penniless orphan any longer, Duchess.'

Her cheeks coloured. 'I didn't mean to imply—'

Then he chuckled, relieving her of the fear that she might have offended him. 'No worries on that score. I can stand the ready, and I'd very much like to offer them that treat.'

'Then, we accept with pleasure.'

'Have you seen the horses there, Mama?' Edward asked.

'Your Aunt Sarah took me once, while the late Mr Astley still performed. They presented "The Battle of Waterloo"; it was quite a spectacle.'

'A battle?' Matthew cried. 'With guns and horses and fighting and everything? That would be splendid!'

'I'm afraid they don't do the battle scene in the afternoons,' Davie said. 'But there are acrobats, and lots of horsemen doing tricks while they ride.'

'Let's feed the ducks fast!' Colin said, picking up the pace.

A few minutes later they reached the verge of the Serpentine, Faith pulled the cloth-wrapped crumbs from her reticule, and the boys began vying to see who could attract the most ducks with their treasures.

Edward, who emptied his handful first, grew bored waiting while his youngest brother painstakingly tossed his bits down, crumb by crumb, giggling at the ducks who rushed around his small feet, gobbling down the morsels.

When one of the ducks, stymied of winning some of Colin's last crumbs, waddled over to nudge at Edward's feet, he picked up a branch and pushed it away. Apparently encouraged by the squawk and flapping of wings that ensued, he began hitting the duck on the back.

Before Faith could say anything, Davie reached out to stay his hand. 'Don't, Ashedon,' he said. 'You mustn't hurt him; smaller creatures are here for us to enjoy and protect.'

'It's only a duck,' Edward said with a shrug.

'Every creature, no matter how lowly, has value,' Davie said quietly. 'Only men with small minds and hard hearts treat cruelly or slightingly those of lesser estate than themselves. A man of high position, as you will one day be, has a responsibility to protect those who are poorer and less fortunate.'

'Like you do in Parliament?' Edward said. 'Uncle Nicholas said your Reform Bill wants to give all men a voice in running their government.'

'That's right. Wouldn't you rather Nurse asked if you wanted bread—or jam tarts—with your tea, rather than just bringing you what she thinks is best for you?' As he nodded, Davie continued, 'Most men don't mind following reasonable rules, but they do like to have a say in making them. Now, are we out of breadcrumbs, Master Colin?'

When her youngest nodded, Matthew gave a shout. 'Now we get to see the ponies! C'mon, Colin, I'll race you back to the coach!'

Rather than run ahead with the others, Edward chose to walk beside them. Her son was even more impressed with Davie than he'd been on that first excursion, Faith realised. But how could he not be? His own father had spent little time with him, never bothering to talk to him about anything that mattered, like a great man's duty to those around him.

Probably because he didn't feel any.

How she wished her sons could grow up with a man like Davie to model themselves after!

'Won't you ride to Astley's with us, Mr Smith?' Edward asked.

'Thank you, Ashedon. If it's all right with your mama, I will. But after we arrive,' he continued, turning to address Faith, 'why don't you send your coach home? No need for the staff to hang about, walking the horses, while we watch the show.'

'Very well, I'll instruct John Coachman,' Faith said, wishing she could take Davie's arm, but too mindful of Edward keeping pace beside them.

The boys were, of course, their excuse to spend time together, but oh, if only she could find some way for them to steal a few minutes alone! How she longed for an obliging screen of trees, a gardener's hut, a conveniently placed empty coach— anything that would allow her to glide close to him, lift her face, and beg another kiss.

Of course, there was nothing in Hyde Park but well-tended pathways…and once they reached Astley's, there would be several hundred additional witnesses surrounding them, she thought, sighing.

Replying, 'No!', rather more sharply than she'd intended when Davie enquired whether something was wrong, she had to settle for the much-less-satisfying pleasure of laying her hand on his arm as he helped her into the coach.

The carriage ride to Astley's was a mixed blessing. Moving her boys on to the forward seat, she was able to sit beside Davie. But trying to maintain a proper distance between them, when all she wanted was to snuggle up against him, strained both patience and decorum, while the bumps that jostled them enough for their knees or hands to touch set off sparks that made keeping away even more difficult.

A sidelong glance at his set jaw and a sensual tension so strong she wondered that even the boys didn't notice something, told her he found this almost-but-not-quite togetherness as difficult as she did.

Still, she would rather burn in his presence than pine for his absence.

Not sure whether to be relieved or sorry when the carriage stopped at their destination—freeing them from frustration, but removing the tantalising possibility that any moment, another rut might throw them together—she let the groom hand her down, while Davie went to obtain their tickets.

Enough amorous thoughts, she scolded herself. *You're a mother, on this excursion primarily for your sons' benefit. Concentrate on making sure they enjoy it.*

Which didn't require much effort, once the boys took their seats in the grandstand and the show began. Totally enthralled, they gasped at riders standing upright on the backs of their galloping horses; a female dressed like a ballerina poised on one foot as her horse circled the ring; others who jumped their horses over fences while standing upright. They marvelled as the manager, Andrew Duclow, performed his famous 'Courier of St Petersburg' stunt, standing astride two white horses while mounted riders carrying the flags of countries travelled through on the journey from England to Russia rode beneath him. With the rest of the crowd, they laughed at the shenanigans of the clowns, applauded the skill of the acrobats, and shouted approval at the finale when a group of riders entered the arena and raced their ponies round and round.

'They will talk about this for weeks,' Faith said over their heads. 'You rose high enough in their estimation for the trip to Brookhollow Lodge; after this, it's fortunate you will be occupied with business, for they would plead with you to take them out again and again.'

'It would be hard to equal the excitement of Astley's.'

'For them, perhaps. I found the end of our day at Brookhollow even more satisfying. I only wish I could repeat *that*—again and again.'

Her words sparked his gaze to an intensity that promised he could deliver exactly what she burned for. Oh, she wanted...she *wanted*. But could she persuade him to it?

The light of his gaze burning hotter, he said, so softly that with all the noise around them, she could barely hear him, 'Repeat that, and dare more.' Taking her hand, he brought it to his lips for a brief caress.

Faith felt the delicious vibrations move up her arm and radiate throughout her body. How she wished they could leave this spot and go somewhere private! She longed with a fervour she'd never before experienced to kiss him, unknot his cravat and place her lips on his bared throat where the pulse throbbed. To peel him out of coat and waistcoat and shirt and rub her lips, her cheek, against his bare chest. Kiss him from his chest downward, unfastening his trousers to unveil him—

Shocked by the explicit carnality of her thoughts, Faith's cheeks flamed. But she was spared the embarrassment of Davie noticing; he had already looked away, breaking that contact between them. Exhaling a heavy sigh, he said, 'But we must be content with less.'

He wanted her, she was certain, but tempting

him to act on that desire wouldn't be easy. Was she even certain yet, despite the force of her desire, that she dared lead him there?

Exhaling a huff of frustration of her own, she turned her attention back to the arena.

What was she thinking, anyway? She was a matron with three sons, not a temptress from the *demi-monde*.

Sometimes, she thought wistfully, she wished she had their skills.

Soon after, the performance concluded. Davie went off to procure their hackney, finding some meat pasties for the boys along the way, which they consumed with gusto. For the length of the drive back to Berkeley Square, they chattered about what a famous time they'd had, what terrific performers the horsemen had been, how beautiful their mounts. Matthew announced his determination to become a skilled rider and open his own amphitheatre, graciously conceding that Colin could join with him, but Edward couldn't, because he would have to be a duke.

Bracketed by exuberant boys, there was no chance for any private conversation. So, when Davie handed her down, after sending her sons up to the nursery, she lingered by the hackney.

'Thank you for another perfect outing.'

He smiled. 'I'm so glad you—and they—enjoyed it. Paragon that you are, no one deserves perfection more.'

'I'm hardly that!' she protested.

'You are to me. The perfect embodiment of joy, purity, and delight.'

She knew she wasn't worthy of such praise, but she couldn't help drinking in an admiration that refilled the reservoirs of self-confidence and self-worth drained so low by years of marriage to a man who'd belittled her.

But the butler still stood at the top of the entry stairs, holding open the door. Hating to end the excursion, she nevertheless forced herself to say, 'I must go now. Thank you again.'

Before she turned away, he caught up her hand and kissed it, the gaze they shared saying they both regretted not being able to end this interlude with the one thing that truly would have made the morning perfect. Faith's lips tingled, imagining that forbidden, longed-for kiss.

Then, with a little nudge, Davie pushed her towards the stairs. 'You must go in, Duchess. Thank you for a wonderful outing.'

'You'll let me know if you have another free

morning?' she asked, wanting to hold on to the magic by guaranteeing she would see him again.

'Yes. Or you may be sure that Lady Lyndlington will rope you into one of her political projects, and I'll see you there, or at another of her dinners.'

'It can't be too soon.'

'I hope it is very soon.' With that, Davie tipped his hat, and she reluctantly turned to walk up the stairs.

As she did, someone stirred the curtains at the front parlour window. Focusing on the movement, she realised with a shock that Lord Randall stood there, watching her as Davie's hackney drove away.

Chapter Ten

Her heart pounding, Faith hurried through the hallway, up the stairs past the salon and up another flight to the nursery, one place she knew her brother-in-law wouldn't follow her. She halted outside the door to the schoolroom, panting from her exertions, but relieved at having avoided a confrontation she dreaded.

Perhaps the Dowager was in the salon with him, or perhaps he simply didn't want to accost her yet, for he'd had enough time, while she skipped up the stairs from the street level, to cut off her retreat, had he wanted to. She could only be glad that he hadn't, and that she was now forewarned that he was back in the house.

For how long, she didn't know; hopefully, he'd borrow more money from his mother and be gone for days again. But she'd have to tread carefully, in case he made a longer stay this time.

Anger fired up, overlaying the dread. She hated having to remain constantly on guard in her own home! She simply had to resolve this intolerable situation.

Only she hadn't yet figured out a way to do that. An enquiry of the Dowager, about which solicitor maintained the documents setting out the rules of the trust established for the boys and the details of how income from the estate was provided to them, was met first with a blank stare, and then a querulous enquiry about why she would need such information.

She only wished she'd paid more attention at the reading of the will, but she'd been so shocked and mortified by the circumstances of her husband's death, all she could think about was how those present must be staring at and pitying her.

Englemere would know; standing in for her deceased father, he'd been involved in arranging the details of her marriage settlement. But with momentous changes about to be voted on in Parliament, he was busy with important work in the Lords. Besides which, he would naturally be curious why she was suddenly enquiring about financial details which had never interested her over the many years of her marriage and widowhood.

Confiding in him would be even more impossible than admitting the tawdry circumstances to Sarah.

Maybe tomorrow, she'd try going through Ashedon's desk—though, as she couldn't remember her husband ever troubling himself over financial matters, the search was unlikely to yield her much.

Better still, why not simply ask Cooper, the butler, she thought, brightening. He would probably think the enquiry strange, but since butlers knew everything, he most likely would be able to give her the name of Ashedon's solicitor.

Heartened, as she leaned against the door, recovering her breath, she imagined the interview with the solicitor. That gentleman, who didn't know her at all, was less likely to think it odd of her to make enquiries, especially when she could tell him, quite truthfully, that she was concerned about how the arrangements had been left for the boys' schooling. She could also explain that her husband had feared his younger brother might try to make inroads upon the estate; wanting to honour his wishes and protect her sons' inheritance, she needed to know just what funds and properties Lord Randall could make use of, and which uses she should report to the trustees, should he overstep his bounds.

She'd spend the remainder of the afternoon here,

with her boys, she decided. She'd need to venture out of the schoolroom to dress for dinner, and then dine with the Dowager, but with any luck, Lord Randall would have cudgelled some funds out of his mother and be gone by then. If the Dowager did coax her darling son to remain for dinner, she would only be interested in talking with *him*, allowing Faith to remain mostly silent, masking the fact that she had no desire to converse with her despicable brother-in-law.

Fortunately, she'd left in the schoolroom the storybook she'd brought up some nights ago, so wouldn't need to retreat to the library to fetch it. By now recovered, Faith opened the door and walked in.

To her delight, her sons jumped up to greet her with a surprise and excitement that grew more exuberant when she told them she meant to stay until suppertime, reading them stories—and would have Cook send up some more bread and tea for their party.

Even Edward smiled at that. Fetching the book, she gathered them around her at the schoolroom table, and began to read.

The degree of relief she felt upon entering the salon before dinner to find her brother-in-law absent told her she'd been dreading the prospect of dining with him more than she'd imagined. Her relief was so great, she bore with unimpaired good humour the Dowager's criticism of her spending the morning out gallivanting with her sons instead of being home to greet Lord Randall upon his arrival, and her selfishness in remaining closeted with them all afternoon, without giving a thought to whether her mother-in-law might need her.

Most unusually, the Dowager continued her complaining after they went into dinner, decrying her son's lack of feeling in deserting her, too, even after she'd most particularly requested that he remain to dine and escort them to the rout this evening. Then, seeming to realise this description of Randall's behaviour did not fit the rosy picture she'd painted of how he would attend and support them, she made an abrupt conversational about-face. Doubtless, she said, he was very busy; after all, a gentleman of his looks, charm and pedigree was highly sought after by hostesses offering the most select entertainments; they could not fault him for not wishing to disappoint such noble ladies to keep company with two old widows.

Her lips twitching with the effort not to laugh at the sudden change in tune, Faith felt an unexpected sympathy towards the overbearing woman. How painful it must be to realise—even if she could not admit the awful truth to herself—that her son visited her only to obtain something, and was unwilling to even occasionally oblige her by spending an evening in her company.

Never would she end up in that sad position, if there were anything she could do to prevent it! Choosing a tutor who included her in his plans for her sons' studies would be the first step. Spending more mornings 'gallivanting about' with them and more afternoons 'selfishly closeted away with them' would follow, too.

For the first time, she saw the Dowager, who along with her son had belittled and criticised her for her whole married life, not as the imposing, elegant leader of society who had always intimidated her, but as a lonely old woman with few true friends, whose one remaining child was indifferent to her.

Perhaps it was a re-awakening of confidence, a spirit healing after years of repression, which provided this fresh point of view. Whatever the reason, Faith felt the sense of a burden lifted. No longer would she dread or resent the Dowager's remarks. Her newly minted sympathy wouldn't prompt her to spend much more time than necessary with her mother-in-law, and she certainly didn't intend to brook any interference in the bringing up of her boys, but she would try to make the time they did have together as enjoyable as she could for the woman.

That resolution stayed with her as the Dowager bore her off to a rout given by one of her society friends, the Dowager Marchioness of Hargrave. To Faith's chagrin, one of the attendees was the woman's daughter, Lady Mary—who never let slip an opportunity to diminish Faith in her sweet, falsely sympathetic voice.

'Dear Duchess!' Lady Mary sang out, coming over to clasp Faith's arm and draw her into her circle. 'Are you in good health? You seem—uncommonly ruddy of complexion tonight. I hope you're not sickening with something. Although I can imagine how difficult it has been to get over Ashedon's sudden demise—and especially the *manner* of it.'

Normally, Faith would have shrunk into herself, returning some monosyllabic reply. But at this moment, it struck her that Lady Mary's remarks *always* focused on Ashedon and his women; might her malice stem from having once been one of them, and then discarded? How it must grate to have been displaced by others of lesser birth and consequence—and to know that Faith, whom she thought so meek and useless, had been able to hold on to him as her husband.

'No, I am in the best of good health, after taking my boys to the Park today for some fresh air. And as we both know, Ashedon hadn't been mine to lose for quite some time.'

Mrs Pierce-Compton, one of Lady Mary's cronies, exclaimed, 'Took your sons to the Park *yourself*? Whatever for? Was their tutor riding in the curricle with Ashedon that day?' she added with a titter.

Fury boiled up in Faith—at the woman's crass comment, at the very idea that she would allow someone so deficient in moral character to instruct her precious sons.

Raising her eyes to meet the other woman's, she stared at her, unsmiling and silent. After a moment, Mrs Pierce-Compton looked away, saying with a weak laugh, 'It was only a joke, Duchess.'

Without a word, Faith turned her back on the woman and walked away, head high, leaving the onlookers gaping. Not until she'd marched into the next room and grabbed a glass of wine from the tray offered by one of the servants did she realise she'd just inadvertently applied Lady Lyndlington's 'technique'.

She had to smile to herself. *You were right, my*

friend. It is effective, and my, how good it feels! Probably the best moment she'd had at a society party since the early days of her marriage, before her husband lost interest in her.

Quite a banner day. First, a new perspective on the woman who'd been one of the banes of her life since her wedding day, and now stumbling into a way to dismiss those who tried to hurt her without resorting to meanness, a way that left her feeling powerful and in control.

Thank you, Davie and Maggie, for helping me regain that confidence.

To her amusement, as it turned out, it wasn't only *her* behaviour that altered. After her cut of Mrs Pierce-Compton, for the rest of the evening, the other matrons who often congregated with her tormentor, piling on disparaging remarks, kept their distance. She was even able to have a halfway intelligent conversation with her host, Lord Hargrave, about the upcoming reform legislation.

All in all, a much more pleasant evening than she'd been anticipating. And if the new degree of respect being awarded her tonight carried over to the other *ton* entertainments she was forced to attend, it would be a banner day indeed.

If it didn't carry over, she told herself, riding high on that new-found assertiveness, she'd just have to deliver a cut-direct to a few more detractors. When it came right down to it, she really didn't care to speak with any of them. If that behaviour reduced the society invitations she received by half, she wouldn't miss them in the least.

Her resolve to be pleasant to her mother-in-law was stretched almost to the breaking point on the carriage ride back to Berkeley Square, during which the Dowager reprimanded her for being impolite to Lady Mary and then went on at length about how poorly she was treated, by the daughter-in-law who embarrassed her with her uncivil behaviour and by her son, who cruelly disappointed her by not appearing at the rout she'd promised everyone he'd attend. It took a great deal of will to refrain from pointing out that, if the Dowager wished to see more of Lord Randall, she should be a little slower in handing him money to fund his gaming habits.

Her high-flying confidence soared abruptly back to earth once the carriage arrived in Berkeley Square. As they walked up the entry stairs, Faith stiffened, instinctively girding herself for the possibility of encountering Lord Randall in the shadows of the stairway or the hall outside her chamber. But to her relief, he did not appear.

Safely ensconced in some gaming hell or some doxy's bed, she sincerely hoped as she latched her chamber door and dragged the chair in front of it.

She fell asleep to dreams of her sons, shrieking with delight at the horses and clowns and acrobats of Astley's. And the handsome, kind, powerfully attractive gentleman who'd given them that treat, whom she only wished she knew how to seduce.

Some time later, she came groggily awake, aware of light spilling over her bed. The dawn sun, she was thinking, when suddenly the sense of someone in the room pulled her into full wakefulness. Sitting up with a gasp, she saw Lord Randall at the foot of her bed, holding a candle.

'How did you get in?' she demanded.

He chuckled, setting the candle on a side table and walking closer. 'If you want to keep someone out, dear sister, you need to bar the door to the service stairs, too.'

She'd told the staff she left the chair by the chamber door to keep it firmly shut against draughts from the hallway, which was at least plausible. Blocking the service entry would not be so easy to explain, alerting the maids and tweenies, coming to lay fires or bring up coffee in the morning, that something was amiss. 'I didn't think you'd stoop to using the servants' stairs.'

'Needs must, sweet sister.'

'I don't care how you got in, just go.'

'I thought by now, you'd be ready to invite me to stay.'

'Do you still not understand?' she asked, exasperated. 'My continuing mention of pistols ought to convey the clear impression that I will never invite you. I'm tired of your little game; it's time that it ceases.'

Fumbling in her bedside table, she brought forth the small pistol. 'I don't want to wake the house and scare everyone to death, but I really have no qualms about using it. And then telling everyone just why I had to.'

'Oh, I don't think you will, sweet sis.' He stepped closer. 'You won't use that pistol, and you won't breathe a word. If you do, I'll just say I was here at your invitation—and who do you think will believe your denial? My mother?' He laughed. 'That low-bred politician who's been sniffing at your skirts? If you're giving him any, or teasing him that you will, he'll be only too ready to believe you're handing it out to whoever asks.'

She hesitated, stricken. She *had* invited Davie's kiss. He told her he thought her the essence of purity. If Randall were to claim she'd lured him to her bedchamber—after she'd tried to tempt *him*—would Davie believe her a wanton?

The thought of losing his good opinion made her stomach lurch.

Randall took advantage of her distraction to move forward and seize the wrist of the hand holding the pistol. 'I think you can dispense with this, my dear. Then you can show me all the little tricks you've been using with your Parliamentary lover.'

She didn't dare struggle, lest the pistol go off inadvertently. 'The only thing I'm going to show you is the door.'

'I think you'll soon be ready to show me a great deal more,' he said, his teasing tone turning harsh as his face set in angry lines, his eyes glittering with lust. 'Put me out of commission for several days with that trick with your knee. You're going to be using those knees to make amends, kneeling before me to kiss and stroke that poor injured part. I can't wait to see how good you are with that sweet little mouth.'

He ran the fingers of his free hand over her lips. Too distressed and infuriated to remain still any longer, despite the risk, she batted that hand away and gave her imprisoned wrist a savage twist, extracting it from his grasp. Thankful that the pistol hadn't discharged, possibly wounding *her*, she placed it down carefully on the coverlet, out of his reach.

'Say what you will, I'll never give you that.'

'I think you'll be giving me that, and whatever else I want. Because I can talk to more than Mama and society. What if I go to those trustees, the oh-so-concerned uncle distressed to reveal the painful fact that my brother's widow is a wanton who brings her innocent boys with her when she meets her lover? A lover so far beneath her, those good gentlemen would be shocked and dismayed. How long do you think they would leave your precious sons in your charge after they learned how you were dragging your title in the mud, consorting with commoners and taking one to your bed?'

Thrown into dismay and confusion by Randall's threat, Faith had no reply. She knew the Dowager, and most of society, would disapprove of her friendship with Davie. Would Lord Randall be persuasive enough to convince the trustees she was a wanton, so abandoned she took her children to trysts? Would even the fact that she 'consorted with commoners' be enough for the trustees to consider taking her sons away?

There would be any number of witnesses who

could testify that they had all been together at Astley's.

'Yes, consider it, sweet sister. If it came to my word against yours, who do you think society—and the trustees—would believe? The son and brother of a duke, living all his life in the most select ranks of society? Or a woman everyone knows as inept and ineffective, never rising to successfully fill the high position to which she'd been elevated?'

He snatched again the wrist he'd seized and yanked her hand over, forcing it to the front of his dressing gown. Shock and fury pulsed through her as her fingers connected with the hard outline of his erection.

'Ah, yes, this is going to be very good. But I can wait. Let you ponder the situation. You may be a failure as a duchess, but you *are* intelligent. You'll soon realise the truth of it. When I come back next, you'll be ready.'

He leaned over and gave her a quick, hard kiss on the mouth. Then, strolling nonchalantly across the chamber, as if they'd just had a pleasant little chat, he moved the useless chair blocking the door and let himself out.

Scrubbing at her lips, Faith leaned back against her pillows, shaking with revulsion and dismay.

A turmoil of thoughts tumbled around in her head. Though she couldn't remember, from the chaotic episode of the reading of the will, who Ashedon had named as his sons' trustees, she found it hard to believe any would be so high in the instep as to consider her an unfit mother simply for having a well-known, well-respected Member of Parliament as her friend, particularly one with close connections to her family. But a claim that she had made such a man her lover, and brought her children along on her rendezvous with him, could well be damaging enough to make them question her fitness.

Sickness churning in her gut, she remembered the housekeeper turning out two maids who were found to be increasing. Though she was almost certain the poor girls had made no attempt to attract her husband's amorous attentions, it was the females who paid the price for that immorality.

With Lord Randall making the accusation, it was highly likely the trustees, drawn from the same rank of society as her brother-in-law and knowing her not at all, would believe him—and not her counter-accusations. Especially since society commonly believed that a man wouldn't make advances unless a woman encouraged him.

Sarah wouldn't believe it—but she was a woman,

without any power. Would Englemere believe in her innocence?

And Davie? She *had* been trying to entice him; indeed, she'd halfway convinced herself to make an all-out attempt to seduce him. Would Randall's assertion that she'd been trying to entice him, too, so shock and disgust Davie that he wouldn't believe her denial, either?

Even worse, she realised that Lord Randall had just checkmated her plan to go to the trustees about him. If she were to accuse him now of making inappropriate financial inroads upon the estate, he would simply claim that she was trying to discredit him because he had refused her advances.

If Sarah couldn't help her, and she couldn't count on Englemere or Davie to believe her, how was she to thwart Lord Randall and keep her boys?

She took a deep, slow breath, forcing her frantic pulse to calm. Just because, at this moment, she had no idea how to do it, she didn't intend to panic.

She'd endured nine years of marriage to a man who'd used and then ignored her. She'd vowed, after his death freed her, that she'd never allow herself to be used or manipulated again. She was not about to let Ashedon's despicable reprobate of a brother coerce himself into her bed and make her break that promise.

There'd be no more sleep for her tonight, at any rate. She might as well spend the rest of the hours before dawn trying to come up with a plan to prevent him.

Chapter Eleven

In the afternoon two days later, Davie hopped down from the hackney at Giles and Maggie's town house, where they were hosting a meeting between officials from the Lords and Commons and some influential representatives of society. At Lord Coopley's behest, they intended to invite those society leaders to encourage their representatives and peers to attend the meetings and the crucial vote soon to come over the Reform Bill.

Excited as he was to see their efforts finally come to fruition, Davie admitted he was looking forward most to seeing Faith again.

It was foolish, and most likely, sooner or later to be the source of anguish, but in every moment not focused on his committee work, his mind was preoccupied by her. And his dreams—ah, in his dreams, she'd completely replaced any strategising about government reform.

In those hazy moments between sleep and wakefulness, his mind and senses were flooded with images of her—the gold of her hair, the precise blue colour of her eyes, the shape of her shoulders, the contours of her cheeks under his hands. The softness of her breasts pressed against his chest, the silk of her hair under his cheek, the velvety fullness of her mouth, the taste of her.

He would come awake hard, throbbing with anticipation, desire and tenderness—only to realise the images, the touch, the taste, were all an illusion. Surprise and disbelief would bring him fully awake, leaving a twist of anger in his gut as passion faded and bitter disappointment settled in its wake.

Conscious, reasonable, he could talk himself out of the disappointment and anger, but in his half-dreaming state, the idea that he could not claim the woman he loved increasingly made him burn with a fierce determination to turn those illusions into reality.

It had become more of a struggle, even when awake, to yield to the hard realities of their world and repress the conviction to claim her that haunted his dreams.

Which was why this afternoon was so precious. In a salon full of other guests, he could see her, talk with her, but with so many witnesses present, have an easier time keeping a tight rein on the growing compulsion to throw caution and principles out the window and make a full-out attempt to win her.

Not as just his lover. As his wife.

Only the harsh truth that marrying her would be a selfish act that would hurt and diminish her allowed him to keep that reckless desire in check. He might have made a place for himself at the tables of political power, but a farmer's orphan could only rise so high.

Handing over hat and cane, he mounted the stairs to the salon, from which emerged a babble of voices. He halted on the threshold as the butler announced him, scanning the crowd for the one face he desired to see above all others.

He spied her at once, standing by Maggie at the hearth, her glance lifting to his as the butler intoned his name. Along with the zing of attraction and the wash of admiration he always felt as their gazes met, he noticed that her eyes looked tired and there were faint lines of strain on her forehead, so fine that anyone who hadn't memorised her features as minutely as he had probably wouldn't notice them.

Whatever had been troubling her that day they went to Astley's had not been resolved.

Which resolved *him* to somehow carve out a few private minutes this afternoon and find out what it was.

He made himself complete the rituals of politeness, going over to greet his host and hostess and the senior members of Parliament before returning, like a lodestone to the north, to the person whose presence drew him most. 'So glad you were able to attend, Duchess.'

'Very good to see you, too, Mr Smith. I was hoping you'd be present.'

He smiled. 'I was counting on seeing you, else I'd not have attended.'

Her cheeks pinked at the compliment. 'I hope to learn enough to be able to speak knowledgeably about the bill, so I may convince any gentleman I encounter at dinners and routs next week to involve himself in the discussion. Lyndlington and Coopley were telling me they believe the bill will be read in within the fortnight, and will surely pass the Commons.'

He nodded. 'I agree. Which means it will come to the Lords soon after. Anything you can do to encourage attendance at so vital a vote will be appreciated.'

'I will do what I can. I did manage to get a few words in about it to my host, Lord Hargrave, at the dinner we attended two nights ago.' She chuckled. 'I've spent so much time at society events with my head down, trying to remain silent and impassive in the face of snide comments, I believe he was astonished to realise I was capable of intelligent conversation.'

'He can't ever have spoken with you before, and thought that.'

'I didn't generally converse with gentlemen. Or anyone, if I could avoid it, for if I did, I was sure to be treated afterwards by a lecture from the Dowager about what I should or shouldn't have said, or belittling comments from my husband, if he chanced to be present. It was easier to say nothing.'

'Another reason to be glad he's gone—even if I shouldn't say so,' he added, holding up a hand to forestall the objection politeness obliged her to make.

After a reproving glance, she said, 'I meant to thank you.' At his enquiring look, she continued, 'Emboldened by your and Lady Lyndlington's encouragement, I even dared confront some of those who made snide comments.'

She must have been recalling the event, for what began as a twitch of her lips turned into a laugh.

Her sudden mirth was like the sun brightening

a grey winter day, he thought, warmed to his toes by her delight.

'When I did confront them, the ladies were even more shocked than Hargrave—and wary of me afterwards. Though the Dowager took me to task on the carriage ride home for incivility, warning that if I couldn't curb my waspish tongue, no one of breeding would invite me anywhere, I think quite the opposite might prove true. Society will be curious to see the novelty of meek little Faith Wellingford Evers behaving as imperiously as a true duchess.'

'You are a true duchess—much as I wish you weren't,' he added softly.

A grave look replaced the mirth. 'I wish I weren't, either,' she said with a sigh, her brow creasing again with worry. 'It's such a heavy responsibility, making sure my sons are brought up correctly. I want Edward to have all the training he needs to discharge his duties to the estate and the tenants, while remaining free of the arrogant sense of superiority that afflicted Ashedon. And his brother,' she added in an odd tone, her eyes flashing with something like anger.

More concerned than ever, he wanted to press her, but Giles was calling the group to order, Maggie begging all the guests to find a seat, so that the distinguished members could present their overview of the pending legislation. Though Davie perched himself on a chair near Faith, he had to wait through the exposition and the question session which followed before Maggie invited them all into the dining room, where light refreshments had been set out.

Seizing the opportunity, Davie gave Faith his arm and escorted her in. 'That was a great deal of information packed into a very short time. How about a stroll in the garden, after your tea and cake? By then, you'll have had time to think through what was presented, and can ask me any questions you might have.'

Though the invitation might have been framed to sound to anyone who overheard it as a helpful follow-on to the discussion, by the brightness in her eyes and her quick smile, Davie knew Faith understood it represented their one opportunity for some private time together. To his relief, she immediately replied, 'That sounds sensible. Over tea, I shall carefully consider everything that was said.'

Impatient for that brief sliver of time alone and determined to coax Faith to reveal whatever it was that brought the troubled look back to her face, Davie scalded his mouth, gulping down tea, munched a cake without tasting it, and had to work hard to curb his edginess while Faith daintily disposed of hers. He was nearly pacing with restlessness when, finally, she announced she was ready for a walk.

As he led her from the dining room to retrieve her wrap, he felt Maggie's speculative look on him. *I trust you to keep your promise*, it said.

Recalling his vow not to think of seducing—or marrying—Faith provoked a ferocious rush of conflicted feelings. Honour demanded he never do anything that might harm her, and reminded him that a promise is a promise. The imperatives of love and desire argued they belonged together, no matter what the world might say.

Should he have given such a promise? Would he be able to keep it?

Shaking off those thoughts, as soon as they'd begun to stroll, he said quietly, 'I don't mean to pry, but I couldn't help but notice you've seemed troubled the last two times I've seen you. Is something wrong?'

The surprise in her eyes before she schooled her expression told him he was right, regardless of whether she confided in him at once or not. Which increased both his worry and his determination to induce her to tell him what was disturbing her.

'Nothing, really. That is, there is something—not

of great import, so you mustn't feel concerned!—but I think I shall be able to handle it. I shall handle it,' she added, the determined note in her voice at odds with the anxious look in her eyes.

While she spoke, she absently rubbed at the wrist of her right hand, where the long sleeves of her spencer met the edge of her short kidskin gloves. As she moved her hand away, Davie noticed a darkened area of skin that looked almost like—a *bruise?*

Without a thought for whether or not it was proper, Davie snatched her arm and peeled down the glove—revealing what was indeed a large, deep purple bruise that appeared to entirely circle her wrist.

Shock and fury blasted out of his mind any intention to try subtle persuasion. 'What is going on?' he demanded.

She blanched before managing a tremulous smile. 'I suppose I can't convince you now that n-nothing is going on?' A sheen of tears, hastily blinked away, momentarily glazed her eyes.

'No, you'll not convince me. In fact...' he gently brushed away one errant tear with the finger of his glove '...I'm becoming more concerned by the moment. I imagine you'll say there's nothing

I can do. But I can listen, at least. Sometimes just sharing a problem lightens the burden.'

She shook her head. 'There you are, being "Davie" again, wanting to solve the problems of the world.'

'Not all the world's. Just yours.'

'I appreciate that. And I can't tell you enough how much your encouragement has…strengthened me. Made me remember the confident, competent person I once was, long ago. The person I want to be again.'

'I'm not happy with encouraging you, if it makes you soldier on alone with a problem others could help you solve.' He touched his hand lightly over the bruise. 'Don't try to tell me you fell against a cabinet. I've been in enough fights to know someone had to have grabbed you hard and held on, to create such a mark. Is the Dowager violent towards you?'

'The Dowager?' she repeated, and laughed. 'Oh, no!'

'Surely not one of the servants!'

'No, nothing like that.' She pressed her lips together, staring into the distance, obviously debating with herself.

'Please, Faith, tell me. How can I go back into that salon as if nothing is wrong, worried that someone might harm you? Do you need to leave London? Should I take you and the boys to your sister's?'

'No!' she cried. 'No, it's absolutely essential that *you* do nothing at all. I…I probably shouldn't even have agreed to walk in the garden with you.'

Struck to the quick, he must have recoiled, for she took his arm, adding urgently, 'I don't mean to hurt your feelings. If I could, there is no one else I'd rather rely on. But…but in this instance, I just can't.'

Stiffly he withdrew his arm, stung far more deeply than he wanted to let her see. He ought to nod, and bow, and return her to the salon—but he just couldn't let it go. 'Before I remove you from my polluting presence, could I at least be informed why my assistance would be inadequate?'

'You know I don't feel that way about you,' she said softly, her eyes filling with tears, which immediately defused his anger. 'Very well, I'll tell you. But before I do, you must *promise* not to intervene.'

Another promise he might not be able to keep?

'If I think my intervention would make the situation worse, then I promise to do nothing,' he said, modifying her request to something he could live with.

She took his arm and led him further away from

the house. 'I told you that first night I'd had an… unpleasant encounter with my brother-in-law, Lord Randall. Shortly thereafter, the Dowager invited him to take up residence with us in Berkeley Square. She believed she would see more of him, but he is generally around only when he needs more money. But on those occasions, he has taxed me to…become intimate with him.'

'The devil he has!' Davie burst out. 'The unprincipled reprobate! Making improper advances to his own brother's recent widow?'

'Well, that's Lord Randall,' she said drily. 'Ever on the lookout for his own advantage.'

'I'll take advantage of his impudence to beat him within an inch of his life!' Davie said furiously. 'Then tell him, if he ever darkens the door of Berkeley Square again, it will be the last doorway he ever walks through without the help of a cane.'

'But that's exactly what you cannot do!' Faith cried. 'You can't confront him, or beat him, or have any contact with him whatsoever. He started by just toying with me, or perhaps he really thought I was desperate enough for male company to take him for a lover. But when I consistently refused, he found a more promising approach. He…he has seen us together, me and you and my boys—coming back from the visit to Sarah's, from the trip to

Astley's. He threatens that if I don't give in to his desires, he'll go to the boys' trustees and claim I am having an affair with you, and am so devoid of proper motherly feeling that I've dragged my sons along while I conduct it.'

'That's preposterous! Surely no one of sense, who knows you, would believe such a faradiddle.'

'But the trustees *don't* know me. Not personally. Probably all they know is what society thinks, that I never cut an adequate figure as duchess, that Ashedon disdained me, and then humiliated me in the manner of his death. After that, they might be convinced I decided to get back at him, dishonouring my rank and his sons, by behaving in the most flagrantly immoral way possible, consorting with a commoner and bringing my sons along to witness it. If you champion me, it just gives more credence to his claims.'

For several moments, Davie paced the pathways with her, his mind feverishly working over all she'd revealed. 'Surely you don't intend to give in to his blackmail, sacrificing yourself to ensure you keep your sons!'

'Of course not. I'd shoot him, as I threatened to, or myself, before I let that happen. But I have some time to figure out a solution. He's delivered his ultimatum, and believes after I think it over, I will conclude I have no choice but to acquiesce to his desires. He said he would wait a while before confronting me again, and I believe he will. First, because he doesn't come to Berkeley Square until he's run out of money, and his mother funded him again just two nights ago. Second, he enjoys this cat-and-mouse game, and will prolong it as long as he can, confident of my eventual surrender.'

'He can't be confident if he's dead.'

'You shooting him is an even worse solution than me shooting him,' she retorted.

'Not really. Either of us could hang for it.'

'I have no intention of dying—either for his murder, or at my own hands, for giving myself to a man I loathe. I will come up with some other plan. But I will not let him force me from my own house, or force himself on me.'

'I applaud that resolution,' he retorted, not in any way convinced. 'But how, exactly, do you mean to ensure that doesn't happen?' He glanced down at her bruised wrist, almost unhinged with fury at the idea of Lord Randall hurting her, threatening her. 'Surely you don't think you're strong enough to resist him, if he did try to compel you.'

She sighed. 'I thought at first I could, but you're right. If it comes to brute force, I wouldn't prevail. So I'll have to see it doesn't.'

She must have been able to tell from his expression how inadequate a response he found that statement—and how much he felt like ripping a branch off the unoffending shrubbery bordering the pathway and breaking it over Lord Randall's head. Halting in the pathway, she took both his hands.

'Please, promise me, Davie,' she said earnestly. '*Promise* me you won't do anything to Lord Randall. Don't trail him, harass him, come to fisticuffs with him—in short, don't assault him personally in any way that would confirm a strong connection between us, giving further credence to an accusation that we are lovers. Any number of people—here today, at Astley's—can testify that we've spent time together, and you are even more an outsider to society than I am. Nothing you assert would be believed over Lord Randall's sworn word.'

'Doesn't anyone in society realise he's a liar, a wastrel, and a reprobate?' Davie spat out.

'Yes. But he was born a duke's son, and that's all that will matter,' she replied bitterly. 'We should go back in. Before we do, you will promise me, won't you? Else I'll worry even more than I am now. And…and I probably can't risk any more outings alone with you and the boys, even to Sarah's.

Much as I hate to concede even that much to Randall, I should probably see you only at gatherings like these.'

She looked at once both so fierce, and so forlorn, it was all Davie could do not to pick her up and carry her back to his rooms in Albany, where he could keep her safe. But she was right, at least initially. He couldn't intervene now, lest he risk giving the despicable Lord Randall more ammunition with which to threaten Faith.

With the loss of her sons. The phrase settled in his chest like a blow.

It would destroy her.

He couldn't do anything that would lead to that.

He couldn't stand by and do nothing, either.

But for now, he would ease her anxiety with a promise, he thought, his mind already racing through possible scenarios. A very carefully worded promise.

'Very well. I promise I will not personally assault Lord Randall.'

Fortunately, she didn't analyse how much leeway that pledge left him. 'Thank you, Davie,' she said, visibly relieved.

'But I want a promise from you in return.'

'What?' she asked, looking wary again.

'If you're wrong, and Lord Randall confronts

you in your bedchamber, scream to raise the roof, shoot first and worry about the consequences later. Or take the boys, today, and go to Sarah. I may be nobody in the eyes of society, but Englemere is a marquess. He can protect you.'

'Your good opinion is everything to me,' she whispered, pressing his hand. 'Knowing that you believe in my innocence gives me the courage to keep on. I won't go to Sarah—yet—but I promise I will shout the house down, if Randall should try to force himself on me. Now, we must go in.'

Knowing he'd pushed her as far as he could, he gave her his arm. Together, they walked back to the house, Davie wondering how he would manage to sit calmly through the rest of this meeting, when all he wanted was time alone to figure out how he would counter Lord Randall's threat without compromising his promise to Faith.

Because he fully intended, before he set eyes on Faith again, to have eliminated the problem of Lord Randall.

Chapter Twelve

Having had difficulty refraining from tapping his heels for the rest of the meeting at Lord Lyndlington's, for the first time, Davie was content to leave Faith with Maggie as the gentlemen made their departures.

'Keep her here as long as you can,' he murmured in Maggie's ear as she kissed his cheek, adding, 'I can't explain now, and don't ask her,' when she moved to arm's length, her eyebrows raised. 'Can you do that?'

'Of course,' she said, giving his hand a squeeze.

'Duchess,' he said, turning to Faith, 'I trust you will try to bend as many ears as possible this coming week, encouraging attendance at Parliament.'

'Yes, Mr Smith. Thank you again for taking the time to walk with me and fully explain some of the particulars.'

'It was my privilege.'

'Mine as well, to talk with so learned and principled a gentleman. Your electors in Hazelwick must have great confidence in you, knowing you are a man who always keeps his promises.'

While Maggie cast a puzzled look from Faith to Davie, he bowed. 'I trust that I keep my promises to everyone,' he said pointedly to them both.

Then, telling Giles he had an errand to discharge before meeting him back at the committee room, he walked out.

Already fairly sure of his destination, Davie chose to walk for a street or two, wanting some quiet time to review his preliminary impressions and confirm a plan of action.

He felt only disgust for a man—he wouldn't dignify Lord Randall Evers with the title 'gentleman,' no matter how high his birth—who would try to coerce a woman into his bed. That the woman the man was trying to coerce was his recently widowed sister-in-law made the attempt even more despicable.

That the woman was Faith made him want to take the man apart limb from limb.

There was nothing that would give him more pleasure than *personally* showing Evers what it was like to be confronted by a more physically powerful opponent. Though he was confident that such a man was a self-indulgent bully, who, once he was opposed by someone who could inflict more punishment than Evers could deliver, would back off and not menace her again, he'd promised Faith not to undertake the punishing himself.

That was disappointing, and he'd need a good, long session boxing with a worthy opponent to work off the frustration of having to honour that pledge.

On the other hand, the man was sly enough, and vindictive enough, that if Davie did assault him, he might make his accusations anyway, counting on his elevated status and the evidence of Davie's abuse to give credence to his preposterous claims. To protect Faith into the future, it was probably wiser that the retaliation for Evers's threat not be traced to him personally.

His authority and opinions might not carry any weight in circles more elevated than Parliament. But there were certain places in which he was well known, his proven competence respected, where he would be able to recruit exactly the assistance he needed.

In this instance, he thought grimly as he hailed a hackney and set off for Bow Street, it was useful to have friends in *low* places.

* * *

Fortunately, for he didn't want to explain to Giles what had taken him so long to 'discharge his errand', Mr Hines was in his office when Davie arrived.

'Mr Smith, good to see you again!' Hines said, waving Davie to a chair. 'All going well in Parliament, I hear? About to strike a blow for the common man?'

'We certainly hope so.'

'As I imagine you are aware, we got a conviction in the case of the man hired to shoot at Lady Roberts—that is, Lady Lyndlington now. With both families involved strongly urging to the judge that clemency be shown, he was transported, rather than hanged.'

'Let me commend you again for how expeditiously your men handled that case.'

Hines nodded, accepting the compliment as his due—which he should; the man was efficient and fanatically persistent in solving the cases brought to him. 'Always glad to help out a man who has given us so much assistance from time to time. So, what brings you to me today?'

'A rather delicate matter, one whose resolution requires discretion and actions that might not precisely follow the letter of the law. Actions, I must warn you, taken against a man of high standing, who could make a lot of trouble for both of us if the business isn't handled properly.'

'So it involves a female,' Hines said, interpreting Davie's euphemisms. 'A woman some high-ranking gent is trying to abuse, like that earl's son in the case of Lady Lyndlington?'

'Something similar. Though I would far prefer to handle the situation personally, if the...actions could be traced back to me, the man in question might be able to make further trouble for the lady. So I'm looking for two or three skilled individuals, who can perform the actual...intervention.'

Hines nodded thoughtfully. 'Them higher-ups been bending the law to suit them for centuries. I reckon it's only fair it be bent a time or two against them—especially if it's to protect a female. I know you got too much respect for the law to ask me for help on this, if the cause wasn't right and just. What type of "intervention" do you have in mind?'

Davie described what he envisioned, Hines making suggestions at various points to improve the plan. Within a half hour, they'd worked out a scenario that satisfied them both with its safety and efficiency, and its ability to be implemented soon, perhaps that very night.

Leaving Hines to put the finishing touches on

the scheme, with directions about contacting him later to launch it, Davie thanked the man again and took his leave. Knowing that he most likely would be able to snap off the problem of Lord Randall like the branch he'd wanted to break in the garden this afternoon, he was able to return to the committee room calm, resolved and full of purpose.

It was mid-evening by the time the committee completed its deliberations, and the Hellions were free for the night. Just as they were finishing up, a boy delivered a note to Davie that greatly relieved his mind.

The very efficient Hines had come through again. They'd be able to put the plan into action this very evening.

'Shall we head off to the Quill and Gavel?' Ben Tawny's question interrupted Davie's thoughts. Rolling his tired shoulders, he added 'After all those hours bent over documents, I could do with a good roast and a large tankard of ale.'

'Before you head off to find refreshment of a more intimate and satisfying sort?' Christopher Lattimer asked with a grin.

'Naturally,' Ben replied. 'You're welcome to come along. Sally has several friends, all of them as voluptuous and playful as she is.'

'I just might,' Christopher said. 'Giles, you're off to your lady wife, I expect. Davie, will you join us for dinner? For as we know only too well, you'll not join us for the festivities after.'

'Certainly not!' Ben said. 'The Saint will return to his empty rooms, to worship at the shrine of "the Unattainable", and find whatever pleasure he can reading musty old legal documents.'

'He's been worse than ever since—for no good reason any of us can tell—he started seeing her again,' Christopher observed.

'Well, having beheld her up close, I can better understand why he's worshipped all these years. Although, Davie, you still know nothing can come of it. Isn't it time you bowed to reality and set your sights on someone more suitable?'

'Isn't it time you both stopped harassing him and let him make that choice?' Giles interposed.

Refusing to be drawn by their banter, Davie simply shrugged. 'I can't join you gentlemen for dinner, either—and not just because you can't seem to stop pestering me.'

'I did refrain from pursuing the Vision myself,' Ben pointed out. 'You owe me something for that, because she truly is delectable. And after all those years tied to a fool like Ashedon, she deserves a little…frolic, with a man who can make sure she enjoys it.'

Finally goaded beyond endurance, Davie sent Ben a thunderous look that had his friend laughing as he raised his hands protectively in front of his face. 'Pax! Don't try that punishing roundhouse punch out on me.'

Reminded of where he wished he could use it, Davie said, 'You push me very close to the edge, but, alas, that's not to be. I do have some urgent business to complete, though.'

'More urgent business?' Giles asked quietly. 'Anything the Hellions can help you with?'

'Not now. Not yet. But if…circumstances develop in that direction, I will certainly let you know.'

'Then all we can do, is hope the enterprise prospers,' Giles said.

'If Davie doesn't need us, I'm ready for dinner. Come, Christopher, let's find a good roast.'

'And then on to more delectable entertainment,' Christopher added as the two friends sauntered out.

Giles lingered, regarding Davie silently until the other Hellions were out of earshot. 'You've been tense as an overwound watch all day. Are you sure I can't help?'

'Not tonight, which I hope will resolve the matter.'

'Then I will hope so, too.' Giving him a clap on the arm, Giles said, 'You've done me a good turn more times than I care to mention. Just know I stand ready to return the favour.'

Davie smiled. 'Considering that, if you hadn't befriended me in that tavern in Oxford all those years ago, I might be toiling away as a lonely law clerk in some barrister's office today, rather than working towards the most significant piece of legislation in the last four hundred years, I think we can call ourselves even.'

'Friends don't keep score. Don't forget the offer, though. I'm off to Maggie.'

'Give her my love.'

'I'll do that.' With a final nod, Giles walked out, leaving Davie in sole possession of the committee room. For a few minutes, he paced the length of it, going over in his mind each step in his plan for the night. Then, satisfied he'd calculated every angle and considered every detail, he squared his shoulders, took a deep breath, and set out.

The initial move had him strolling into an area of London he seldom visited, a slip of a lad trailing him. Until recently, when the government sinecures he'd been awarded had begun providing him with a steady income, he'd not possessed enough blunt beyond what was essential to pay for his food and lodging, to think of wasting any on gaming. Not that, he thought, looking askance at the knots of young men swaggering down the street from gaming hell to gaming hell, their fine garments proclaiming them as gentlemen of privilege, he could ever have been persuaded to throw away good coin on games of chance.

Solid farm boy that he was, he thought with a wry grin, whenever he got a penny to spare, he'd saved it to invest in good English land—and now possessed a fine small estate, a fact that gave him far more satisfaction than the lucky outcome of a frivolous game.

A moment later, he reached his destination. With his imposing size and prosperous look, he was easily granted access to Aphrodite's Dice, a hell known both for its deep play and its lovely—and available—women. When the proprietor, spying a gent who might be a new pigeon for plucking, tried to induce him to join in some game of chance, he politely declined, informing them he was there as a friend of Mr Hine's.

The man's eyes widened before he nodded. 'Very good, sir. Would you like a glass of wine while you wait?'

Accepting that, he followed the proprietor, who led him into the next room and nodded towards a table. There sat Lord Randall, rolling a pair of the dice featured in the establishment's name, the glass of brandy in his other hand continually replenished by the scantily attired lovely at his side.

'The preparations are all made. Did you want to have a word with the gentleman—before?' the proprietor murmured.

'Not as yet.'

'As you wish.'

Giving him a short bow, the proprietor exited, and Davie turned to watch Lord Randall. It appeared, as arranged, he was currently winning, for the stack of counters in front of him had been steadily growing. Intent on the play, his eyes glazed with the feverish look of the hardened gamester, he was oblivious to all else, even the blandishments of the lady wielding the brandy decanter, whom he pushed away when, from time to time, she leaned over to whisper in his ear.

After one particularly successful run, he gave a crow of triumph, leaning back to seize the hand the harlot had rested on his shoulder and pulling it down to rub at his groin. 'Feel that power, Letty?' he crowed. 'Stronger and sweeter than brandy.

You'll be getting a mouthful, soon as I finish off this round.'

Davie only hoped the man hadn't used such crude terms with Faith. The very thought made him clench his fists, and he had to force himself to remember all the good reasons he couldn't just walk over and punch Lord Randall in the gut.

Since he'd turned down the offers of the other young ladies who strolled up to accompany him to the card tables, the faro bank—or upstairs—they soon left him alone. He found himself pitying not only the unfortunate women who had to service such clients, but the gaming-crazed young men who seemed unable to walk away from the tables until they'd spent their last coin.

Imagine, he thought—watching as one well-dressed gentleman dropped almost five hundred guineas—having that much blunt, and just tossing it away.

Finally, the moment for which he'd been patiently waiting arrived. Lord Randall, happily finished at his table, pawed up his winnings and staggered upright, leaning on the shoulder of his doxy. As he crossed the room towards the stairway to the chambers above, he finally spotted Davie, and halted.

A slow smile on his face, he patted the doxy on

the bottom and said, 'Go on up, honey. I'll meet you in a trice.' Giving her a push towards the stairs, he sauntered over to Davie.

'Well, well,' he said, subjecting Davie to a slow, insolent inspection from his boots to the crown of his head. 'You're that guttersnipe politician who's been sniffing around my brother's wife, aren't you? Wonder they let so low-born a cur in the place. Might have to take my custom elsewhere.'

'I'm sure they'll be delighted if you do. The women, at least.'

'Ah, yes, women.' He smirked. 'Ashedon's doxy wife, in particular, eh? Can't blame you being interested—she's a choice little morsel. So hot-blooded, I'm having trouble holding her off! But she's not available—at least, not until I'm done with her.'

Gritting his teeth against the compulsion to knock the varmint to his knees with one well-placed blow, Davie made himself reply calmly, 'I think you will be "done with her" very soon. Tonight, as a matter of fact.'

'I will, will I? When I haven't truly started yet? No, indeed!' Randall struck an exaggerated pose, hands on hips. 'You're thinking you can make me?'

'I won't need to. Your conscience is going to persuade you it's only right to stop harassing your brother's widow.'

Randall burst out laughing. 'What, she tell you tales? Say I "threatened" her, or some such? Thing is, she's so unsophisticated and simple, she exaggerates or misrepresents what she hears.'

Davie nodded. 'I'm rather unsophisticated and simple myself. But I understand what a bruised wrist represents. So you're not going to see her again. In fact, you're not going back to Berkeley Square—ever.'

Randall's smile faded. 'You know, you're not so amusing any more. Why don't you leave, before I have the proprietor eject you? And if you have the audacity to come around me again, trying to tell a duke's brother how to treat his women, I've got a little warning for you. Persist in this, and I'll tell the trustees overlooking her brats about the little trysts between you two. Yes, I've seen you, bringing her and the sons back in the carriage. Don't think the trustees would hold with a duchess rutting in the gutter with a commoner—while her dear children watch. I'm guessing they'd whisk those boys away faster than she could find herself a handkerchief to boo-hoo in. Face it, guttersnipe. You can't help her. You can only destroy her.'

'Whereas you don't *care* if you destroy her,' Davie said, calling on all the willpower he possessed to keep from pummelling Evers then and there.

Randall smiled again. 'True. But unlike you, I get what I want.'

As Evers waved a hand dismissively, Davie added, 'Perhaps. You'd have to be alive to get it, though. Bullies who try to abuse innocent women often suffer unforeseen...accidents. Goodnight, Evers.'

After the insult of neglecting to accord him his title, Davie turned on his heel and walked away. Having confirmed all that Faith had confessed and more, it was time to initiate the second part of the plan.

Unfortunately for the fury and contempt raging through him, he would have to play a much less active part in that.

Forewarned by the proprietor, the men Davie had hired were stationed by the door as a drunken Lord Randall was helped down the back stairs of the gaming hell some time later. From the place in the shadows where he stood beside his horse, Davie gave the nod, and the driver of the waiting carriage pulled his vehicle up to the bottom of the stairs.

''Ere's your hackney, governor,' one of the men said.

'Get you back to your lodgings all right and

tight,' the other said, grabbing Lord Randall's shoulders and heaving him up the step.

'D-don' need lozzings,' Randall slurred. 'Hav'a house. Berkeley Square.'

'In good time, governor. In good time.' After pushing Evers into the cab and closing the door behind him, the two men hopped up on the box beside the driver and gave Davie a wave.

The carriage set off, Davie mounted quickly, and quietly followed.

After a winding journey from the dubious streets behind Covent Garden to a nicer part of town, the carriage entered through the gates of Hyde Park, continuing through the deserted gardens until it reached a place near the verge of the Serpentine. There, the vehicle halted.

While Davie dismounted and took up his position a short distance from the vehicle, the two men climbed down from the box and opened the carriage door.

'Wakee, wakee, my lord,' one said. 'Time for your walk.'

'Wa—walk?' Evers's drowsy voice repeated.

'Yes, walk. Preacher says, contemplation's good for the soul.' With that, the man reached inside and yanked Lord Randall from the coach.

The full moon illumined them as Randall stumbled out, the second man caught him neatly and held him upright while the first pulled a sack over his head and down his body, securing it with a quick knot of rope about his upper thighs.

'Wha—what are you doing?' Evers cried. Shock and the cool air apparently dissipating some of the drunken haze, he flailed his imprisoned arms inside the sacking restraining his upper body.

As Davie watched, the two men half-pushed, half-dragged the protesting Randall over to the Serpentine, threw him in, and waded in after him.

After a moment, Evers found his feet and surfaced, gasping. 'Whatever do you—?'

Each man taking an arm, they knocked his feet out from under him and tossed Randall into the water again.

Breathing even more raggedly, he emerged a second time. A note of panic in his voice, he cried, 'What do you want? I can pay—'

The two seized him and submerged him a third time—and a fourth, and a fifth.

When they finally allowed him to remain on his feet, Randall sobbed, 'P-pay you! Wh—whatever you want! J-just let me go!'

At Davie's signal, the two grabbed Randall again, dragged him back up the bank, and tossed him to the ground.

'Wh—why are you doing this?' he cried. 'I haven't done anything! You must have the wrong man!'

'Don't reckon we do,' the leader said. 'Heard a lot about you. Lordling's son and brother. Living off his mama in a smart house in Berkeley Square. Got the right of it, don't I?'

'But what—?'

'Threatening his sister-in-law. His poor, widowed sister-in-law. Just ain't right. A man don't do such.'

'*He* sent you!' Randall cried. 'That pox-ridden politic—'

The second man struck Randall on the jaw before he could finish, knocking him to his knees.

While he scrabbled to regain his balance, the leader said, 'Don't need no names. And nobody sent me. Heard a mate repining over a mug of ale, ya see? 'Bout a fine lady being threatened by a greasy muckworm—that would be you—and how angry he was, not being able to grind the muckworm under his boot like he wanted, on account of the muckworm maybe making more trouble for the lady. Now this mate, he's done me some powerful good turns over the years. So when I heard him so agitated 'n' all, I thought to meself, why not do him a favour back, and take care of this for him?'

At his nod, the second man hauled Evers upright. The leader reached out to grip Randall's shoulder with one large paw, his hold punishing enough that Randall cried out. Leaning closer, he said, 'Had to sympathise, ya see. Got a daughter of me own— prettiest thing a man ever laid eyes on. So pretty, a fancy man tried to snatch her for a bawdy house. I 'bout lost my mind when I found her missing, but with the Lord's blessing, I found her right quick. And that fancy man? Well, he won't be snatching no more girls, ever again.'

'No names!' Evers agreed, his voice pleading. 'Just let me go. I'll pay you! And I'll leave the bitch alone, I promise!'

'Here, now, show the lady some respect!' the first man said, nodding to the second man, who punched Evers again.

This time, Lord Randall didn't try to stand back up, but remained cowering on the ground. Between Evers's sobs, the first man continued, 'Don't want your mama's money. Don't believe a muckworm's promises, neither. No, we'll have a little agreement, jes' between me 'n' you. You'll take those winnings Aphrodite's Dice allowed you tonight, and leave London. Go far away as you can get. I hear Calais is a good town for cheap living and high play. And you'll stay there a good long while.

Till my agitation with you simmers down. Understand?'

He nodded to the second man, who hauled Randall back to his feet. 'I understand,' Randall sobbed. 'Leave London, tonight. Won't come back.'

'That's right. Good to know even a muckworm like you has some sense. But just in case you get to thinking, after we drop you at that lodging house to get your spare duds, that maybe instead of leaving, you'll go complain to your mama, or the constable, or some such, remember this. We knew where to find you tonight. When a man don't pay his valet, or his servants, or any what provide him with coats and hats and boots and such, there's a lot of folk eager to tell whatever you want, to get a few coins back on what's owed them. If you don't leave London, I'll know, and the next time I toss you in the water, there'll be a rock in that sack with you. Doubt anyone will miss you, 'ceptin them what you owe money to. Now, think you can remember that?'

'Yes,' Randall gasped. 'Please, just let me go!'

'Dunno,' the man said, his tone considering. 'Not sure your memory's that good. Mebbe need another dunking to strengthen it some.' At his wave, the second man knocked Randall to the ground and started dragging him back towards the Serpentine.

'No, please!' Randall screamed, struggling futilely in the confining sack. 'I'll remember. I'll leave tonight!'

At his leader's nod, the second man halted. The leader walked over to where Evers struggled on the ground and knelt next to him.

'Sure you'll remember? No more trouble for the lady? No recriminations for my mate?'

'No! Nothing! I hope I never lay eyes on either of them again.'

'Ah, yes—yer *eyes*. Now, if after a time you should come to think, from the safety of whatever rat's nest you run to, that you might send yer *money* back to London and try to get someone to find me, save the coins. Oh, someone'd take them, all right. But you'd get nothing else for them. I'm a rather well-connected gent in certain parts; you have no power and no influence there. If you was to want to come back and settle up yerself—now, that's a meeting I'd relish. Got lots of sacks, and there's plenty of lonely riverbank. But I don't think you're up to that. Better you just take your winnings and get your miserable muckworm self out of London tonight, and stay gone.'

'I'll go. I'll stay gone. Just take me away now!'

'Sure you don't need a little more water cure to help your memory?'

'No, no, I'm sure! Please! Just let me go!'

When Randall stopped to take a breath, the leader said, 'Very well. Being a fair man, I'll give you a chance to hold up your end of the bargain.' He clapped his hands, summoning the coachman, who dismounted and came running.

'Take him to his lodgings,' he told the second man. 'And keep watch. Don't report back until you know he's left London.'

While Randall moaned and whimpered, the second man and the coachman half-led, half-carried him to the carriage, dragged him up the step, and tossed him in. After securing the door, the two men scrambled back up on the box, and a moment later, the coach drove off.

Once it was well away, the leader walked over to where Davie waited in the shadows. 'Where do the toffs come up with such scum?' he asked. 'Right tempted to toss him in the water again and leave him.'

'Glad you didn't,' Davie said. 'I wanted him cowed, not murdered. Though I doubt anyone but his mama would miss him, doing away even with a reprobate like Evers would cause too many problems. My conscience would have required me to fish him out, and I'd have been hard-pressed to make myself do it.'

'Never can tell for sure, but I think he's gone for good. I'll have Jack watch him for a week or so, and keep Hines posted.'

'He'll write his mama and beg for more money, once what they let him win tonight runs out,' Davie said. 'But I don't think he'll be back to make accusations. Sadly, there are too many other women in the world for a man with money to bother, to keep pursuing just one, especially after you made him such a convincing case for moving on. Thank you.'

Davie held out his hand, and the leader shook it.

'Figure what I owe you for the gaming hell, the carriage, your men, and the surveillance, and let Hines know.'

'Some for the lads and the gambling house, but nothing for me,' the man said. 'Putting the fear of God into him was my pleasure. Wasn't bamming when I told him about me daughter. Wish I could bag up all the varmints that prey on females and toss 'em in the river! Good luck to you and your lady. You'll be getting us common men our day in Parliament soon, right?'

'I will keep pressing for it,' Davie promised. Tipping his hat to Hine's operative, he walked back to his horse, while the man disappeared into the night like the phantom he was.

Reasonably sure that Randall had been dealt with

for good, Davie rode back towards Albany, as satisfied with the results of the night's manoeuvrings as he could be, without having been permitted the satisfaction of personally planting a few blows in the middle of Lord Randall's smirking face.

Now he had a more delicate task to accomplish: figuring out how to tell Faith what he'd done, and convincing her to visit Sarah until he was sure his ploy had permanently removed the threat of Lord Randall.

Chapter Thirteen

Encouraged by a note from Hines confirming that Lord Randall had indeed left London that night, followed by a second indicating their man had watched Evers boarding a packet bound for Calais, Davie was able to curb his impatience to see Faith again until a favourable opportunity arose. Which it did in the afternoon three days later, when he learned from Giles that the ladies were going to call on an elderly peer, an old friend of Lady Maggie's father, who'd turned over his estate to his son and lived in a grace and favour apartment at Hampton Court.

'Are you going to escort Maggie there?' Davie asked.

'Yes. Maggie and the Duchess will go to charm Lord Harvey, and I'll come along to provide any details he may demand about the legislation. His lordship's not as healthy or vigorous as he once was, but still takes an interest in Parliamentary doings,' Maggie said. 'With the vote to come next week, we need to involve as many peers as possible.'

'Sure he'll vote with us?'

'Maggie says he's a realist. If we can convince him the vote must pass, he'll want to have a part in doing what will prevent further unrest and distress in the country.'

'Do you mind if I accompany you?'

Giles studied him for a moment. 'Wouldn't it be better if you did not?'

'Not this time. I have some information of a... confidential nature for the Duchess that shouldn't be trusted to a note. The visit to Lord Harvey will allow me to convey it to her personally, upon an occasion in which our meeting will not excite any comment.'

'This "confidential information" is related to the "business" you were so keen to take care of several days ago? Which, I assume, prospered, since you've seemed much more your normal self since then.'

'Yes, and, yes.' Davie gave him a wry smile. 'Thank you for trusting me on this, and making no attempt to pry. And especially for not making any mention of it in front of Christopher and Ben, who would have no compunction about pressing the matter.'

Giles nodded. 'I figured if the Hellions could be of any help, you'd ask, and if we couldn't, it was none of our business. Especially as it seemed to relate to the Duchess.' He hesitated. 'Do you… have some notion of what you envision for that association?'

'There's where I'd wish it to go, and where it will likely end,' Davie admitted.

Giles clapped a hand on his shoulder. 'If there's anything I can do…'

'Noted. When do we meet the ladies?'

Giles consulted the mantel clock. 'We'd best leave now. The Duchess was to take tea with Maggie at Upper Brook Street, with our carriage ordered to come around after.'

Anticipation and trepidation rising in equal measure at the idea of seeing Faith soon, Davie rose with Giles and went to get his hat and coat. Some time after the meeting, he'd ask Faith to walk with him in the gardens.

It had better be a long walk, he thought wryly. Because after he confessed what he'd done, she might hand him his *congé* this very afternoon.

When they joined the ladies at Upper Brook Street, the light that sparked in Faith's eyes and the warmth of her smile at his unexpected appearance soothed the ever-present ache in his heart with an uplift of joy. Driving deep the hunger to touch and taste her that also leapt to the forefront the moment he saw her, he tried to convince himself he could be satisfied by a life where he met her only as a friend.

'Mr Smith! What a surprise!' she said, coming over to him as Giles and Maggie shared a hug.

Wistfully wishing he had the freedom to share the same with Faith, he said, 'Not an unwelcome one, I hope.'

'Indeed not! I'm so pleased you'll be joining our little expedition this afternoon.'

'You've been well, I trust?' he asked, knowing that Lord Randall had not been around to bother her, and hoping that she'd been able to suppress her anxiety over the threat he posed. 'You look more rested than when I saw you last.'

After this afternoon, she would have no more reason to lose sleep. The certain knowledge that he had eliminated for good the threat posed by her brother-in-law made it worthwhile to have acted without her knowledge or approval, even if it created a breach between them.

Her safety was more important than anything else.

'Yes, thankfully, there have been no...disturbances these last few days.'

'Shall we go?' Maggie turned to ask. 'I told Lord Harvey in my note that we'd be there in time for a late tea. So many of his generation have already passed, he doesn't get many visitors, so I know he'll be waiting for us.'

'Then let us leave at once,' Faith said. 'We'll find an opportunity to talk later, Mr Smith?'

'Certainly. Perhaps we might stroll in the garden after the business is complete, to give Maggie some time for a private chat with Lord Harvey?'

Faith's eyes brightened. 'We could walk in the maze! I haven't wandered through it since I was a child, but I remember being enchanted by it. Although, you are so tall, you may be able to see over the hedges.'

'I've never been; you must show it to me. I promise not to peek and spoil the suspense.'

With that, the ladies collected gloves and wraps and descended to the carriage. Thinking it wiser to avoid the temptation of sitting beside Faith—and any potential awkwardness on the drive back, if she should be furious with him—Davie chose to make the transit on horseback. Not wishing to mar even this limited contact being impatient or anxious, he forced his sense of urgency beneath the surface. Once they were out of the congestion of the city, he rode beside the carriage, keeping up a running conversation with the denizens of the coach, as he had when he'd escorted Faith and her sons to Lady Englemere's.

The day being warm and pleasant, the trip was enjoyable, with autumn wildflowers nodding beside the lanes and just a touch of chill in the air to warn of the approaching change of season. Their vehicle and Davie's horse dispatched to grooms at the palace, they proceeded to the apartment occupied by Lord Harvey, where they found the genial gentleman and tea awaiting them.

After introductions were made all around, the ladies launched into their mission of charming the elderly peer, accomplishing it so successfully that Giles's announcement of the radical changes about to happen in Parliament drew nothing stronger than an exclamation of surprise from Lord Harvey. As Giles presented the major points, he asked a series of sharp, penetrating questions that made Maggie remark with a laugh that she was glad the more knowledgeable gentlemen had accompanied them.

Content to let Giles explain their position, Davie curbed his impatience to get Faith alone and simply appreciated the joy of being around her, watching her with even more than his usual intensity.

The enquiring angle of her head as she listened

to Lord Harvey pose a question, or Giles answer it, reminded him again of that summer of debate they'd shared. So full of dreams and purpose they'd been, he thrilled that Sir Edward's patronage would allow him to take part in turning his ideas for a new England into reality, she giddy with anticipation to enter the adult world.

She was just as lovely as she'd been that summer, a girl poised on the brink of becoming a woman. She still lit up the room, and his heart, with her smile. But the struggles of her marriage and the responsibility of motherhood had created layers of reserve and complexity that made the woman even more fascinating than the girl. After enduring heartache, disappointment, and disparagement, she'd raised that little chin, and with a militant sparkle in her eyes, ultimately refused to be defeated by the neglect of her husband, the disapproval of society, the criticism of her mother-in-law—or the crude threats of a reprobate.

Which just emphasised the need for him to be eloquent this afternoon. His newly confident Faith wouldn't be dictated to, or metaphorically patted on the head and told what he'd done without her approval was for the best. He would need to persuade her that his actions had been well thought out, fitting—and effective—in order to preserve her trust.

Would he be persuasive enough?

With tea consumed, Lord Harvey having reached the end of his questions and the personal chat between their host and Lady Maggie beginning, he was about to find out.

'Shall we have that walk now, Mr Smith?' Faith asked, turning to him, obviously eager to begin the stroll he both anticipated—and dreaded. He absolutely hated to spoil their precious time together bringing up something that was sure to make her angry. But he'd rather have her distressed with him, than to have stood by and done nothing as she'd begged him to, and have her still at the mercy of the infamous Lord Randall.

Wraps and coats collected, they exited Lord Harvey's apartment and strolled across the palace grounds to the entrance to the maze.

'Isn't it lovely?' Faith exclaimed, examining the handsome stand of boxwood at the entrance. 'I don't think even you will be able to see over it, Davie.' Taking his arm, she said, 'Though it would be amusing to discover who could solve the key and reach the centre first, I simply can't bear for us to part, and waste this opportunity to be alone, far from prying eyes and listening ears!'

'I doubt we'll be overheard, though we might still be observed from the upper storeys of the palace,' Davie noted. With her perfume infiltrating his nose and the touch of her hand on his sleeve setting his body into a full clamour for more, he was struggling to keep her enchanting presence from distracting him from the serious matter he had to discuss.

'The trees will block the view—or well enough. Oh, Davie, it's so good to be with you again!' Taking his arm with both hands, she marched him at a quick step down the first avenue and around the corner, into the sheltering walls of the maze.

And then before he was aware what she intended, she reached up and pulled his head down for a kiss.

Desire incinerated surprise the instant her lips touched his. Prudence, discretion, the confession he was about to make—all cindered as well, as his whole universe narrowed to the woman pressing her lips to his.

He wrapped his arms around her, drawing her close, sighing as the softness of her bosom contacted his chest. Though he was so starved for the taste of her, he wanted to possess and plunder, he kept himself still, letting her set the pace.

And discovered there was something intensely erotic about letting her initiate and probe and explore, opening his mouth only when she demanded entry, meeting her tongue with his only after she sought it out. Her little gasps and sighs filling him with a tenderness almost as vast as the passion they inspired, he opened to her as she pressed deeper, the vibrations created by the sensuous plush of her tongue rubbing his so intense, he thought he might reach his peak from her kisses alone.

Devil take it, how he wanted her! So much, he blessed this narrow walk, bordered on either side by nothing more comfortable than evergreen shrubbery, else he might lose all control and take her right here, right now. But her artless passion deserved wine, and wooing, and fine linen sheets, and hours in which to show her how much he desired and cherished her.

She must have been near the brink, too, for heedless of time and place, she wrapped her arms around him and pulled him closer still, bringing his throbbing erection tight against her belly. Knowing if she gave any indication of moving that sweet mouth to the part of him most desperate for her caress, he'd be well and truly lost, he somehow found enough will to break the kiss.

Not enough will to release her, though. They stood with their arms wrapped around each other, the only sound their ragged, panting breaths and the distant call of a bird. Finally, with a sigh, she pushed away.

'Though ending that before it went any further was prudent, it doesn't make me feel any less like slapping you,' she said, taking his arm and starting to walk again.

'Slap away. I didn't like ending it any more than you did.'

She took a shuddering breath. 'Maybe we ought to talk about…going to a place where we wouldn't have to end it.'

Not allowing his mind to explore the meaning behind that comment, Davie said, 'Before we talk of anything else, I have a confession to make, as well as a prediction that I hope will leave you much relieved.'

'A confession? Oh, dear—I'm not sure I like the sound of that.'

'Although, to be prudent, I'd like to have you take your boys and go visit Lady Englemere for a few days, I'm nearly certain your problems with Lord Randall are over.'

It took her only an instant to comprehend the implications. Halting, she dropped his arm and turned to face him. 'What have you done? Oh, Davie, I begged you not to intervene! You haven't shot him, have you? Or beaten him to a pulp?'

'No, though it required a great deal of restraint to resist beating him to a pulp.'

'But you did confront him—thereby providing him all the ammunition he needs to accuse us to the trustees! Which, unless you truly did murder him, he's sure to do. And after you promised me! I wish I *had* slapped you! Now I'll never be free of his menace! And if he ends up getting them to take my boys away, I'll hate you f-for ever!'

Her furious voice breaking as tears started in her eyes, she turned on her heel and stalked away from him. In two strides, he caught up and grabbed her arm.

'Wait, Faith, let me explain! I didn't break my promise.'

She looked up at him, confused and miserable. 'But—didn't you just tell me you'd confronted Randall, hurt him, after I most particularly begged you not to?'

'I promised not to physically assault him myself—and despite the utmost provocation, I did not.'

'But you did confront him.'

'I—talked with him. Predicted that he would cease his unwelcome attentions of his own free will, since it was the right thing to do. Which, in a way, he has. True, there are people at the gaming hell who could testify to seeing us together. But we parted without any altercation, so even if he were to return at some point and try to make an issue of it, no one could claim to have witnessed anything more than a conversation.'

"If he should return at some point?" she echoed. 'What, you had him kidnapped and transported?' A reluctant smile tugging at her lips, she sighed and laid her hand back on his arm. 'You'd better tell me the whole.'

Briefly he summarised the events at the gaming hell and beside the Serpentine, concluding with the reports that Hine's operative had seen Randall safely embarked to Calais.

'I only wish I could have witnessed his dunking in the Serpentine!' she said, laughing as if she were envisioning it. 'I might have been too tempted to let him drown, though.'

'I was tempted as well, I assure you. But a dead duke's son would cause too much trouble.'

'Oh, Davie, what a marvel you are! And so very clever about wording your promises! I shall have to remember that.'

'You didn't truly believe I would just sit on my hands and let him threaten you?'

'Yes—no. Other men might have. But not you,

Davie. I should have known you would find some way to thwart him.'

I would die to protect you, he thought. Suppressing the words, he said instead, 'Randall's just a bully, Faith. Purposeless, idle, and too much indulged. That sorry breed only preys on the weak. I learned enough about them when I got to Oxford. I wasn't quite so strapping then, but I was still strong enough. They soon learned not to bait the "farm boy", and took their mischief elsewhere.' He smiled. 'My education in fisticuffs progressed rapidly.'

'But you said—ah,' she said, making the connection. 'You stood up for the other boys.'

He shrugged. 'It was only right. Outsiders should stick together. Although, after Giles took me up, I never felt like an outsider again, even though I was. And am.'

'That knack served you—and me—excellently well in this circumstance.'

He chuckled. 'Yes. I doubt Lord Randall will forget the events of that evening for a very long time.'

'Do you think he wrote his mother? She's not complained about him abandoning her, yet. Although, it's not at all unusual for him to disappear for days at a time, without sending her any word, although ostensibly he's living in her house. My *son's* house, I should say.'

'He was warned not to complain to anyone. Being mostly concerned with his own hide, I doubt he'll contact her until he runs out of money. I'm reasonably sure he will remain in Calais for some time, and when he does return to England, he'll avoid you.' Unable to help himself, he added, 'By then, you'll probably have a new champion.'

Suddenly, with a gasp, Faith halted. Taking both his hands, she looked up into his face, her expression eager. 'I just realised the full extent of what you've accomplished! Not only are my boys safe, but now there is truly an opportunity for...for *us*. To come together as one. Oh, Davie, I know it's shocking of me to propose it, but I...I want you so badly! I admire and honour and esteem you as the dearest friend I've ever had, but I want more. More of *this*...'

She flung her arms around him and pulled his head down for another kiss, one that started already hot and needy and quickly intensified. One hand twined in his hair, she pursued his tongue, laving, sucking, urging him deeper. With the other, she slid her hand between them to stroke the iron rod of his erection.

The pleasure was so intense, he thought he would

shatter on the spot. But he couldn't, wouldn't, have her making love to him in a garden within view of the palace, where anyone who looked out an upper-storey window might see them.

It still took him several minutes to find the strength to break the kiss. 'Darling Faith, not here,' he gasped.

She leaned against him, trembling. 'Yes, you're right. Not here. I'll come to you at Albany. Or I have money, I can hire a house. We'll have a place to be together, where we can do away with the sham of "Mr Smith" and "Duchess", and be the lovers we were meant to be. I've known it must happen, somehow, since that first summer—haven't you? Oh, Davie, please say "yes". All I've ever known of passion is to be taken by a man who just wanted to breed sons on me. Won't you give me the joy of being loved by a man who truly cares for and desires me?'

His friend. His lover. He'd known it all along, but hearing what she said—or rather, what she didn't say, cut deeper than he'd imagined possible. *She'd take him as a lover, but he wasn't good enough to be a husband.*

Ruthlessly he squelched the anguish and made himself focus on reality. 'There's nothing I desire more, but you must realise, my darling, that eliminating Lord Randall doesn't make our situation that much safer. He's not the only peer who might find a relationship between a commoner and a duchess with minor children objectionable enough to bring it to the attention of their trustees. And this time, it could be someone more reputable, more credible than Lord Randall.'

She waved a hand dismissively. 'With all the affairs going on amongst members of the *ton*? I doubt any would care enough to make a point of it. Would you deny us a chance for happiness over so unlikely an event?'

'Happy, yes—but for how long? A week? A month? Before someone found out, and society started to point fingers? Because it *would* get out, you know that. We'd have to end it, and it would end badly. With you disgraced. Possibly even threatened again with losing control over your sons. And what if you were to conceive? Forcing you to hide away somewhere to give birth in secret, and then give up the child. *My* child. How could I bear for you to give me a son neither of us could ever acknowledge?'

He waited, still unable to relinquish the slender hope that she might suggest the one way they could prevent that from happening. When instead, she drooped against him, crestfallen, he reined in the urge to ask for her hand.

Eliminating Lord Randall hadn't changed any of the hard facts about their relative positions. Marrying him would still be a huge step down in the world for her, turning her into an object of derision. Exiling her from association with her class. And quite possibly, resulting in the loss of her sons.

He couldn't take advantage of her longing and his desperation to urge her into a union she would almost certainly come to regret. A regret that would cripple him with remorse for persuading her into it. A regret that would force him to carry for the rest of his life the burden of knowing he was not considered "good enough".

He'd worked too hard for too many years to remove that taint.

The heat of passion drained away, replaced by an anguish that cut inside like two opposing hussars with blades clashing. 'I won't be the means of diminishing you.'

Two tears slid silently down her cheeks as she stared up at him. 'Then, you'll offer me…nothing? Nothing to live for, to look forward to? Not even a chance for happiness, however fleeting?'

Anger, hurt, desire and the sense of impending loss churned inside him. Much as his body urged him to accept, to salvage something rather than nothing, he knew that having her and giving her up again would destroy him. 'I won't be your "temporary diversion", Faith,' he said, unable to keep the bitterness from his voice. 'Such an affair would be an affront to *my* honour, as well as yours.'

Uttering a curse so vile it startled him, Faith stamped her foot. '*Honour!* How often men dredge up that word to provide noble camouflage for refusing to do—or not do—what they want? With the immorality so rampant in the world, you'd object to our having an affair? Using "honour" as your excuse for denying two people who care for one another any chance to be happy? Oh, Davie, of all times for you to revert to your…your *bourgeois* principles!'

Frustration and rage won out over the hurt and despair. 'Yes, I am *bourgeois*,' he shot back. 'I still care about things like decency and loyalty and honour. I'm sorry that failing displeases you.'

Knowing he couldn't bear any more, he turned and stalked away.

But instead of giving him the space he needed to mourn and lick his wounds, she ran after him. 'Please, Davie, don't go! I'm sorry, I'm so sorry!'

She caught up and grabbed his sleeve, forcing him to halt. 'You'd think by now, I'd be used to humiliation, but having you refuse me, deny what I wanted so desperately—I just…lashed out. I won't importune you, or throw myself at you again. Please, promise me you'll remain my friend. I…I don't think I can go on, else.'

Furious, agonised, he stood, refusing to look at her, battling against the raging desire to throw honour and conscience to the winds and accept her offer. Even now, he could envision the rendezvous, a snug little house where Faith waited for him, clad only in a wrapper. Opening her arms to him when he walked in and picked her up, laid her on the bed where he would cherish every inch of her with kisses and caresses, finally claiming the body of the woman he'd loved for so long.

Better to shrug off her hand and keep walking, then accept "friendship" with its twin burdens of temptation and heartache.

She reached up to angle his face towards hers. 'Please, Davie,' she whispered.

But when he looked down at her, those tear-filled eyes, the misery on that dearly beloved face, he was as lost as the first time he'd set eyes on her.

With a deep sigh, he cupped her face in his hands. 'Never doubt that you are the most lovely, desirable creature on the face of the earth. That it tests my willpower to its utmost limit every time

I am alone with you—yearning for what must not be. If there were any justice in the world, you would have been married to a man who appreciated how beautiful you are, inside and out. Yes, I'll remain your friend. But I cannot be more than that, so please, don't tempt me any further. If I broke the vow I made to protect you, I would end up hating us both.'

She kept nodding her head up and down as he spoke. 'Yes, yes, anything. Whatever you want. Just...promise you'll never a-abandon me?' she asked, her voice breaking again at the end.

His heart turning over, he held out his arms and she rushed into them, clinging to him, burying her head in his coat. Her slender body trembled, and he knew she was silently weeping.

Damned if he did, and damned if he didn't, he thought despairingly, loving the feel of her in his arms, hating that he was the source of her sorrow. Heartbreak was written all over this agreement, but he didn't know what else he could do.

Spurning her when she needed him was unthinkable.

At length, she pushed back, giving him a watery smile. 'I know I should have more resources on my own, and I shall do better, I promise. Just now I was at a...rather low ebb.'

He offered his arm and she took it. 'We shall just have to go about rising the tide.'

'As long as our boats travel together—even if we can't travel in the same one.'

'You must start by doing me that favour I mentioned. As you know, the vote on the Reform Bill should take place any day now, and it's certain to pass the Commons. We'll all of us be occupied then, rallying support for a swift passage in the Lords, so I'm likely to be tied up for the next several weeks. We know Randall has left England, but just to be safe, would you pay an extended visit to Lady Englemere? Rebuild your intimacy with your sister and her family, so you will feel comfortable calling on them in future, should the need arise. Tell the Dowager you want to give your sister a break from the sickroom and spend time with your recovering niece, while you let the cousins become further acquainted. I imagine you want to do all that anyway.'

She nodded. 'It would certainly be nice to be out of the house, once the Dowager starts to worry over Randall's absence. Like you, I don't believe he'll bother to contact her until he is out of funds.'

'With Aphrodite's help, he has a healthy stake with which to begin life in Calais.'

She shook her head, her expression wry. 'I ought to repay you that, at least.'

'Absolutely not. The blunt means nothing; all I truly regret losing was the opportunity to go a few bare-knuckle rounds with him before he was sent on his way.'

'A few rounds?' She stopped walking and took one of his large hands in her small one. 'Randall wouldn't have lasted more than a minute against this.' She raised his hand to her face, rubbing her cheek against it before kissing his knuckles. 'Dearest Davie, can you even imagine how safe you make me feel? How much I treasure you?'

With everything in him, he wanted to pull her back into his arms and hold her for ever. Resisting the urge to embrace her one last time, he took her arm instead and resumed walking.

At least, she felt safe—and treasured him. It wasn't nearly what he wanted, but it was something. It would have to be enough.

As they reached the entrance of the maze, Faith halted again, turning to gaze back over her shoulder. 'I will dream of this, and imagine you gave me a different answer,' she said softly.

'I can't control your dreams.' *Or his own*, he thought.

Would he curse himself later, for letting high

principle squander a priceless opportunity? Faith would keep her word, he knew. She'd not invite him into her arms and her bed again.

Honour wasn't honour if you invoked it only when it was easy or convenient, he told himself.

Repeat that homily in the chill of your lonely bed, his outraged body replied.

Chapter Fourteen

After attending the entertainment the Dowager wished them to grace with their presence that evening, as their carriage carried them back to the Berkeley Square town house, Faith realised for the first time in several weeks, she was returning home without a sense of dread.

She descended from the coach in a state almost of euphoria, feeling as if an enormous burden had been lifted from her shoulders. She could go to the nursery and read to her boys, or retreat to her chamber and read to herself, even tiptoe into the library later in her robe and night rail to pour herself a glass of wine, without fear of encountering Lord Randall's insinuating voice or groping hands.

Or his threats against her and her children.

Bless you, Davie, she mouthed silently as she ascended the stairs.

Though they were probably asleep by now, she'd

celebrate by running up to the nursery to see if the boys were awake, sharing her joy with them—and inform them that, faithful to the promise she'd made Davie, they would soon have a prolonged visit with their cousins—the possessors of those oh-so-desirable dogs, horses and trees. Smiling, she was about to continue up the stairs to the nursery when the Dowager's voice recalled her.

'My dear Faith, you'll sit with me in the salon, won't you? I've been so worried about Randall. He's not been home in days, nor have we seen him anywhere when we've gone out in society. I was almost certain he'd be at the Blanchards' tonight, as they are our most particular friends.'

With true nobility, she refrained from pointing out that it was not at all unusual for Lord Randall to disappear until his funds were exhausted, nor, while he was flush in the pocket, did they ever see him at respectable *ton* gatherings.

'Of course, if it will make you feel better.' But, she promised herself, if the Dowager started criticising her while she fretted about her son, Faith was going to instantly develop a headache that required she take to her bed.

'Pour me a sherry, won't you, dear? I'll just send a note with the footman round to his lodgings. Sweet boy that he is, he might be feeling he's imposed too much on us, visiting so often—as ridiculous as that sounds! I'll reassure him that we miss him, and can't have him with us often enough.'

You'd be welcome to join him in Calais, Faith thought.

It shouldn't take the footman long to make the transit to and from Berkeley Square and the rooms near Bond Street where Lord Randall resided, when he wasn't sponging off the estate. The interlude would give her the opportunity to warn her mother-in-law of her upcoming trip.

Bringing the Dowager the requested glass, she poured herself one and waited until the woman finished writing her note. With that dispatched, Faith said, 'I shall be off myself, as soon as I've confirmed a convenient date with my sister. My niece has been ill, you may recall. I promised Sarah when I made my first visit that I would return for a much longer one. It will give me an opportunity to become better acquainted with my niece and nephews, let my sister have a break from her sickroom duties, and allow the boys to enjoy their cousins' company.'

'Must you go now?' the Dowager said with a frown. 'Lady Blanchard told me tonight that her husband said this Parliamentary session will be ending soon. With all the best families heading to the countryside for the autumn shooting, there will be such a dearth of good company in town! We must enjoy the parties while they last. Surely you can visit your sister later. You have a duty to your family here, you know.'

'Duty to family is very important,' Faith replied patiently. 'But while you have many friends in town to visit with at various entertainments, my sister has only me close enough to assist with her convalescing daughter. My other sisters are all busy with their families at their estates, far from London.'

'Your responsibility to the ducal line should take precedence,' the Dowager said repressively.

While her husband was alive, much as her soul resisted such coercion, she would probably have acquiesced, as he certainly would have seconded his mother's comments—probably with an added slur on how inadequately she performed her duties as duchess.

Wonderful, she thought, how *freeing* his absence was.

But for one thing, she could almost be happy with her life now.

While the Dowager chattered on about the missteps she'd noted among the attendees tonight, and recounted all the latest gossip she'd obtained,

Faith's attention wandered back again to the interlude in the maze this afternoon, an episode to which her thoughts returned every time she wasn't physically occupied doing something else.

Her cheeks burning at the memory, she could still hardly believe what she'd had the audacity to propose. The burn went deeper as she recalled the humiliation of being refused.

But 'humiliation' wasn't truly an accurate description. Davie's denial hadn't denigrated her in the dismissive, contemptuous way her husband had delighted in. Her overwrought reaction stemmed from disappointment, devastation even, that Davie, who'd shown her more appreciation and concern than anyone since her family growing up, had refused her what she wanted so badly.

Indeed, he'd taken pains to affirm it wasn't the woman, or her desirability, he was repudiating. She knew with absolute certainty that Davie desired her and a liaison between them as much as she did. But Davie, honourable-to-the-core Davie, wouldn't take what he wanted, when he knew that doing so would put her good name, reputation, and relationship with her children at risk.

And he was right, much as she hated to admit it. They were not living isolated in some wilderness; in the London of servants and merchants and gossips avid to discover the latest *on dit*, there was no such thing as a 'secret' hideaway, where they could go back to being simple Faith Wellingford and Davie Smith, two kindred souls sharing friendship, as they had that halcyon summer.

Sharing friendship, and so much more, she thought, recalling the kiss she'd all but forced on him. Not that he'd refused it. Oh, no, he'd let her play with his lips, his tongue, taking, retreating, opening himself to her fully. Even as she explored him, she'd sensed the strength of the passion he was restraining, felt the thrill of trying to provoke him beyond the limits of his control.

He'd been teetering on the brink of succumbing as she stroked him. A shudder of arousal and longing went through her as she recalled the hard, thick length of him under her fingers, sharply outlined where it pressed against his breeches. The tremor intensified as she imagined his member teasing at the entrance to her hot, moist centre, then entering her, filling her. She could almost weep with disappointment that she hadn't managed to break through that barrier of restraint and succeed in uncovering him, tasting him…mounting him.

Right there in the maze? Where, as he'd rightly said, a casual observer looking out one of the palace's upstairs windows might have been able to see them?

No, he'd been right to stop her. Right to turn her down. An affair between them would eventually be discovered, probably sooner than later. Even with Randall gone, the risk of someone finding that relationship objectionable enough to broach the matter to her sons' trustees was serious, and losing them too great a catastrophe to contemplate. No matter how much she wanted Davie.

But her sons wouldn't be young and in her care for ever. Sooner than she could imagine—as had happened for her sister Sarah and her eldest, Aubrey—they would be grown and going on with their lives.

Might there be a time for her and Davie then? she wondered, her flattened hopes rising on an updraught of excitement. Truly, the only consideration preventing her from making a full-out assault on Davie's sense of propriety was the threat of losing the boys. The prospect of being 'disgraced' didn't worry her in the least—she'd been a source of mockery among the *ton* ever since her wandering husband made his disdain for her obvious. She didn't care a fig for society's opinion of her, and being banned from participation in its entertainments would almost be a blessing.

Her growing excitement halted abruptly as she considered the man Davie had become. She knew he'd loved her since that long-ago summer. But he was no longer a gangly boy on the cusp of manhood, a powerful intellect who'd attracted a prominent patron, but was otherwise an obscure unknown of no wealth or family. With his sponsor's support, and through his own wits, efforts, and skill, he'd become a force in the Commons and one of the intellectual leaders of the Reform movement.

He'd also grown into a powerfully attractive, virile male. Considering that fact, Faith was astonished some ambitious girl hadn't already manoeuvred him into the parson's mousetrap. As his wealth and fame increased over the years, he'd likely be married long before her boys were old enough for her to be able to truly do whatever she wanted.

As she reached that dismal conclusion, a knock sounded at the door, interrupting the Dowager's monologue, followed by the entry of the footman she'd dispatched with her note.

'Well, Johnson,' the Dowager said sharply as the man simply stood there. 'Did my son give you a reply?'

'Weren't there, Your Grace. I knocked and

knocked, thinking his man would answer, but he never did. Finally, the landlord came round and said Lord Randall had scarpered—run off, Your Grace.'

"'Run off!'" the Dowager echoed. 'What do you mean?'

'Lord Randall don't live there no more. The landlord took me up to the rooms to have a look-see, telling me he woulda seized and sold anything Lord Randall left, to cover the unpaid rent, but there weren't nothing. No clothes, no rings or snuff boxes or personal items. Looked like he'd left in a hurry, too—drawers standing open, old newspapers spilled on to the floor. The landlord pressed me, wanting to know my direction—I think he wanted to task whoever sent me with paying the rent—but I didn't tell him nothing.'

'Gone? How could that be? Where could he have gone, with no word to me?' the Dowager cried, wringing her hands. 'Oh go away, man!' she added with exasperation as the servant remained standing. 'You are dismissed.'

'Well done, Johnson,' Faith said quietly before the footman could exit. Her mother-in-law might not appreciate the man's cleverness in preventing Lord Randall's creditors from descending upon them, but she certainly did. 'Stop by my study tomorrow morning, and there'll be a coin or two for your efforts.'

The footman's face creased in a smile. 'Thankee, Duchess. Your Grace.' Bowing, he left the room.

'Honestly, child, I can't imagine why, when you indulge in such reckless generosity, you haven't already run through the household accounts,' the Dowager said sourly. 'Rewarding that impudent fellow, when he didn't even fulfil his duty by actually delivering my note!' Jumping up, she began to pace. 'And where could Randall have gone, and why? Oh, I shall be beside myself until I know his whereabouts, and have word that he is unharmed!'

With an effort, Faith refrained from retorting that Lord Randall was a far greater charge on the household budget than giving a vail to an employee who persisted in discovering her son's circumstances, when he might well have simply knocked once and left. Reminding herself that the mother's anxiety was genuine, despite the worthlessness of the child she worried over, she told herself to hold on to her patience.

And might there be just a wee bit of guilt tempering her indulgence, because she knew Randall's true circumstances but would not reveal them?

She shrugged it off. Randall was perfectly capable of informing his mother of his plans, if he so chose. That it caused his mother distress because he had failed to do so was not her fault.

'I can't imagine what could have caused him to—to flee in the night, taking all his possessions, with no warning to me!'

'He is very fond of gaming,' Faith observed. 'Perhaps he suffered…sudden and distressing reverses.'

'Yes!' the Dowager cried, halting. 'That must be it. Naughty boy, he confessed the last time he visited that he has, on occasion, resorted to moneylenders when he found himself, as he put it, "up Tick Creek without a paddle", and did not find me at home to provide assistance when he called. He must have been anxious to escape the presumptuous importunings of such a person, or his lackeys! There could be no other reason for him to decamp so suddenly.'

That might not be the reason this time, Faith thought, but if Randall had indeed borrowed from a cent-per-center, such an individual would be none too dainty about the tactics he used to recover his loans.

'Even so, where would he have gone, if he did not come here?' the Dowager wailed. Then she stopped short, her worried countenance clearing. 'Ashedon Court, of course! Clever boy! Some un-

savoury individual might track him here, but they'd
never venture that far out of London. Have your
maid begin packing at once, and tell the nursery
maids to prepare the boys, too. I shall get Talbot
working now, so we can leave for Ashedon Court
as soon as possible. I shall not sleep a wink until I
am certain about the safety of my dearest Randall!'

With that, she swept from the room, apparently
not giving a thought to the fact that Faith might not
wish to drop everything and hurry off to Ashedon
Court with her.

She was about to follow her mother-in-law out
and tell her that she would visit Sarah while the
Dowager travelled to Derbyshire when a new notion occurred.

She knew for certain that Randall wouldn't be at
the ducal country house. Even if he quickly tired
of Calais and made his way back to England, she
doubted he'd return to an estate in the middle of
the countryside that he'd several times pronounced
a dead bore, in which he didn't intend to spend a
moment's time until he was buried in the family
crypt. So she needn't fear running into him there.

And she'd longed for years to take her boys into
the country, acquaint them with the rhythms of a
life she so much preferred to the city routine of
London. Edward, in particular, needed to learn

about the land and tenants whose care would be his duty and heritage.

Instead of rusticating at Sarah's, why not accompany the Dowager to Ashedon, spend some quiet, unhurried time there with her boys, soaking in the peace and beauty she'd missed so much? Meanwhile, she could see to hiring a new tutor, employ a groom to teach the boys to ride, and maybe show them a few tricks about catching fish, catching frogs, and climbing trees she remembered from a long, carefree youth spent running after her brother Colton.

Davie had warned her he'd likely be too busy the next few weeks to find some 'unexceptional' occasion to see her. After their fraught meeting yesterday, she probably needed some time apart to reorder her thinking and convince herself to keep her promise and not try to seduce him again the first chance she got. To persuade herself that she could be content with friendship for the present, while she nurtured the hope they might share something more in future.

As long as he didn't marry. Needy for him as she was, she wouldn't attempt to seduce a married man. Not that her honourable-to-the-core Davie would allow himself to be seduced, once he'd pledged his troth to some other woman.

Dismissing that outcome as too dreadful to contemplate, she forced herself to concentrate on the immediate future. With him so occupied with his duties in Parliament, it was unlikely that some ambitious female would lure him into a liaison now. Surely she could bear being parted from him for a *few* weeks.

He'd already helped her recover much of her former energy and confidence. It was up to her to continue the process, and being in the countryside she loved would further fuel that recovery.

After they were safely arrived at Ashedon Court, she thought with another tweak of conscience, she'd make amends for her bad behaviour by having the Dowager receive an anonymous note informing the woman of her son's whereabouts.

She'd write the note tonight, with instructions that it not be posted until after their departure.

If, after receiving it, her mother-in-law wanted to pursue her son to Calais, she could go with Faith's blessing, but not with Faith's escort.

Oh, to be able to spend several weeks in the country! she thought, the idea filling her with enthusiasm. Having the boys all to herself, to dine with and read to and take walking and fishing and riding. Perhaps she'd even have the gamekeeper start showing Edward how to use a pistol.

She could rise in the morning to fill her lungs with sweet country air. Ride for as long as she liked, without having to worry about returning to dress for callers. And, praise Heaven, delight in evenings spent reading or placing games with her sons instead of being forced to endure boring *ton* parties being polite to sharp-eyed matrons who, though wary of her now, still watched her every move, looking for something to ridicule or criticise.

The only thing that would make a country sojourn more perfect would be having Davie beside her—in her life, in her bed. With a deep sigh, she recalled how safe and cherished she'd felt, wrapped in those powerful arms. The giddy delight of tasting, teasing, stroking him, pushing the limits of his passionate restraint. The heat and burn that simmered deep within whenever she was near him.

Just thinking of him, she burned anew.

But since the ultimate means of satisfying that desire wasn't possible—yet—she might do well with a period away from Davie's frustration-inducing presence. In the meantime, she would do her best to enjoy the unexpected opportunity the Dowager had just given her to introduce her sons to country life.

Chapter Fifteen

In the evening a few days later, Davie hefted a mug of ale with the other Hellions in the boisterous taproom of the Quill and Gavel, as they and the other patrons, most of them Members of Parliament, celebrated the passage through the Commons of the Reform Bill.

'Almost ten years since we envisaged this, sitting in that dingy taproom in Oxford,' Ben cried. 'Here's to Davie, our intellectual light, to Giles, master manipulator extraordinaire, to Christopher, the voice of doom who helped us find and eradicate the flaws. To the Reform Bill!'

'To the Bill!' they all repeated, raising their mugs.

'We still have a lot of work to do, even if the Bill passes the Lords without alteration,' Christopher pointed out. 'Voting requirements need to be standardised from district to district, and we absolutely must work towards universal suffrage.'

'Yes, towards a day where a farmer's orphan won't need aristocratic patrons to be able to participate in government,' Davie agreed.

'You're a long way from being that penniless farmer's orphan now,' Giles said. 'As a man of property with several sources of wealth, and a growing reputation as a visionary political thinker, *you* have no need for aristocratic patrons any longer.'

Davie waved a deprecating hand. 'If I am even close to being that, it's due to the support and assistance of you all. From the day Giles took pity on the outcast sitting alone, nursing the single glass of ale he could afford at the cheapest of Oxford's taverns.'

'Giles is right,' Ben agreed. 'You're no longer an indigent outsider, but a man of influence within the circles of power.'

'At heart, I'll always be that farm urchin,' Davie said with a laugh. Then, those words instantly transporting him back to his contentious interview with Faith, he fell silent.

She'd accused him of clinging to bourgeois values that prevented them from having a chance for happiness. She'd been right—but in a different way than she'd meant, or he'd realised at the time.

Yes, he prized honour, loyalty and the sanctity

of marriage. But, as Christopher and Giles had just reminded him, he was no longer a lowly orphan, alone and powerless. Without false modesty, he could agree with their assessment that he was now a man of substance and a politician of growing influence and authority.

So why, when it came to Faith, was he acting as if he were still that penniless farm urchin? Believing himself unworthy of her hand because he had been born so far beneath her station?

He wasn't and never would be an aristocrat. But the steps they'd achieved with the passage of the bill today would provide the framework on which they would continue to build, towards an England where every man had a vote and every man's vote mattered, where one's birth meant less than what one made of the opportunities one was given. He didn't truly believe himself inferior to the wretched Lord Randall, or even the admirable Marquess of Englemere, simply because he hadn't been born with a title, did he?

If he, who was fighting to change society, didn't think he was equal to the best of those who did have titles—Giles and Lord Witlow and Englemere—how could he hope to sway the opinions of other Englishmen?

The only Englishmen whose opinions mattered

on this point *now* were the trustees for Faith's children. If he were to claim her, would they consider her an unfit mother, for marrying too far beneath her?

He didn't know. But Englemere, with his connections throughout society, would probably not only know who had been named as trustees, but also be well enough acquainted with them to give an accurate assessment of how those men would view Davie's pretensions to the hand of a widowed duchess.

If Englemere should confirm that Davie could marry Faith without threatening her control over her sons, he could act. It wouldn't change the fact that, in today's England, marrying him would be seen by society as a big step down in the world. But as long as proposing to her wouldn't compromise her control over the sons who meant so much to her, he would feel free to finally reveal to her his deepest desire, and let her make the choice.

Did *she* think him the equal of Englemere and Witlow?

She certainly could have no doubt about the strength of his affection. He knew she felt at least a fondness for him. And she certainly desired him, he recalled with a deep sense of satisfaction.

But she'd have to feel a good deal more than just

'affection' to be willing to jeopardise her position in society.

Ask, and he faced the serious risk that she might turn him down.

Did he dare do so now, if Englemere cleared the way?

Or was it better to hang on to friendship, rather than attempt to take the relationship in a new direction, be refused, and lose everything?

For if he proposed, there would be no going back to simple 'friends'.

All, or nothing at all?

But he didn't have to answer that yet. First, he needed to track down Lord Englemere and discover whether he could, in good conscience, dare to move forward.

A finger-snap right in front of his nose brought him suddenly back to the present. He turned to the owner of those fingers, who was looking at him quizzically.

'So lost in contemplating our satisfying victory that you've forgotten where you are?' Ben asked. 'Or have the celebratory shouts left your throat too dry to speak? Let's refill your mug and take care of that!'

'No, don't,' he replied. After his spellbinding realisation, he was suddenly on fire to find Lord

Englemere and discover whether he might hold the key to his future in his *own* hands. 'As Christopher reminded, we still have much to do—and the first step is getting the bill passed in the Lords. I'm going to hunt up Englemere and get his estimation on where we now stand.'

'Tonight?' Giles asked, giving him a puzzled glance. 'You don't think you could spare one evening to celebrate with the Hellions, before we move on to the next battle?'

'Englemere might be at Sir Edward's, if he didn't go back to Highgate Village.' He managed to manufacture a smile, which he hoped would deflect any curiosity over this sudden urgency. 'It shouldn't take long to stop by, and I imagine you will be celebrating all evening.'

'Can't promise not to drink all the ale before you get back,' Ben warned.

'Guess I'll have to take that risk,' he replied. 'I'll look for you here, later.'

'I may be off to Maggie before you get back, but I'll be looking forward to hearing what you learn from Englemere,' Giles said. But the assessing gaze he levelled on Davie told him his friend didn't completely believe his impromptu excuse for leaving.

If it all turned out well, he would explain the

whole to Giles later. But with the outcome so uncertain, he didn't want to voice his hopes even to his closest friend. Giles would do anything to help him, he knew—but only Englemere, and Faith herself, could help with this.

Having to exercise all the willpower he possessed to stroll out at a leisurely pace, rather than in a tearing rush, Davie crossed the taproom and exited on to the street.

Once there, he jogged at double-time to the nearest hackney stand.

After the short transit from the Quill and Gavel near the Houses of Parliament to Sir Edward's town house in Moulton Street, Davie ran up the steps, filled with both excitement and trepidation. What happened in the next few minutes might well determine whether he would live with heartache for the rest of his life—or have at least a chance to build a future with the woman he'd loved for almost a decade.

Nothing, not even the satisfaction of passing the reform legislation over which he'd toiled for that decade, could compare to the euphoria engendered by that prospect. The very idea was so intoxicating, he hardly dared think it.

One step at a time. First he needed to determine whether proposing to Faith was possible.

The butler, knowing him to be a frequent guest, told him that the family was in their private parlour, but despite the lateness of the hour, he would notify his master that Davie had called.

'Is Lord Englemere with them, Shelborn?' Davie asked, his stomach churning with anticipation and dread.

'Yes, Lord Englemere will be spending the week, before he returns to Highgate. Political dinners, I gather,' Shelborn confided before bowing Davie into the formal salon and going off to inform his master of Davie's presence.

Too agitated to take the seat Shelborn had led him to, Davie paced the room. He was reasonably sure the butler would return with an invitation for him to join his mentor and Englemere, bringing closer the moment when he would discover whether his hopes could be realised or not.

A few minutes later, Shelborn returned to escort him to the private family parlour on the floor above. Anxiety and anticipation speeding his steps, Davie entered to find Sir Edward, his wife Lady Greaves, and Lord Englemere playing cards.

'Welcome, Davie!' Sir Edward said. 'Will you join us in a hand? Or are you too energised after your victory in the Commons today to sit still that long?'

'It was energising,' Davie affirmed. 'So much so, that I indeed find myself eager to move on to the next step. With that in mind, I stopped by on the hope that you would be here, Lord Englemere, and I might claim a few minutes of your time to get your estimation of the situation in the Lords, now that the chamber has learned of the bill's passage by the Commons.'

'If you gentlemen are going to talk politics, I shall go check on the children,' Lady Greaves said with a smile. 'There is no such thing as "a few minutes", once you start on that!'

'Please, don't let me break up your game,' Davie protested. 'If you don't mind chatting, my lord, I'm happy to wait on your convenience.'

'Considering how wretched my hand is, I'm willing to end the game now, before these gentlemen complete their most unchivalrous rout of me,' Lady Greaves said, tossing down her cards. 'Ned, dear, I'll see you when you come up later. Englemere, I wish you a goodnight, and will see you at breakfast tomorrow.'

With that, Lady Greaves rose, gave her husband a kiss and Davie a shake of the hand before walking out.

'Would my assessment be of any value, or would you rather be closeted with Englemere?' Sir Edward asked.

'No, please stay,' Davie said. Before Englemere could begin to answer his query, he interrupted to confess, 'With apologies, I didn't really seek you out to talk about politics. My urgency concerns a much more personal matter.'

'If it's more personal to you than the politics you've lived and breathed these last ten years, it must be important indeed,' Sir Edward said with a smile.

'It is,' Davie affirmed. 'Will you withhold any comment until I've told you the whole, no matter how...presumptuous you may think me? At that point, I will be most grateful for your candid opinions.'

After exchanging a puzzled look with Sir Edward, Englemere said, 'Agreed. So, tell us the whole.'

'I'm sure it doesn't come as any surprise to either of you that I developed a great admiration for Faith—the Duchess of Ashedon—that first summer I served as your secretary, Sir Edward. Over the years, my affection and admiration have remained undiminished, nor have I subsequently met any woman I consider her equal. As you may know, after the Duke's death, we…rekindled the friendship we formed all those years ago. A renewed association with her has only strengthened the feelings I've held for so long. To the point that, I feel I must dare trying to move the relationship beyond mere friendship.'

Sir Edward and Englemere exchanged another glance. 'You mean, you want to *marry* her?' Englemere asked.

Relieved that the Marquess hadn't immediately shown him the door for his effrontery, Davie said, 'Yes, I would like to propose to her.'

'Do you believe she returns your affection?' Sir Edward asked.

'I know she cares about me. Whether she cares enough to marry me, I won't know until I ask. Although she cannot be unaware of my feelings, up to now, I have been very careful not to say anything that might hint I desire more than friendship. I'm now prepared to risk revealing my heart. However, I would not ask her to consider a marriage the trustees of her children would find so ill judged they would question her fitness to raise her sons, and decide to remove the boys from her care. What I'd like to learn from both of you, is how you feel the trustees would react, were she to marry me.'

He held up a hand, forestalling any comment.

'I'm not so naïve that I don't realise society would be shocked, even outraged, by such a marriage. But after years of work in Parliament, I believe I now occupy a position of sufficient authority and prestige that the trustees would find nothing objectionable in my *character*. Still, no amount of Parliamentary good works will turn me into a peer. I'm willing to let Faith decide whether or not she cares enough for me to face possible exile from society. But do you think my Parliamentary position good enough to satisfy the trustees?'

After a few minutes of shocked silence, during which Davie could hear his own heartbeat thudding in his ears, Sir Edward said slowly, 'You cannot doubt that we both esteem you personally, Davie.'

'I don't doubt that. But you both came to know me through rather...unusual circumstances, and our long association colours your opinion of my worth. Are you acquainted with the Duke of Ashedon's trustees? Enough to predict *their* assessment of my worth?'

'Having no inkling that his demise was imminent—' Englemere grimaced, doubtless remembering the tawdry circumstances of the accident '—Ashedon did not arrange for trustees before his death. At the time the estate was settled, Chancery appointed three men to serve in that role—his cousin, the Marquess of Trent, one of his maternal uncles, the Earl of Sandborn, and the family solicitor, Mr Campbell.'

'Sandborn?' Davie echoed, his anxiety ratcheting down a notch.

Englemere smiled. 'Yes, Sandborn, one of your staunchest supporters in the Lords. There would certainly be no objection to your suit from that direction, or from the solicitor. Trent, however, is as starched-up as they come, and might well have reservations about the duchess's remarriage to a commoner.'

'Must the trustees be unanimous in their approval?' Sir Edward asked.

'I don't know,' Englemere admitted. 'I have no expertise in matters of guardianship. However, Sandborn would offer strong support, and I'd be willing to put in a good word as well.'

'As would I,' Sir Edward said.

'So,' Davie began, trying to rein in his eagerness, 'you think I could try my luck, without any harmful repercussions from the trustees, if she should accept my suit?'

After exchanging glances, the two men nodded. 'We do,' Englemere said.

Hope, buried so long and so deeply, rushed out

in a flood of excitement that had him leaping to his feet with a whoop of joy. 'Thank you!' he cried, shaking Sir Edward's and Englemere's hands in turn. 'She may send me away with my ears ringing for my presumption in asking for her, but at least now, I can dare to do so.'

'Hardly presumptuous, Davie,' Sir Edward said with a laugh. 'You're a landowner and a highly respected member of Parliament—not a factory labourer living in a garret, or some womanising fortune-hunter.'

'I don't care about her fortune at all—let it be tied up in her sons,' Davie said. 'My income doesn't compare to a duke's, but I can support her comfortably enough.'

'Far more important to me than you supporting her,' Englemere said quietly, 'is that you will *love* her. Something that bastard Ashedon never did. After all the misery he caused her, she deserves some happiness. If she believes she will find it with you, you'll both have my blessing, and Sarah's.'

'Mine and Joanna's, too,' Sir Edward said. 'We've grieved for her over the years, and would love to see her happy at last. *Both* of you happy at last,' he amended.

'Don't worry about the trustees,' Englemere said. 'If necessary, Ned and I will bring them around.'

Such a rush of joy and enthusiasm filled him, he might be one of those Montgolfier hot-air balloons, released from the tethers binding it to earth to soar up, up, up into the sweet, pure air.

'Thank you both,' he said, shaking their hands again. He knew he was grinning like a village idiot, but he couldn't help it. He could barely restrain himself from turning cartwheels across the parlour rug.

'You're not going to try your luck at once, are you?' Sir Edward said as they walked him to the door.

'I would like to—but it's probably too late,' Davie said, trying to throttle back the compulsion to seek her out at once. 'I don't want to ride out to Brookhollow Lodge and wake them all up in the middle of the night. That is, I assume Faith and the boys are with Lady Englemere?'

The Marquess shook his head. 'Not that I know of. Were they supposed to be?'

This wasn't the time to reveal the machinations of the despicable Lord Randall—and Faith might well wish them never to be revealed. 'She mentioned she would like to take the boys out for a longer visit some time soon. I haven't seen her for several days, and thought she might have already left London.'

'As far as I know, they are still in town,' Englemere replied. 'But although the trip from here to Berkeley Square is short, it would probably be better not to invade that house at this late hour, either.'

'If you're going a-wooing, better to send a note and flowers ahead, with a request that she designate a convenient time to call on her,' Sir Edward said. 'Give you a chance to work out a pretty speech, too, so you don't just blurt out a proposal. Ladies do like pretty words.'

'Faith likes honest ones. Say what's in your heart—that will be enough,' Englemere advised.

'Good luck, Davie,' Sir Edward said. 'I hope Faith does accept you. She couldn't choose a finer man. Whatever you do, you do with your whole heart and soul.'

'If she does me the honour of becoming my wife, she'll have both in her keeping for the rest of my life,' Davie affirmed. Nearly bursting with hope, pride, urgency and impatience, he bowed to them both and strode out of the room.

Chapter Sixteen

Well aware that he was too agitated to return to the Quill and Gavel without the other Hellions immediately demanding to know what was wrong, Davie took himself back to his rooms at Albany. Sleep being equally impossible, he passed the rest of the night alternately pacing and rehearsing his proposal to Faith.

'Work out a pretty speech,' Sir Edward had advised. Though Davie had thought out carefully what he wanted to tell her, he suspected that, driven by the love he'd finally allowed to escape the shackles with which he normally confined it, once he gazed upon her face and knew that his whole lifetime's happiness would depend on how she answered him, he would probably forget every word.

So calamitous was the possibility of her refusing him, he almost decided not to visit her at all—yet.

Should he indulge in the delight of her presence—
as a friend—a few more times before he risked everything on the possibility of her accepting him?

But if she did, why delay that joy and live in an
agony of uncertainty any longer than he must?
If she were going to refuse him, better to know
straight away, and start figuring out how he
would salvage the shattered remnants of a life that
stretched in a frighteningly long void ahead of him,
if he contemplated a future without her.

How had he progressed so quickly, he marvelled, from feeling blessed just to share a few
outings with her before she was caught up in her
life again, to knowing that the rest of his life would
be blighted if she wouldn't share hers with him?

Whenever that drastic transition had occurred,
it was far too late to try to retreat into the safety
of friendship.

That being the case, better to learn at once what
his future held.

Sir Edward had also advised sending a note with
flowers, asking her to set a time for their meeting. Probably advice as valuable as his prompting
Davie to prepare a speech, but he was no more able
to follow it. Waiting the whole of the night had
been interminable enough; as soon as it was po-

lite to make a morning call, he would go. If Faith accepted him, he'd deluge her with flowers after.

Some time after dawn, he bathed and shaved, wishing he'd allowed the nattily dressed Christopher to persuade him into ordering a new jacket and trousers the last time his friend had dragged him along on a visit to his tailor. Dressing with care, he went out for a breakfast of steak and ale, of which he ate only a few mouthfuls. Sipping at the ale, he checked his pocket watch every fifteen minutes until, finally, it was late enough to be permissible to call on a society lady.

His heart pounding so hard he felt light-headed, he left the inn and took a hackney to Berkeley Place. Hoping he would find Faith without encountering her dragon of a mother-in-law, he'd trotted up the front steps before he noticed the knocker was off the door.

Surprised and puzzled, he made his way around to the mews and crossed the back garden to the kitchen, where his vigorous knocking finally roused an elderly servant. After reprimanding Davie for pulling her away from the task of putting the house under holland covers, she sourly informed him that the Dowager, the duchess and her sons had departed London two days ago for their country estate in Derbyshire.

After he pressed several coins into the old woman's hand, which sweetened her manner considerably, she was prompted to add that while the Dowager had decided all sudden-like that she must go to Ashedon Court, the young duchess had said she welcomed the chance to let her boys spend some time in the country. Asked her opinion of how long the family would remain away, the woman replied that the duchess had said, with Parliament set to adjourn soon, they probably wouldn't return to London until the following spring.

Thanking the woman as he dropped one more coin into her hand, Davie walked thoughtfully back to the news. From the sound of it, the Dowager must have discovered her son was missing— and suspected he might have fled into the country. Unskilled at subterfuge, Faith would probably not have tried to persuade her mother-in-law there was no urgency in determining her brother-in-law's whereabouts, but simply acquiesced to the Dowager's plans and accompanied her to Ashedon Court. If Lord Randall should suddenly return to London, Faith would be as safe from him, buried in Derbyshire, as she would be staying with her sister Sarah in Highgate. Besides, she'd several times mentioned how much she missed being in the country.

Still, he'd begun to wonder, with a touch of panic, why Faith had not let him know she'd left town, when he recalled having told her he would be fully occupied over the next critical few weeks, pushing for passage of the Reform Bill. She probably thought she would have time to send him a note from Ashedon Court, explaining her change in plans, before he could discover her absence.

He was tempted to follow her immediately, to make sure there was no more alarming explanation for her silence…but there was the matter of the pending vote in the Lords. Driven as he was to speak with her and discover his fate, he couldn't dismiss the duty to see to its fruition the work to which he'd devoted the last ten years of his life.

He was hardly the only member of the Commons who'd be pushing for the Lords to pass the bill, he argued with himself. Surely others could keep the pressure on for the week or so it would take him to take care of *his* pressing business in Derbyshire.

He could go to the Quill and Gavel, and hope to find his fellow Hellions at a strategy session before their usual afternoon meeting in the committee room. Ask their opinion on how long it would take for the Bill to come to a vote in the Lords, and if they thought he'd have enough time to go to Derbyshire and return before the vote was taken, he would do so.

His course of action decided, he set off for the hackney stand.

To Davie's relief, he did in fact discover the Hellions in the private parlour they often bespoke when they were working outside the committee rooms. However, as he should have expected after his precipitous departure the previous evening, before he could get a word out, Ben rounded on him.

'Good thing I didn't save you any ale! Was Englemere so loquacious you couldn't get away, or did you forget you'd promised to return and give us his assessment?'

So preoccupied was he with his own personal quest, it took him a telling few seconds to refocus his mind and pick up the thread of that discussion. By the time he had, three speculative gazes were fixed on him.

'Unless discussion of the Reform Bill wasn't what set you running off,' Christopher said before he could answer.

'Isn't it time you trusted us enough to let us know what's really going on?' Giles asked quietly.

Well and truly caught, Davie blew out a frustrated breath. But Giles was right. Though there was nothing, besides advice, with which his friends could help him on this, on a matter of such importance to him, he ought to tell them what was happening.

'Very well,' he acquiesced, taking a chair. 'Get me some ale, and I'll explain.'

In a few succinct sentences, he related the quick progression of his renewed relationship with Faith, from unexpected meeting, to offering assistance, to the desire he had increasing difficulty controlling, to his epiphany last night, after which he'd sought out Englemere to determine if he could ask for her hand and still remain the man of honour and integrity he took pride in being.

His summary complete, he braced himself for derision. 'If you wish to make some crack about "pursuing the Unattainable", now is the moment.'

'It doesn't sound as if she is "unattainable" any longer,' Ben said quietly. 'And I'd hope you'd give us more credit than to assume we would mock your efforts, now that the relationship has turned from an impossible dream to a courtship that may actually win you a bride.'

'Englemere and Sir Edward did affirm the trustees could have no objections, I trust,' Giles said.

'They believed two of them would not. The third,

a stickler for rank, would require some persuasion, but they thought they could win him over,' Davie confirmed.

'They should remind the stickler that Prime Ministers are often ennobled,' Giles said with a smile. 'You may end up with a title higher than his.'

'No, he'd turn it down,' Ben said. 'We're focused on abolishing the importance of titles, after all, not collecting them. Except for you, of course, Giles. You can't help being born a viscount who is destined to become an earl.'

'Thank you for excusing me,' Giles said drily. 'There's nothing wrong with titles, as long as men are judged and promoted for their own efforts, not merely because of an accident of birth.'

'So, when are you going to try your luck?' Christopher asked. 'Though she'd be a fool to turn you down.'

'After suffering through a decade of marriage to Ashedon?' Ben inserted. 'If she has any sense at all, she ought to jump at the chance to wed a man who'd actually mean his vows to love, honour and "keep himself only unto her".'

'I hope she will—if she loves me enough. That's the unknown, of course. Until I spoke with Englemere and Sir Edward last night, I didn't feel I could hint at wanting anything more than friendship.' Davie made a wry grimace. 'She's fond of me, I know, and friendship might be all she's interested in.'

'Then she *is* a fool,' Christopher said.

'Not necessarily,' Davie countered. 'She's a duchess, remember. Marrying a commoner would outrage a large part of the society in which she's moved all her life, and probably close many doors to her. That's a lot to ask.'

'If she loves you, I don't think that will matter,' Giles said.

'I hope not. I expect I shall find out soon. Which is what I came to ask you—'

'If you wanted our permission to address her, you have it,' Ben interrupted, a twinkle in his eye.

With an exasperated glance, Davie continued, 'I wanted to ask you how long you think it will be before the Bill will come up for a vote in the Lords. Faith isn't in London at present; I learned just this morning that she and the family have gone to Ashedon Court, in Derbyshire, and don't plan to return until next spring. I'd like to follow her to Ashedon immediately, if you think I'd have time to travel there and back before the Bill comes up for a vote.'

'You want to leave London?' Ben asked incredulously. 'With the most important vote of the last four hundred years about to happen? When we need every penetrating wit and every persuasive voice to convince the members of the Lords that the bill must and should be passed *now*?'

'I appreciate your desire to lay your proposal before the lady with all speed,' Giles said, frowning. 'But truly, Davie, there couldn't be a worse time for you to be away. It may be longer than a week before the vote is taken, but returning in time for that is less important than the work that needs to be done by all of us now, to ensure that we get the proper result once the votes *are* counted.'

'Here, here,' Christopher said.

Their advice was hardly unexpected, but Davie found himself resisting it. He'd given all of himself for years to the fight to create a better nation. Couldn't he be allowed a few *days* to pursue something of such compelling personal importance?

For several moments, none of them spoke, the only sound the tick of the mantel clock and the muffled voices from the taproom beyond. Finally, Ben broke the silence.

'No one knows better than you how important the next two or three weeks will be. If you still feel you must go to Derbyshire anyway, then go. I think I speak for all the Hellions in saying you'd travel with our best wishes and our blessing.'

Surprised it was the rake Ben, who'd never remained with the same lady more than a few weeks, rather than the faithful married Giles, who understood the strength of his compulsion, Davie nonetheless felt validated and humbled by their trust.

And he also knew, despite their approval, that he'd found his answer.

More than anything in the world, he wanted to make Faith his wife. But he could no more square with his conscience abandoning his duty to his country to pursue a personal matter, than he could have pressed Faith to become his wife, if doing so would have put her at risk of losing her sons.

'Thank you all for the vote of confidence,' he said at last. 'But...I guess I'll stay. We've waited ten years to alter the fate of the nation; I suppose I can wait another few weeks to find out my own.'

Giles reached out to shake his hand. 'Thank you. We all appreciate the sacrifice you're making.'

'It's only a few weeks' delay, Davie,' Ben said with a grin. 'Who, in that short time, could appear out of nowhere to carry your lady off from an estate in *Derbyshire*?'

'There had better be no one,' he retorted, exceedingly glad he'd made sure Lord Randall was tucked away in Calais.

But despite their high hopes and best efforts, it was an angry and frustrated group of Hellions who reassembled in the private room of the Quill and Gavel two weeks later, the day after the Reform Bill was voted down by the House of Lords.

'I still can't believe it!' Ben cried, banging his fist on the table. 'All that effort spent persuading a majority of the peers to pass the bill now, lest they incite the violence of a populace that so overwhelmingly supports it, and then this!'

'Even the most intransigent had agreed to abstain, if they couldn't in good conscience vote for it,' Christopher said.

'Only to have the clergy bring out their members in such numbers, the Lords Spiritual were able to outvote the Lords Temporal, and defeat it,' Davie said disgustedly. 'I stayed in London, talking to peers for days on end, for *this*? I should have left for Derbyshire two weeks ago.'

'The clerics back at Oxford called us "hell-bent" for daring to propose eliminating their seats in the House of Lords,' Ben said. 'Mark my words, if they haven't stirred up a devil's brew of trouble themselves, by opposing this.'

'I hope you're wrong about that, Ben,' Christopher said, looking weary. 'Where do we go from here?'

'I've heard there will be a call for a vote of confidence in Grey's government,' Davie said. 'He'll win it, and then advise the king to prorogue Parliament. All he's pushed for these last few years is getting that bill passed, and since it can't be reintroduced in the same session, he'll want to call a new one.'

'That will give you enough time to travel to Derbyshire and back,' Ben said. 'At least something positive will happen from proroguing the session.'

'Yes, we'll wish you luck—' Stopping in midsentence, Giles smoothed the front page of the newspaper he'd just opened. 'Hell and the devil, Ben, I'd hoped you were wrong, too. But it appears you weren't.'

'What do you mean?' Christopher asked. 'What's happened?'

The other three crowded around as Giles swiftly scanned the paper. 'News of the defeat of the Reform Bill must have spread through the countryside. According to the *Morning Post*, there have been riots in Derby, Nottingham, Dorset Leicestershire, and Somerset. The palaces of the Lord Mayor and the Bishop of Bristol were destroyed, the Bristol jail broken into and prisoners freed. Rioters even set fire to Nottingham Castle and Wollaton Hall, Lord Middleton's home.'

'Wollaton Hall!' Ben repeated, turning to Davie. 'Isn't Ashedon Court near there, outside Derby?'

Shock iced his veins, followed by the burn of anger. 'It is,' Davie affirmed grimly. 'Excuse me, gentlemen. I'm leaving for Ashedon immediately.'

Grabbing up his coat, Davie barely heard his friends' offers of encouragement and assistance as he rushed out, ticking off in his head the tasks he must complete in order to leave for Derbyshire. Hovering at the edge of his mind was the horrifying vision of Faith, his lovely, innocent Faith, menaced by crowds of angry men who didn't know the warmth and charity of the lady, but only that she lived in a house bearing a ducal coronet.

If she were harmed, he couldn't be responsible for what he might do.

Chapter Seventeen

Two days later, Faith sat on a bank of the stream that divided the Home Wood at Ashedon Court, the skirts of her oldest gown tucked under her, watching as her boys fished. Sunlight spangled the trees drowsing in the afternoon breeze with a gold that brightened leaves just beginning to turn to their autumnal hues of red and yellow.

Edward, become quite proficient after nearly a month of practice, baited a hook for Colin, even the younger boy now expert in detaching his catch from the line. Looking on fondly, she thought how much more like a normal, happy eight-year-old her eldest had become, after three weeks out of the city and away from the influence of the tutor who'd been trying to turn him into a miniature of his arrogant, self-absorbed father.

To her guilty delight, Faith wasn't having to counter the Dowager's influence, either. Several days after their arrival in Derbyshire, the letter she'd penned in a disguised hand in London was delivered, informing her mother-in-law that a 'concerned friend' had seen Lord Randall board a packet for Calais. Alternately relieved to know her son was well and alarmed that he had departed to the peril of foreign shores, the Dowager had dithered over whether she would follow her son to offer succour, remain at Ashedon Court in the hope that he would join them there, or return to London. Finally choosing London as the most likely place Lord Randall would try to contact her—and no more a lover of country life than her son—she'd immediately begun preparations to return to the metropolis.

She'd harangued Faith about accompanying her to resume the duties required of a duchess in London society. To which Faith had sweetly responded that she had a higher duty to remain with her son at Ashedon Court, so the young Duke might become better acquainted with the land and responsibilities that were now his.

The Dowager hadn't been happy, but she'd recognised a winning trump card when she saw it. Left with no more ammunition to attack Faith's determination to remain with the children, she left in a huff, accompanied by an entourage with enough grooms, outriders and footmen to satisfy even their former tutor's concept of the consequence due a duchess.

As the clomp of hoofbeats and jingle of harness faded as the Dowager's coach disappeared down the Long Drive, for the first time since her marriage, Faith had felt entirely free.

Since that morning two weeks ago, she'd let herself drift through the days like thistledown blown on the wind. Rising early to take a bruising morning ride; sharing breakfast with the boys in the nursery; teaching them lessons that continued outside, as she identified trees and plants, fish, frogs and insects. Often, as they had today, they brought along a picnic lunch and fishing rods, ending the tutoring walk by throwing some hooks in the stream or, in Colin's case, climbing the nearby trees.

They'd also, during their rambles, stopped by the nearer cottages on the estate, introducing the tenants to the new little Duke—and overhearing several muttered comments about how the occupants wouldn't have recognised the old one, seldom as he came to the estate. The assessment troubled her; Wellingford hadn't been nearly so vast a property, but she'd grown up knowing all the families who worked the land, and she wasn't even the heir. She vowed that, before he saw London again, Edward would be able to say the same about his tenants.

During her rides, she'd got to know the grooms, and engaged a younger one with a sharp eye and a friendly manner to begin teaching the boys, to their great delight. Just last night, she'd penned the last notes to the prospective tutors recommended by Englemere, inviting each of the top three candidates to visit at Ashedon Court for a personal interview.

Back in the countryside she loved, for the first time in ten years free to manage her own time where her actions were not dictated, observed, or criticised by anyone else, she could almost feel herself growing stronger, more relaxed, and confident. The ability to read, think and act solely according to her own inclinations was setting her firmly back on the path to the person she'd once been, the path on which Davie had started her the night he'd rescued her in that Mayfair lane.

Ah, Davie. The only problem she hadn't resolved was what to do about Davie.

She'd penned him a note the night of their arrival at Ashedon, explaining her sudden change of plans, and received a brief one from him in return, approving her actions and wishing her a happy sojourn in the country. He'd added that, once the

Parliamentary session came to an end, he might pay her a visit at Ashedon.

The prospect filled her with excitement—and flung her into an agony of indecision. Here, in the open countryside, there were scores of forest bowers, shepherd huts, shady glens where there were no armies of servants, tradesmen or gossips with prying eyes to observe or report. Even the mansion at Ashedon Court was vast enough, nearly all its several dozen chambers unoccupied, that a midnight tryst in a guest bedroom could take place with almost no chance of discovery.

If he did visit, should she hold fast to her promise not to try to seduce him again? Could she? She might feel stronger and more resilient than she had in a decade, the continual disparagement that had taken such a toll on her sense of confidence and self-worth gradually fading into unpleasant memory, but she still couldn't do without Davie's friendship and support. If she lost that, trying to entice him into her bed, she wasn't sure how she would go on.

But she also wasn't sure how she could resist attempting seduction, when she wanted him so badly, wanted so much to experience the loving embrace of a man who truly cared for her—and sensed that, if she pushed just a bit harder, she might shatter the iron will restraining him and catapult him into responding.

The very idea sent a wave of arousal and excitement through her. Oh, how vividly she could envision it: his mouth on hers, his large, gentle hands tugging loose the hooks, undoing pins, freeing her from her garments so she stood naked before him. His mouth at her breasts, his hands parting her, caressing her; his lips back against hers, his tongue stroking hers as he entered her, thrusting that magnificent, rigid member deep inside again and again until she shattered, the incomparable pleasure of it carrying him over the brink with her...

She wouldn't hold him very long, of course. He would tire of her, as men did of the women who pleasured them, and move on. Would it be worth it to have him for that little space, knowing she could not have him for ever?

Was it worth risking, knowing that if she pushed them into becoming lovers, it was unlikely she'd be able to hang on to his friendship afterwards?

And so, round and round the two possibilities rolled in her head, as they had since the moment she'd had enough peace and time to think about them. Deny herself the pleasure she wanted so badly, the pleasure she knew he could give her?

Or seize it, and risk losing the friendship so essential to her well-being?

Colin's cry of delight as he captured another fish brought her back to the present. With a regretful sigh, she let go the dreams of lying in Davie's arms, which, sadly, were likely to remain only dreams for a very long time. At least now, she had the joy of being with her boys, their days together structured just as she wanted them.

'Put that fish in the basket, too,' she called, rising to shake out her skirts. 'We should start back.'

Laughing at the chorus of protests, she said, 'Sorry, boys! We'll fish again tomorrow, if the weather is good, but remember, we planned to stop by the widow Banks's cottage on our way back. Matthew, will you carry the basket we brought for her?'

Subsiding with sighs, the boys dutifully gathered their gear, and after carefully adding their latest catch to the other three trout today's expedition had won them, they set off.

'Why does Mrs Banks need us to bring her bread and soup?' Colin asked, skipping along beside his brother.

'Because she'd old, and sick, looby,' Edward replied.

'Why doesn't her maid or cook help her?' Matthew asked.

'As a farmer's widow, she doesn't have a maid or a cook,' Faith explained. 'Usually, there would be children to help—'

'Like Mr Smith said, when he told us about having lots of chores on the farm when he was growing up?' Matthew interrupted.

'Yes, exactly.' How like Davie, to explain so vividly Matthew still recalled his remarks. How wonderful it would be, if he were here to share all this with them!

Pushing that unattainable desire out of mind, she said, 'Yes. But apparently all of Mrs Banks's children left to work in Manchester. One of Edward's most important tasks as owner of Ashedon is to know which of the tenants are old, or sick, or in need, and take care of them.'

'And I will, Mama.' Straightening to his full height, Edward reached out to Matthew. 'Let me carry the basket.'

'What can I take, then?' Matthew asked, reluctantly giving up his charge.

'Why don't we give her our fish?' Colin piped up. 'Fish is good to eat, isn't it, Mama?'

'That would be very fine,' Faith said, warmed

by her son's spontaneous generosity. 'We'll see if she has anyone to cook it for her.'

'Can you cook fish, Mama?' Matthew asked. 'I know you can climb trees.'

Her thoughts flashed back to several impromptu barbecues with her brother Colten, fresh fish grilled over open fires they'd put together beside the banks of the trout stream at Wellingford. 'It's been a long time, but I suppose I still know how. Very well, we'll cook a fish for Mrs Banks, if she feels up to eating it.'

'If it was jam tarts, I might not give one away, but she can have one of my fish,' Colin confided, setting Faith to chuckling.

A short walk later, they reached the Banks cottage. The fields beyond it were fallow, the widow obviously not feeling up to working the land for some time. The cottage itself also looked neglected, Faith noted. She must remind the estate manager that it required fresh roofing thatch and a thorough inspection of the soundness of the timbers in the windows and framing.

Nodding to Edward, she let him knock at the door. 'Mrs Banks, may we come in? We've brought some things for you,' he called.

But instead of the frail widow, the door opened

to reveal a husky, broad-shouldered young man, dressed in the rough clothes of a labourer.

'Who are you, and what do you want with my gran?' he asked, scowling at them.

'It's all right, son,' they heard the widow's weak voice from within. 'It's the Duchess and her sons. Please, Dickon, let them in.'

The man didn't move aside. Looking Faith up and down contemptuously, he said, 'Come to play Lady Bountiful, have ye, after paying no heed to nobody for years? Too late for that now, I reckon. As for you, little lordling, your grip over this land won't last much longer.'

Knowing her husband's lack of involvement in the estate, the man probably had a right to his grievance. But furious at his tone and manner, Faith looked him in the eye, saying coldly, 'Mrs Banks is ill, and we have food and provisions. Would you deny them to her?'

After a moment, the man looked away. Moving aside reluctantly he said, 'I s'pose you can bring them in.'

Head held high, Faith ushered her boys past Dickon, Colin, his eyes wide, clinging to her skirts. Ignoring the man who followed them in, as if he expected they would do his grandmother some harm, she walked over to the pallet on which the old woman lay and took her hand. 'How are you today, Mrs Banks? We've brought some bread and soup. And the boys caught you some trout, if you'd care for one.'

'And how do you expect her to eat it?' Dickon asked. 'She ain't got no cook to fix it for her, Your High-and-Mightiness.'

Faith looked back over her shoulder. 'She might once have had children who would care for her. But since apparently they don't any longer, I can cook it.' She looked back down at the old woman. 'If you fancy it now, Mrs Banks.'

The old lady smiled. 'A taste of fresh trout? Ah, Your Grace, can't say when I last had that!'

'You shall have it today, then. Boys, would you go outside and find some wood? There isn't any by the hearth.'

Ignoring the woman's grandson, who was now loitering uncertainly beside the woman's pallet, Faith walked the few steps to the hearth, hunting among the meagre supplies for a pan in which to cook the trout, and hoping she would remember how to gut and prepare it. She'd spent years being disparaged by a duke; the last thing she wanted was to have this arrogant commoner laughing at her ineptness at frying fish.

A few minutes later, sticks and branches in hand,

the boys hurried back in. 'Mama, there's so much smoke in the sky!' Matthew cried.

'Smoke?' she repeated, frowning. 'Where?'

'Coming from the direction of Ashedon Court,' Edward answered.

Putting down the pan, she followed the boys back outside. As they'd described, there was indeed a large pillar of dark smoke rising in the distance, from the place where the ducal palace stood.

Alarm fluttered in her chest. Sticking her head back inside the door, she called, 'I'm sorry, Mrs Banks, but there appears to be a problem back at Ashedon Court. I'll just leave the bread and soup, and come back later to prepare the fish.'

'You go on, then, Your Grace,' Mrs Banks said.

'Come on, boys, at the double-quick,' she said, breaking into a trot herself.

Only to have Dickon follow and stop her with a hand to the shoulder. 'You oughtn't go back, ma'am! Take the boys and head for the village. There's only trouble back there.'

For a moment, Faith stared at him incredulously. 'Not go back? That's my son's house afire! With a score of servants working inside, we must make sure everyone has got out safely, and organise a party to fight it.'

Shrugging off his hand, she made a scooting motion at the boys and picked up her pace, consumed with worry. The heart of Ashedon Court was an Elizabethan Great Hall, whose ancient hornbeam timbers would ignite like paper in a bake oven. Fortunately, the flanking wings were of brick and the roof was slate, which would slow a blaze. But where had it started—?

'You don't understand,' Dickon cried, trotting after them. 'This fire—it weren't no accident. It were set, deliberate.'

Astonished, she stopped to face him. 'Set? Why?'

'Lords like your husband saw fit not to pass the Reform Bill. We aimed to show 'em we'll not bow to their refusal no more.'

'Were the servants warned first?' she demanded. 'It wasn't their fault the Bill didn't pass.'

He looked away, not meeting her gaze. 'Dunno.'

Furious, she turned back towards Ashedon Court. 'A right fine victory it will be for your lot, if the under-butler gets trapped in the wine cellar when the roof falls in, or some maid in the attics! We'll go to the village and leave the house to you, but not until I know everyone's safely out.'

Dickon trotting by her side, Faith and the boys ran for Ashedon Court, the volume of smoke increasing as they neared.

As they burst out of the cover of the Home Wood and ran up the Long Drive, Faith was relieved to see the fire appeared to be in the stable block, not in the main house. By the time they reached the turn where the drive split, one trail leading to the stables, one to the house, she halted, panting. She was about to continue to the stables to check that all the horses had been led out when she realised that a crowd of men had gathered in the courtyard before the manor house, their angry shouts just discernible in the distance.

They must have spotted her, for several broke away and headed down the drive towards her. While Dickon beside her swore, Faith drew in a trembling breath and gathered her boys behind her.

This must be what Davie had meant, when he said Parliament *must* pass the Reform Bill. She'd just never imagined the repercussions of failure would touch her, and her boys, here.

Suddenly, she heard the sound of galloping hooves approaching on the Long Drive behind them. Ranging her sons behind her to face this new threat, she braced herself, wishing a bit hysterically that she had her riding crop, or even one of the sticks the boys had gathered for the fire, with which to defend them.

Her heart racing so hard she could scarcely

breathe, Faith clenched her teeth and waited as the horseman reached them and vaulted from the saddle.

'Lord have mercy, are you all right, Faith?' he cried.

Faith gazed up, astonished. 'Davie?'

Chapter Eighteen

Relief at finding her unharmed making his knees weak, all Davie wanted was to throw Faith on the back of his saddle and carry her to the safety of the village. But he couldn't take her and the three boys, and he knew she'd never leave without them.

Noting the stream of men now approaching them, he calculated the distance to the stables, and realised he couldn't get them there and harness a vehicle to take them away before the crowd reached them.

'Who are you?' he barked to the labourer who hovered at her side. If the man were part of the mob, keeping her here until the others could arrive, he could at least dispatch that threat.

'Banks,' the man answered. 'She were helping my gran. Don't think the two of us can hold 'em off, but we can slow 'em down.'

'We won't just slow them—we'll stop them,'

Davie replied. Setting free his nervous, rearing gelding, who was more likely to trample them in his smoke-induced anxiety than provide a means of escape, he told Faith, 'The village knows what's happening, and the fire engine is on its way. Is there anyone you can trust at the stables?'

'Yes. Abrams, the groom who is teaching the boys to ride. He'll help us, I'm certain.'

'Take the boys and go at once. Tell him to ready a gig or a farm wagon, whatever he can put a horse to the quickest, and drive you to the village.' When she hesitated, he said, 'I know you are worried about the servants at the main house. But your first concern must be the safety of your sons.'

Her face clouded, she nodded quickly and gathered the boys. 'Come along, my dears. I'm afraid we'll just be in the way here.'

'Will you come with us, Mr S-Smith?' Matthew asked, his voice breaking.

Fury coursed through Davie anew, that Faith's home and perhaps safety had been put at risk, that her precious sons had been frightened.

'I'll come to you in the village afterwards.'

'Sh-shouldn't I stay, Mama?' Edward said, his words at odds with the anxiety on his face. 'This is my land, you've been telling me, and I'm responsible for the safety of its people.'

While Faith's eyes filled with tears, Davie said, 'You can delegate that task to me today, Ashedon. If you will allow me the privilege.'

The boy gave him a short nod. 'I—I will.'

The faint sound of jingling harness had Davie looking over his shoulder. To his relief, an open farm cart approached from the stables, pulled by two shying horses the driver was struggling to control.

'Abrams!' Faith cried, spotting the vehicle. 'It's all right,' she told Davie. 'He's the groom I told you about.'

'Here, Your Grace,' the man said, pulling up the team. 'Climb up with the youngsters, and I'll get you safely into the village.'

Without waiting for Faith to reply, Davie lifted her to the bench, while Dickon quickly assisted with the children.

'Take her to the inn. I'll come later.'

'No!' Faith cried. 'Just to the edge of the drive. If things…get out of hand, we'll continue, I promise. But I'll not leave Ashedon Court's people to the mercy of these rowdies unless I absolutely must.'

While Davie would prefer to countermand her, the mob was on foot, and as long as the cart kept its distance, the groom would be able to get her safely away, if necessary, before they could catch up.

He hoped it wouldn't be necessary. Much as he'd like to break a few heads, it would be much better if he could defuse this situation before it got any more out of hand, resulting in far too many angry farmhands being hung or transported.

'Very well. But make sure it's a safe distance,' he told the groom.

'It will be, I promise,' the man said, and set the vehicle in motion.

Watching until the wagon halted a good distance away at the curve of the drive, Davie turned back towards the manor house.

The first members of the crowd were almost on him.

Seeing his imposing size—and no doubt the furious determination on face—the first three halted, wisely hesitant to take him on by themselves. Spying a large boulder set decoratively at the juncture where the drive branched towards the stables or the house, Davie trotted over and scrambled up on it, until he stood a half-a-man's height taller than the men gathering below.

Knowing the importance of projecting authority and confidence, he simply stood, holding the men below by the power of his presence, not attempting to speak until the majority had arrived from the courtyard. He had an orator's voice, born for addressing a crowd, and as they assembled below him, he drew on every bit of it.

'Men, you have a just grievance, and good cause for disappointment. But this is not the way to express it, or to bring to reality the goals we all share.'

'*We* share?' one of them shouted. 'We seen you with the Duchess!'

'Aye, you're just one of their lackeys!' cried another. 'A pet canary, singing for them in the Lords!'

'We aim to show 'em we won't put up with them tunes no more!'

'Why don't we pull him off his perch?' the first man shouted.

As several of the men moved forward, Davie braced himself, ready to play Big John to their Robin Hood at the river. But to his surprise, Banks put up his hands, warding them off.

'What, you turned traitor?' the first man snarled. 'And you tole us you was jest goin' to check on your old granny.'

'I did! But I don't hold with threatening women and boys. Besides, the Duchess was taking care of my sick gran.'

'It's not the Duchess or her children with whom you have a quarrel,' Davie said. 'You want your outrage to be heard, but continue in this way, and all you'll hear is the snap of the rope at the end of a hangman's noose. You're local men, aren't you?'

'Aye, most of 'em,' Dickon said.

'Which means you could be identified, arrested, tried, and hanged or transported. That will not aid your cause, nor keep your families clothed and fed, until we pass the legislation we all want.'

'What would the likes of *you* know about it?' one of the men jeered.

'A great deal. I'm David Tanner Smith, a Member of Parliament for Hazelwick, and I've been working towards the passage of a reform bill for ten years. I know you are all impatient that progress has been so slow. But it does continue, and the bill will pass. From there, we'll move on to address the next great issue, opening the vote to all. But only if we do not give those who oppose us reason to brand us as hooligans, intent only on destroying property and the social order.'

While there were mutterings about how the social order ought to be destroyed, the fire in the crowd had been banked. Already a few, doubtless having second thoughts about the wisdom of attacking a ducal property, were drifting off.

'How do you mean to get the bill passed, when all of them that killed it still sit in the Lords?' one of the instigators demanded.

'Because they may not be the only ones sitting,' Davie said. 'If it seems likely the Lords will vote down the bill in the next session, Grey will pressure the king to create new peers, enough to flood the Lords with supporters who will get the bill passed.'

At that moment, a horseman appeared at the corner of the drive, galloping past the farm wagon carrying Faith and the boys, and charging up the rise towards them. As the rider drew closer, Davie recognised him as Walter Downing, the Member of Parliament for the local district.

His arrival created a flutter in the crowd, some stirring as they identified their Parliamentary representative, a few more guiltily slipping away.

'Men, what's going on here?' he demanded as he reined in.

'Letting our displeasure be known,' one of the leaders returned with a surly look.

'Surely you don't mean to jeopardise all our progress by doing something foolhardy!'

'Is it true, what that man's telling us?' the leader asked, jerking his thumb at Davie. 'That Grey and the King will make sure the bill passes in the next session?'

'That man?' Downing said, belatedly looking up. 'Why, it's Mr Smith! I don't know what brought you here, but if you've kept these fellows from rash action, I thank you!' Turning back to the leader, he said, 'Henries, Mr Smith is one of the leaders of the Reform cause. Whatever he predicted, you can count on it!' Looking towards the column of smoke coming from the direction of the stables, he frowned. 'But what have you done here?'

Just then, the crowd's attention was deflected to the farm cart now driving back towards them, saving Henries from an answer. To Davie's displeasure, as he wasn't convinced the danger had been completely defused yet, Faith herself handled the ribbons.

'Your Grace!' Mr Downing cried as she brought the cart to a halt before them. With an aggravated glance towards Henries, he said, 'I hope the...disturbance today hasn't alarmed you.'

'An unfortunate...accident at the stables, I'm afraid,' she answered. 'But Abrams tells me all the horses were got out safely, and the fire engine from the village is on its way. I expect these men heard of it, and came to help. If you gentlemen could hurry on and man some buckets while we await the fire engine? Much of the building is stone, so I hope we can salvage the main part.'

'Off with you, men,' Downing said, waving them towards the stables. Most took to their heels immediately, apparently eager to put the incident behind them.

'So you are not inclined to summon the magistrate and…press charges against anyone?' Downing asked.

Faith turned a long, hard glance on the several ringleaders. 'Not at this time. I hope they're now convinced there is a better way to move forward.'

'Magnanimous of you,' Downing said. 'Henries, Markham, and you others, why don't you thank the Duchess, and go help the bucket brigade?'

After a chorus of mumbled 'Thankee, ma'am', the men set off, even the recalcitrant Henries finally offering Faith a grudging nod. As he strolled away, they heard the bells of the fire wagon in the distance.

Downing looked up to Faith and tipped his hat. 'Thank you, Your Grace, for a forbearance and understanding that, frankly, would not have been forthcoming from your late husband. I must admit, as I rode out, I feared the day would end with half the local farmhands headed for gaol and a hanging.'

As Davie clambered down from the rock and strode over to stand by the farm wagon, Mr Downing came over to shake his hand. 'Thank you, too, sir. I've heard the tales from Derby and Bristol and even as near as Wollaton. We don't need that here, or we'll never get that blasted bill passed!'

They all turned as the fire wagon appeared at the corner of the drive and laboured up the rise towards them. 'Now that the brigade is arriving, Mr Downing, why don't you encourage most of the men to return home?' Faith said. 'Abrams, take the wagon back, please. I'll walk to the house with the boys, and come back to the stables after I check on the staff.'

'Very good, Your Grace,' Downing replied. 'Thank you again.'

As the MP set off, Faith turned to the man who'd helped Davie hold off the crowd. 'Mr Banks, a special thanks to you, for coming to our aide. Your granny raised a responsible young man.'

'Man enough to admit when I been wrong. Thank *you* for looking after Gran. I'll see what I can do at the stables.' After doffing his cap to Faith, Banks waved down the fire wagon, hopped aboard and rode along as it passed them and headed towards the stables.

'Let me accompany you to the house,' Davie said, helping Faith and the boys down from the wagon. 'Just in case any recalcitrants are lingering in the vicinity.'

'Thank you, Mr Smith, the boys and I would appreciate that.'

Though he was finally able to draw an easy breath, Davie wouldn't be completely satisfied until he'd verified that the house was safe. Anger still stirred in his blood at the thought that those ruffians had threatened her and her boys—but how brave and magnificent she'd been, facing down that crowd!

'How did you happen to come to Ashedon today, Mr Smith?' Faith asked as he fell in beside them, arms held stiffly at his sides to resist the urge to sweep her into an embrace, just to feel the steady, normal beat of her heart against his chest.

'We read in the papers about the disturbances in the countryside after the defeat of the bill. When Wollaton was mentioned, I knew I had to come check on you. So you must excuse my dirt.' He motioned to his mud-splattered attire. 'I rode straight through.'

'From London?' She looked back at him, startled. 'You must be starving, as well as exhausted! We'll find something for you in the kitchen—assuming that mob didn't ransack the place.'

'If they did, you may have to reconsider not pressing charges. We need a new England, but not one built out of coercion and law-breaking,' Davie said grimly. 'I haven't worked the last ten years of my life for that.'

A few minutes later, they arrived at the main house and skirted the front to go to the kitchen wing. Rapping at the door, which unaccountably appeared locked, they were admitted by the butler bearing a fireplace poker and the cook brandishing a rolling pin, while several maids wept in the background.

'Your Grace! Thank the Lord! You are unharmed, I hope?' the butler asked.

'We are all well,' Faith replied. 'What of you in the house? Is everyone safe? Goodness, what a smell of smoke!'

'Oh, ma'am, I thought they would murder us!' one of the maids wailed.

'They first sought admission at the front door, which I locked after refusing them. They tried to force their way in here, but Mrs Pierce and I were able to prevent them. They did manage to set fire to part of the roof—'

'Trying to burn us alive!' the maid wailed again.

'But I sent the footmen up. They were able to put it out before it spread from the kitchen wing, but I fear it may take a long time to air the smoke from the rooms.'

'Thank you, Knoles, and Mrs Pierce, for your

bravery and resourcefulness! Despite the turmoil, might there be something in the larder for Mr Smith? A close friend of the family, he read about the disturbances in the newspaper, and has ridden straight through from London to offer us assistance.'

'Of course, Your Grace, I can manage something,' Cook said. 'Susie, Mary, stop your snivelling and give me a hand.'

'Mr Smith, you were the one standing on the rock, addressing the crowd?' the butler asked. 'I could see you from the upper windows.' When Davie nodded, the butler said, 'We owe you a great debt. The crowd might have decided to rush the doors, or tried harder to set this building afire, had you not deflected them. Whatever you told them must have been very persuasive!'

'Dismay at their rash actions had begun to set in by then, and common sense to reassert itself. Mr Downing's calming presence finished the matter,' Davie said. 'I would appreciate a quick bite, Mrs Pierce, and then I'm off for the stables. I'll send the fire brigade down to check the roof, once they have the damage there contained.' Turning to Faith, he said, 'Why don't you take the boys up to the nursery, out of all the commotion?'

'Can I go to the stables with you?' Matthew asked. 'I like commotion!'

'Later,' Faith intervened. 'We don't want to distract the men from their work.'

'The housekeeper is making a survey of the main and bedchamber wings now, Your Grace,' the butler said. 'To see how far the smoke spread, and determine what needs to be repaired.'

'Very good, Knoles. I'll take the boys out of harm's way. Mr Smith, thank you again for your intervention. One hopes the crowd would have come to their senses before inflicting any more… damage, but I shall always credit you with making sure of that.'

Her eyes telling him she'd like to say—and do—more, she simply pressed his hand. A sudden tremor running through him at the thought of what an angry crowd might have done to her, Davie felt that reassuring touch all the way to his bones.

'We'll talk later, Mr Smith,' she promised as she gathered her sons. 'Upstairs with you, now, boys! I bet Mrs Pierce will find something nice for your tea, as well as Mr Smith's!'

'So I shall, Your Grace,' the cook said as Faith ushered the children out. 'Mr Smith, Knoles will

show you to the morning room. I'll have something sent up in a trice.'

'Just a quick nibble in the servants' hall will do
for me, if that won't disturb your work,' Davie said,
watching Faith walk out. *Why did it always seem
as if the light in the room dimmed, once she'd left
it?* 'I'd like to get down to the stables as soon as
possible. By the time I get back, the housekeeper
should have her report ready, and we can help the
Duchess decide which repairs are needed first.'

Mrs Pierce nodding her agreement, he followed
the butler to the servants' hall. Not until they'd
sorted out the uncertainties left in the wake of
today's disturbance, and he assured himself that
Faith and her sons were truly safe, could he think
about broaching the question he'd been wanting
to ask her for the last three weeks.

Chapter Nineteen

After an afternoon spent assessing damage and penning quick letters to Giles and Lord Englemere detailing the situation, Davie arrived back at the main house to find Faith had already dined and was about to tuck her sons in for the night. Invited to accompany her to give them the latest news, for, she said, their conversation all afternoon had concerned him and the extraordinary events of the day, he gladly followed in her wake as she took the stairs up to the nursery.

Acutely conscious of her lovely form beside him, torn between impatience to get her alone and uncertainty over whether he should wait a while longer before delivering his proposal, or try his luck at once, he followed her up.

The boys' exclamations of delight at seeing him were gratifying, if counter-productive to their mother's desire to settle them to sleep. 'I'm glad to see you, too, boys, but I shouldn't have come to bid you goodnight, if I'd thought I would keep you from your bedtime. It's been a long day, for you and your mama, and you all need to rest.'

'All the horses are safe, aren't they?' Matthew asked, as the boys subsided against their pillows.

'And the dogs?' Colin added.

'Yes. All the livestock are unharmed. Much of the stable wing will need rebuilding, but we found space in barns on the neighbouring farms to house the dogs and horses while the work is done.'

'Can we continue our riding lessons?' Matthew asked.

'I imagine you can, but that will be up to your mama.'

'You were very brave, Mr Smith, staying there to face the crowd,' Edward said.

'It's easier to be brave when you know you are right, and that by standing firm, you can protect people.'

'I was scared!' Matthew admitted. 'Maybe when I grow as big as you, I won't be.'

'I'll bet you won't be,' Davie replied with a chuckle.

'Mama, why did you tell that man the crowd came to help us, when they came to burn the stables?' Edward asked.

'Sometimes people get so angry, they do things they regret. The penalties under law for destroying property and threatening people are very harsh,' Faith explained. 'Having them arrested would hurt their families. I wanted to give them the chance to reconsider their behaviour, and do better in future.'

'Why *were* they so angry?' Matthew asked.

'Laws have changed, and many people lost the right to use common land to grow vegetables or keep a cow or chickens. That's made it hard for them to feed their families. They wanted to elect officials who could change that, and a few days ago, the new law that might helped do that was voted down. They felt they had lost something precious, and been betrayed in the bargain.'

'You mean like someone wanted to take away all their jam tarts, and leave them only a fish?' Colin said.

Faith smiled. 'Worse than that. Take all the jam tarts, all the fish, and leave them hungry.'

'I'd be mad, too,' Colin decided.

'So you see, they weren't angry at you, just disappointed that they'd not received the help they expected. They acted hastily, without thinking first, as we all do sometimes,' Davie said.

'So…we'll be safe here, tonight?' Matthew asked.

'I would never let anything happen to you or your mama,' Davie promised.

With a little sigh, Colin snuggled into his pillow. 'I think I can sleep now.'

'Good,' Faith said, kissing him on the forehead. 'Tomorrow will be better.'

'Can we go fishing again?' Matthew's drowsy voice asked.

'Perhaps. I'll have to talk with the staff. We might have to tend the dogs while they start the rebuilding on the stables.'

'Building!' Matt's sleepy eyes opened wider. 'Can I use a hammer?'

'Very possibly. But now, you must sleep.'

'Thank you for helping us today, Mr Smith,' Edward said. 'I was happy to let you protect Ashedon Court for me.'

'And I was privileged to do it,' Davie replied solemnly.

'Goodnight, boys,' Faith said.

'Goodnight, Mama. Goodnight, Mr Smith,' they chorused.

Together they tiptoed out the nursery door and walked down the long hall. 'How about a brandy?' Faith asked. 'I might even join you in one.'

'An excellent idea. If you will guide me to the

library. Otherwise, I may wander all night without finding the way.'

Chuckling, she led him down the hallway, across a landing that overlooked the Great Hall, down a staircase into another wing. The odour of smoke increased notably as they proceeded.

Wrinkling her nose, she said, 'Thank heavens the smoke penetrated only as far as the central block. I don't think we could sleep, if the smell were as strong in the bedchamber wing.'

'I'm just glad they didn't succeed in setting fire to the whole place.'

'True,' she agreed, walking into the library and pouring him a brandy from the decanter on the sideboard, then pouring one for herself.

'You were serious,' he said, raising his eyebrows.

'Indeed,' she retorted. 'There's something about watching your stables burn down, your house being torched and your children menaced, that creates quite a thirst.'

Some of his earlier anxiety for her safety recurred, sending a shudder through him. 'Thank the Lord it didn't go any further.'

She nodded. 'Thank Him—and you. When you jumped down from your horse this afternoon, I was never so glad to see anyone in my life! Just having you nearby makes me feel safer.'

He bit his tongue on the urge to propose here and now. Instinct warned that, with things just returning to a semblance of normalcy after a day of chaos, it wasn't the moment to suggest she disrupt her whole life again. 'I hope I can always keep you safe,' was all he allowed himself. 'In fact, let me urge you to accompany me back to your sister at Highgate Village. I don't believe there will be more trouble, but I wouldn't like to risk it. You'll need the stable rebuilt and a complete airing of the main house before it's truly habitable again; you could have that visit with your sister while the work is underway. By the time it's complete, we should be close to finally passing the Reform Bill, ending any further threat for good.'

After sitting thoughtfully for a moment, she nodded in agreement. 'It would be better to move the boys from any possible danger, and no one could enjoy living in this smoke. Large as this manse is, it will take for ever to fully air it out.'

'Hire as many as you can from the village to help. They'll be glad of the wages, which will also sweeten the mood of the surrounding area.'

'Another good suggestion.' Taking one last sip of brandy, she set down the glass. 'Suddenly I'm weary. Will you walk with me back to the bedchamber wing? I wouldn't want you to get lost and end up sleeping on a trestle in the Great Hall.'

Now that they were alone, in the intimate camaraderie of candlelight and darkness, the desire always simmering beneath the surface intensified. The mere mention of 'bedchamber' made his member leap in anticipation. Having her escort him to his chamber was probably a very bad idea.

Before he could answer, she continued. 'I have to admit, I still feel a shiver down my spine, every time I turn my back.' She shook her head. 'I'm as bad as Colin! But I've never experienced such... naked animosity. It was...unsettling. How magnificently you handled the crowd, though!'

'Nothing like a little reminder of the gallows to make men reconsider their rashness,' he said wryly, finishing his own brandy.

While she blew out the candles on the sideboard, he picked up a brace, then escorted her from the darkened room. Shadows danced along her face as he walked her down the hallways, the battle between desire and good sense intensifying with each step.

He was barely able to breathe by the time she halted in front of a door. 'This chamber is mine,' she said, her voice as unsteady as his heartbeat.

'Would you go inside with me, and make sure no rioters lurk in the corners?'

His mind immediately played with the words of her request, bringing up images of another sort of penetration. His mouth too dry for speech, he merely nodded before opening the door and walking in, Faith trailing behind him. After making a circuit with the candelabra, shedding light across a sitting area, the hearth, a dressing table...and then back to a wide, four-poster bed, he set the candelabra on the bedside table and made himself walk back to the open door.

Halting there, he had to swallow twice before he could get any words out. 'Goodnight, Faith. Sleep well.'

She stepped over, closed the door and turned to face him. 'Oh, Davie,' she whispered. 'You don't really mean to leave me all alone tonight, do you?'

He *ought* to, but desire seemed to have snuffed out reason as completely as Faith had extinguished the candles in the library. He simply stood, unable to make himself quit the room, every bit of will engaged in keeping himself from picking her up and carrying her to the bed.

'Don't go,' she whispered again. Reaching up

to cup his face in her hands, she leaned up and kissed him.

And, as always, he was lost.

In the time it took him to register the touch of her mouth against his, her kiss turned from tentative to frantic and demanding. Anxiety relieved, passion long denied—whatever it was, it drove him as powerfully as it did her. Opening to her, he scoured her tongue with his own.

She clung to him with one arm, trying with her other hand to raise her skirts high enough to wrap her legs around his. Still kissing her, their mouths locked, he picked her up and carried her to the bed. Perched on the edge, she yanked at his neckcloth, unravelling the knot and pulling the length free, jerking the neckline of his shirt open until she could slide her hands up and under, the imprint of her fingers sizzling against his bare skin.

As he leaned her against the pillows, driving his tongue into her, she pulled his hands to her breasts, gasping into his mouth as he rubbed his thumbs across nipples so rigid, he could feel their hardness through the layers of chemise and gown. She sought his hardness, too, trying to grasp and stroke the erection straining against his trouser front, fumbling for the buttons.

Knowing he'd never last if she touched him there, wanting her satisfaction to be complete and overwhelming, he pushed her hands away. Apparently misunderstanding his intent, she began tugging up her skirts.

But he was a large man. Not knowing how long since she'd last been loved—not wanting to know—and intent on giving her pleasure unmarred by discomfort, he helped her pull up the skirts, bunching them around her hips until the pale skin of her thighs gleaned in the candlelight. But instead of uncovering himself to straddle her, as she urged, he caressed his fingers up her legs, over her knees, across the bare skin of her thighs, over the softness of her stomach.

She cried out, thrusting her hips against his hand. And so he moved his fingers lower, stroking across her cleft, where she was hot, and wet, and oh so ready. Bending to kiss her again, his gentle fingers massaged and caressed, back and forth across that tender ridge in time to the thrusts of their tongues, until a few seconds later, she reached her peak and cried out, going rigid in his arms.

He let her sag back against the pillows, laying his cheek against her head while they both gasped for breath. But before he could move away and ease himself on to the pillows beside her, she thrust her hips against his hand again.

'More, my darling?' he whispered, giving her a tender kiss.

'More, please,' she whispered.

Quite ready to continue, he trailed his fingers from her centre down one bare thigh, up the other and back. Bending to kiss her again, he slid one slick finger into her warm depths. He felt the tremor within her as she gasped and angled her hips to invite him further. Stroking deeper, he inserted another finger, then another, stretching her, filling her, sliding in and out until, her hands clutching his shoulders, she shattered again.

This was bliss, he thought, gathering her against him, kissing her damp forehead, exulting at the response he'd drawn from her. But he shouldn't be surprised that his tree-climbing, crowd-confronting, tender-hearted Faith was as passionate as she was fiercely loving.

While he reclined in a euphoria of pleasant, if unsatisfied, satisfaction, she stirred against him. 'Ah, Davie, that was wonderful,' she murmured. 'But I want to feel you inside me. All of you. Now. Please.'

As she spoke, she worked open the buttons of his

trouser flap, freeing the straining erection. Stroking him, she said, 'I think you want that, too.'

Her hand still on him, she lowered herself against the pillows and urged him down over her. So close to breaking under the stimulation of her touch, he knew he couldn't hold back much longer, he gasped, 'No, not like that!' Gently removing her hand, he rolled to his back and held out his arms to her. 'I'd crush you, sweetheart. Ride me instead.'

'Willingly.'

And not only was she willing, wicked wench that she was, she retained enough of the presence of mind he was fast losing to be able to tease, straddling him and running a finger along his swollen length before guiding him home. Even then, she eased herself down on him gently, inviting possession one slow bit at a time, until he was nearly mad from restraining the wild motion his body craved.

But once she'd fully sheathed him, ah, then, she too abandoned any pretence of patience, moving with him in hard, frantic thrusts that soon had them both spinning into the abyss together.

Some time later, Davie drifted awake, floating happily in the grip of the most splendid dream he'd ever had—making love to Faith, falling asleep with her cradled in his arms, awakening to the warmth of her beside him, her soft breathing the only sound in a chamber gilded by flickering candlelight.

In the moment he realised the experience was real, not just the most vivid dream he'd ever had, a sense of awe and wonder suffused him.

He must convince Faith to marry him. Having tasted such magnificent joy, how could he go back to the dull greyness of a life without her?

Then she stirred and smiled up at him. "Oh, Davie, I've never been so happy.

'Nor have I, my darling,' he said, smiling back.

'Well, that is, I could be a *little* happier. If we dispensed with all these annoying garments.'

He grinned. 'Happy to oblige, my angel. Shall I blow out the candles first?'

'No, don't.' Her merry eyes grew serious. 'I want to see you. All of you. Oh, how often I've dreamed of it! I want to see every bit.'

Everything within him stirred and tightened at her request. 'Only if I can see all of you in return.'

To his delight, despite her boldness earlier, a shy blush coloured her cheeks. 'If that would please you.'

'How often I've imagined it,' he echoed her response, that prospect the ultimate fulfilment of all his many dreams.

'Then imagine no more.'

She eased from the bed and offered him the laces at her back. Swiftly he undid them, helped her out of her bodice, then her skirt. When she turned, the outline of her breasts clear under thin linen of the chemise, he had to halt long enough to kiss them, his member stirring as he cupped each full, heavy round. He had to stop again after he'd pulled off her chemise to suckle the soft pink nipples into rigid points, before caressing his way down her legs as he stripped off stockings and garters.

When she stood before him, fully naked, he could only stare, mesmerised. 'You're even more lovely than I imagined.'

'My turn,' she said, her voice trembling. Distracted by her nakedness, he was scarcely aware of shrugging off his jacket and vest, kicking off the already-unbuttoned breeches, peeling down his hose, until a draught of wind that rattled the shutters sent a cold breath of air to prickle his skin.

All he cared about was her molten gaze, fixed on him. 'What a wonder you are,' she whispered, running her fingers over the breadth of his shoulders, his chest, down arms and thighs whose muscles tensed at her touch. 'So big, so powerful. Such pleasure you give me.' Before he could guess her intent, she bent and kissed his erection.

Dizzied by the intensity of his response, he clutched at her shoulders to steady himself. Before the pleasure of it made him lose his balance entirely, she pulled him over to the bed, driving him mad again as she suckled and caressed. Knowing he was nearing the peak, he moved away from her, breaking contact.

Ignoring his body's protest, he slid to his knees before her. 'I want to taste satisfaction on you,' he whispered. The sloe-eyed seduction of her gaze spurring him on, gently he parted her legs and plied with his tongue the tender areas his fingers and shaft had pleasured, until she was pressing against him, sobbing for release.

She motioned him back on to the bed, pulling him up, pushing him back against the pillows, sheathing him to the hilt in one swift thrust. There was no pretence of teasing this time, just urgent, relentless movement that drove them both to completion.

Sated, dazzled, Davie subsided against the pillows. Exhausted after the anxiety of the day and his long hours of riding, he tucked Faith against his chest, blew out the candles, pulled the blankets over them, and fell immediately into the most contented sleep of his life.

Chapter Twenty

Smiling drowsily, Faith snuggled into the warm, solid shape beside her. She couldn't remember, she thought with a sense of awe, ever feeling so safe and cherished, so completely happy and at peace. So *satisfied*.

And then she remembered. Davie, making love to her tenderly, completely, thoroughly. Davie, here in her bed.

Wasn't he? Suddenly terrified it was only a dream, she sat up abruptly, panic draining away to leave only delight when she saw he was, indeed, still lying on the pillow beside her, arms crossed behind his head. A beam of morning light illumined his face and the blue, blue eyes watching her, full of tenderness and the same sense of wonder she felt.

She leaned down to kiss him, sure in the whole history of the world, there had never been a sweeter, more beautiful awakening. 'You *are* still here,' she said as she released him.

'I am.' He reached up to trace the line of her jaw with one finger. 'Where I've wanted to be for so long. Where I never want to leave.'

She caught his finger and kissed it, then slipped it into her mouth and suckled it, drawing a groan from him and sparking a delicious flutter in her nether regions. Which, though oh-so-satisfied, seemed to indicate they were quite ready to begin the activities of the night all over again.

She took his hand and cupped around her bare breast. 'Last night was…magnificent. Amazing. I never dreamed such pleasure existed.'

He stroked her breast, drawing his hand up to caress the already rigid nipple. 'All for you.'

She whimpered, leaning into his stroking fingers. 'Now I understand why men and women have affairs.'

He stopped abruptly, his smile fading, and drew himself up against the pillows. Pulling her into his arms, he said, 'I don't want to have an affair with you, Faith.'

Alarmed by that blunt statement, she pushed away so she might watch his expression. 'You don't? How can you say that? You couldn't be so cruel as to dismiss me after only one night! Surely you care more for me than that!'

'That's just it. I don't want one night—I want *every* night. I want you in my life, in my arms, in my bed, from now until the day I die. I love you, Faith, totally and completely. I have, I think, almost from the moment we met. Won't you marry me, my darling?'

Shock washed the drowsy sensuality clean away. 'Marry you?' she gasped. 'But I had no idea—'

'Surely you had *some* idea. True, I never spelled out what I really wanted for us. At first, I didn't think I had the right. But the night the Reform Bill passed, I realised in the new England we wish to create, if I truly believe I am the equal of any man, I should act like it. In fact, with Lord Randall, and with the crowd today, I've been of *more* use to you than I would have been, had I been born a peer. The rioters would have ignored—or attacked—a nobleman, leaving you in danger.'

She shook her head wonderingly. 'I can't think of another man who could have accomplished what you did.'

'The only reason I hesitated to press my suit was my concern over the boys. Before I came to Derbyshire, I talked with Englemere and Sir Edward, to ask their opinions about how your children's trustees might react, should you marry me. They felt certain they would not disapprove—at least, not enough to remove your sons from your care. It only remains to determine if *you* believe I am your equal, and if so, to decide if you love me enough to suffer the other consequences.'

'Other consequences?' she echoed, still too shocked to really take in what he was saying.

'The titters from those who believe you've married far beneath you. Cuts direct from people who cross you off their guest list. Your own mother-in-law might refuse to receive you any longer.'

She laughed. 'I would rather call that a "blessing"! You should know more than anyone how little I would miss anything about society. But... marriage?'

Suddenly, she saw not Davie's dear face but Edward's, the night he proposed. How ardent he'd seemed, how completely intent on convincing her that he wanted her and only her, to be his wife and bear his children, his alone for the rest of his life.

How long had that ardour lasted? How much was it her fault that it had not?

'Unless you believe I'm not...good enough,' his voice recalled her.

'*You* not good enough?' she said incredulously, looking back at him. 'How can you even think that?'

Her avowal earned a fierce hug and an even more ardent kiss. 'Then you'll accept my hand?' he said as he released her.

Much as she hated to disappoint him, warning bells were sounding in her head like the voice of Cassandra predicting doom.

'I...oh, I don't know! You know I care about you. But...you've wanted me a long time. Loved me a long time. I...I fear you have created a vastly over-rosy image of me, as some sort of paragon, something I could never live up to. I'm not very special, really. I don't embroider, or sing, or play, or make clever, witty conversation. I fear I would end up... disappointing you, and I couldn't bear that.'

Fortunately, since she found herself perilously near tears, he did not laugh at her, or make some dismissive remark. Instead, he took her hands and looked straight into her eyes. 'You are special to *me*. A shining star who brightens the life of everyone around her. Who else would climb a tree, just to make her son smile? Or stand before an angry crowd who threatened her sons, and yet show mercy? A woman scorned and belittled by society, by the family that should have cherished her, who reacted with calm resignation rather than hate and vindictiveness. I've felt that way about you since the first day we met. My heart rejoices every time I see your smile, or hear your laughter. I expect some day, our world will have created machines to embroider, or play music, or even to sing to us. But I don't think there will ever be as beautiful a spirit as yours, or one whose sensitivity and compassion make my heart rejoice every time I see her.'

Davie—dear, dependable, compassionate Davie—hers to cherish for the rest of her life? Sensual, passionate Davie, the most magnificent lover she'd ever known?

It seemed…unbelievable that he would want to marry her. Despite what he vowed, could she really believe she could keep him in love with her for ever?

Accepting his hand meant that he would *be* in her life for ever—whether or not he still loved her. Unlike Edward, Davie would be faithful, kind and courteous, even if his affections towards her cooled.

She'd almost not survived becoming the wife Ashedon barely tolerated and regarded with contempt. She knew she could not survive becoming the object of Davie's faint disdain and polite disinterest.

The distress and turmoil of her emotions must have been painted on her face, for with a sigh,

Davie let her go. 'I can't do more than promise my love. You have to believe it. Believe in us. If you can't, there's no point going any further. I won't be your lover, Faith. I will only be your husband.'

She fought to keep the tears back. The last thing she wanted was to drive him away. But did she dare ask him to stay?

While she wrestled with a response, he said, 'Don't marry me because you know I love you—only if you need and love me, and can't imagine being happy in a life that doesn't include me. Clearly, I've shocked you, and rather than press for an answer now—and force one I may not like—don't tell me anything, yet. Think about it carefully. If you decide your answer must be "no", I will accept that, and never importune you again. You'll have my respect and admiration for the rest of my life.'

'But not your friendship?' she asked, fearing she knew the answer.

His smile now was strained. 'That would be too…hard.'

With that, he rose from the bed and walked around, collecting and donning clothing scattered in haste during the night. Torn between accepting his suit at once and drawing him back to her bed, and letting him go so she might think about this when her heart wasn't pounding so hard with fear and distress, her head hurt, she simply watched. The urgency of making the right decision made her feel almost physically ill.

When he'd finished dressing, he came back to the bed. Looking at her face, he sighed. 'Dearest Faith, the last thing I wanted was to upset you. Take all the time you need. I'll be waiting. I've always been waiting for you.'

This time, she couldn't keep back the tears. 'W-won't you kiss me goodbye?'

He gave her a wry smile. 'I'll kiss you "hello", and much more, when—if—you accept my suit.'

'Will I see you again?'

'Like this?' He swept his hand to encompass the room. 'Not unless you agree to become my wife. Before I leave, I'll have a word with the estate manager, letting him know you'll want to have workmen from the village come in to assist with repairs to the stables and the main house, if you'd like.'

She nodded, feeling at the moment entirely unequal to making any decisions at all. 'Yes, that would be helpful.'

'Very well. I'll be at the Bow and Snare, in the village. Send me a note when you and the boys are ready to depart, and I'll ride over to escort you.'

'What shall I tell the boys, when they ask why you've gone?' she asked, grasping at one last straw to keep him here.

'Tell them I'm making arrangements to escort them to their cousins, for more riding, fishing, and tree climbing. They'll be delighted at the prospect. As I imagine you will, to spend some time with your sister. Goodbye, my darling Faith.' With that, he turned and walked out the door.

She sagged back against the pillows, still shocked and stunned. Should she scramble into her clothes, ready to guide him out if he got lost in the maze that was Ashedon Court?

But, no, competent Davie would have no trouble in daylight, navigating his way out. And he'd likely be long gone by the time she could summon her maid and hurry into her clothes.

Maybe instead, she'd replay in her mind the glorious night he'd given her—and not think about the paralysing decision he'd left her with.

But she didn't have to decide right away, she told herself, trying to unseat the leaden weight that pressed at her chest every time she thought of having to make that decision. She'd have time with Sarah, unhurried time to think over Davie's unexpected proposal.

There was no question she cared for him—perhaps more than she'd ever let herself realise, until he revealed his desire to build a life with her. But did she dare accept him—and believe in a happiness which had never in her life been anything but fleeting?

A few days later, Faith sat in the sunny morning room at Brookhollow Lodge in Highgate Village, awaiting the arrival of her sister Sarah for breakfast and the private chat she'd been in desperate need of since Davie's surprising proposal—had it only been four days ago?

Despite the bustle of preparing the boys for the trip to her sister's, giving final instructions to the servants at Ashedon Court, and consulting with the chief workmen and the steward who would be overseeing the repairs, and then the long journey, taken in short stages so as not to tire the boys, the urgent question of how she should respond to his proposal was seldom far from her mind.

He'd not made the choice any easier, falling back, as he'd promised, into the role of helpful friend, freezing out any attempt she made to take his hand, forestalling any chance to snuggle close on the carriage seat by riding beside the vehicle all the way. At the inns where they'd broken the journey, he'd arranged for rooms and meals with

calm efficiency, while skirting her efforts to ma-
noeuvre him alone in a hallway or stable yard to
claim a swift, reassuring kiss.

Was he trying to show her what it would be like,
were she to refuse him and allow them to dwindle
into fond, but distant friends? Or was he giving her
a glimpse into what life would be if she accepted
him, and after a year or two or five, he finally realised she was only a modestly accomplished, or-
dinary woman, and fell out of love with her?

Would she end up, ultimately, more wretched
with him than without him?

All she knew was the polite distance he'd maintained between them on the trip to Brookhollow
had driven her mad with regret, longing, frustrated
desire, and uncertainty.

Take all the time you need, he'd said. But she
must decide, soon. She couldn't exist with this decision weighing so heavily on her, she could hardly
breathe.

She ought to make the decision on her own. She
hadn't consulted anyone about personal matters for
years—hadn't had anyone to consult. Until she'd
found Davie again—but he couldn't help her now.

The last time she and Sarah had discussed something this important to her future, she'd blithely
dismissed her elder sister's plea that she wait be-

fore rushing into marriage with the Duke. This time, she intended to listen closely to the advice of the wise older sister who knew them both so well—even though the final choice would have to be hers alone.

Sarah's arrival interrupted her tortured thoughts. 'Sorry I'm late—another minor crisis in the kitchen.' She came over to give Faith a kiss before pouring herself some coffee. 'Did the boys settle in well last night?'

'Yes, although they are so excited about spending time with their cousins, I'm betting they scarcely slept a wink.'

Sarah turned a penetrating glance on her. 'Nor did you, by the looks of it. What is troubling you? I wouldn't be surprised if you're suffering bad dreams, after the scare you had at Ashedon Court! Please God, such uprisings will soon be behind us.'

'It was frightening, I'll admit. Though Davie did a wonderful job, settling down the rioters and restoring order.'

'I can't tell you how anxious we were after we heard about Wollaton! Englemere was just setting out for Ashedon when we got Davie's note that you were all safe and well. We'll never be able to thank him enough for taking such swift action.'

After choking down the one sip of coffee she

could manage without having it rise back up her throat, Faith traced a nervous finger on the polished mahogany table. 'That wasn't all the action he took. Before we left for Brookhollow, he...he asked me to marry him.'

Her eyes widening, Sarah set down her cup. 'He proposed to you! Though, when I consider it, I shouldn't be surprised. One would have to be blind not to have noticed how much he's cared for you, as far back as that first summer with Ned and Joanna. And when he escorted you here recently... well, one could torch kindling with the heat evident between you. He might not be what the world would consider a good match, but one couldn't hope to find a man of finer character.'

'He's the most excellent man I've ever met.' *Which made the idea of living without him even more devastating to contemplate.*

Sarah leaned closer, studying Faith. 'You didn't tell me how you answered him. From the distress on your face, I take it you haven't yet decided. I know there would be those who'd claim you'd be failing in your duties to young Ashedon and the estate to remarry so soon, but there are trustees and stewards to oversee all that. Certainly, accepting Davie would mean a huge loss of consequence, but I don't think the prestige of being a duchess ever mattered to you. I know how he feels about you. The only thing that does matter is how you feel about *him*. You certainly seemed lighter, happier, more at ease than I'd seen you in years when you came here with him. Does he make you happy?'

'Oh, yes! I feel more like myself with him—the self-confident, assured, happy self I used to be—than at any time since the early days of my marriage. It isn't that.'

'Do you love him?'

Faith nodded slowly. 'I…I think I do. How could one help loving a man who is so strong, principled and compassionate? Not just with me—with everyone, from the poorest crofter to the indigent factory worker. I'm so in awe of all he's accomplished, and admire so much all he wants to do for this country.'

'And you love the way he kisses you,' Sarah added with a naughty twinkle.

Faith felt herself blushing, glad her sister hadn't guessed how far beyond a kiss they'd already gone. 'Yes. That, too.'

'Than why do you hesitate?'

'He's so…wonderfully attentive, and caring, and ardent. So convinced he wants me for his wife, to love and cherish the rest of his life. Just like Ashedon was, during our courtship and the early days of our marriage. I believed with all my heart that our love would last for ever.'

'But it didn't,' Sarah said gently.

'No,' Faith replied, that small word inadequate to express the depth of devastation her marriage had become.

'The difference, you see—what Englemere and I suspected and what time proved—was that Ashedon never really loved you. Oh, he made a good show of it, I'll grant you. Flattered and indulged all his life, he was brought up to believe only what he wanted was important, with no thought given to the feelings or needs of anyone else. He wanted a convenient, pliable wife—that she adored him, he took as his due. So he played the part that would gain him what he wanted. Do you believe Davie is only playing a part?'

'No. I think he truly loves me, and I know he would never humiliate me as Ashedon did. But loving him, giving myself to him…and having him eventually grow distant, as Ashedon did, while remaining faithful and kind, as his character would compel him to, would be even worse than Ashedon's treachery.'

Wanting Sarah to understand, she made herself continue. 'In my heart, I'd known for a long time, years maybe, that Ashedon no longer cared about me, if he ever had. Then, a few months after Colin's birth, I caught him as he was going out for the evening and asked if I could go with him, or if he might consider remaining at home, so we might spend the evening together. "Why would I want to spend an evening here?" he said. "You've no wit, no conversation, to balance against your appalling country manners. Now that you've done your duty and provided me with sons…well, the charms of an *ingénue* are highly overrated." It wasn't just his words, cruel as they were—it was the *look* on his face…'

Nausea rose in her throat and her stomach twisted as she remembered it. 'Disgust, contempt, disdain. As if an insect had crawled upon his plate.'

Sarah reached over to take her hand. 'Oh, Faith! I'm so sorry.'

'I thought I should die, sitting there as he left me. Just…stop breathing, and fade into nothingness. But the nursery maid came running in, saying Colin was crying to be fed, so I got up, and walked out, and went on. Oh, Sarah, if Davie ever looked at me like that, I *would* die.'

'But you know he loves you! Why would he ever be so unkind?'

'The entire time he's known me, I've been the "unattainable ideal". The golden girl, destined to marry to a duke, mistress of a great house, descendant of an ancient line—someone far above him. What will he do when he's around me long enough to realise I'm just…ordinary?'

'Davie has never been impressed by the pomp and circumstance of aristocracy—quite the opposite! He's called to what he sees in *you*, Faith. The sweet and loving spirit we all cherished as you were growing up. But it isn't his love you must believe in, it's yourself. I hate that Ashedon destroyed your confidence in your own worthiness. Davie believes in the joyous, confident person you can become again. But you're not going to be happy anywhere, or with anyone, unless *you* believe in it.'

A knock at the door interrupted them, a kitchen maid curtsying to relay the latest event in the continuing crisis below stairs. Rising, Sarah pressed Faith's hand. 'I'm sorry, I must go. Trust in him, and yourself, Faith.'

Faith shook her head. 'I was so wrong before! Do I have the courage to risk it?'

'All life is a risk.' Sarah leaned over to kiss her forehead. 'Don't let Ashedon punish you a second time, the doubt he instilled keeping you from seizing what could make you happy. If you truly believe Davie *would* make you happy.'

She certainly endured enough years of misery,

Faith thought as she watched her sister walk out. But if she took a leap of faith with Davie, would she be claiming that elusive happiness—or only grabbing more misery with both hands?

Restless, unable to eat a bite, her head throbbing, Faith threw down her napkin and exited the room after her sister. She headed for the garden, hoping to walk out some of her anxiety without encountering anyone with whom she'd have to attempt the unlikely job of masking it.

Trust in Davie's love? Trust in herself? How could she embrace such a choice with confidence? No one could predict the future; there were a thousand things that could and probably would happen to erode the bond between them, creating annoyance, dissension or distrust.

Could she imagine anything that would destroy her love and admiration for Davie? Even if he were to cease the wonderfully tender actions towards her that so boosted her confidence, the caring and compassionate man he was would still command her love and admiration. She could with utter confidence predict he would never act towards anyone with selfish disregard for their welfare, or sacrifice others to achieve his own ambitions.

Look how he'd tried to protect even the men who'd tried to burn Ashedon Court from the con-

sequences of their rash actions. He could have ridden in with the magistrate at his heels, ready to
send them all to jail and a harsh punishment.

No, she could not imagine losing her love for
him. As for his *loving* her...the mere memory of
his touch set the banked fires of her desires flaming.

Did she think him so naïve, so self-deceiving,
that he did not believe as completely in whatever
it was he saw in her?

All life is a risk, Sarah had said. Where had she
misplaced the reckless confidence she'd possessed
as a girl?

After the heartbreak of Ashedon, she'd retreated
deep within herself, going through the motions
of life, giving herself only to her boys. If she sent
Davie away, she could retreat back into that world
of shadows and that safe half-existence. Protected
from pain. Protected from joy.

Or reach out with both hands to embrace it.

Wouldn't it be worth claiming a few months or
years of joy, even if she eventually lost it—than
never experience it at all?

Yes, it would, she decided. She would never be
the sort of clever, accomplished woman she felt
could fascinate a man for a lifetime. But she could

summon up enough courage to claim this man, for now. For however long she could hold him.

Maybe, God willing, for ever.

Finally decided, she pivoted around and headed back to the house. She didn't want to waste another moment.

An hour later, her children confined to Sarah's care, with the admonition that, with luck, she wouldn't be returning to Brookhollow for several days, Faith mounted her borrowed horse and set off for London. Calm now after the raging storm of her uncertainty, her only anxiety was finding Davie—and making sure her initial refusal hadn't made *him* change his mind.

The journey to London accomplished much more speedily on horseback, at Sarah's suggestion, Faith looked in first at the committee rooms in Parliament, then went to check at the Quill and Gavel. Finding neither him nor any of the Hellions at either place, she stopped to see Maggie—who, after asking what was wrong, accepted Faith's plea that she not enquire further, and gave her the address she requested of Davie's rooms at Albany. Leaving with an assurance that, once all was settled, Maggie would be the first to know, Faith set out again.

Lamplighters were illumining the encroaching darkness when Faith, having left her horse at a nearby livery, at last entered the courtyard at Albany. Boldly talking her way past the porter with a claim of needing to consult Mr Smith at once on a matter of great personal urgency—quite an accurate assessment, actually—she paced down the hallway.

Standing before his door, knowing he was within and that her whole future hinged on what happened in the next few minutes, she hesitated. Trying to banish the anxiety that made her dizzy, she told herself to focus instead on the wonder that was Davie, and how glorious it would be to be held in his arms again.

With a firm knock, she walked in.

Wondering why the porter hadn't announced the visitor who had just entered, Davie looked up from his newspaper, ready to toss a disparaging remark at Ben or Christopher or Giles. He had to blink twice to make sure he wasn't dreaming, when instead, Faith's lovely form filled his vision.

Jumping to his feet, he went over to meet her. 'Faith, what are you doing here? Why didn't you send me a note, I would have—'

Seizing his shoulders, she cut off his protest by

pulling him down for a fiery kiss that made him forget, for a moment, that she'd just risked her reputation by paying a forbidden call on a bachelor establishment. When they finally broke the kiss, he had to struggle to make his mind focus on anything beyond his body's urging that he carry her into his bedroom.

'I trust this means you've decided to accept my proposal?' he asked, sure—*almost* sure—but greedy to hear her say the words aloud.

'Yes, I'll marry you. I'm only sorry I made you wait so long for my answer.'

Wild exultation was running through his veins, feeding the barely banked fires of desire. 'Thank you, God,' he whispered, gathering her against his chest, the very idea that she was agreeing to marry him so spectacularly wonderful he couldn't quite get his mind around it. For long moments, he simply held her, imprinting into his brain the marvellous feel of her in his arms, the even more marvellous news that he would be able to keep her there.

The reality of the situation finally penetrating both desire and delight, he gently pushed her away. 'But you mustn't stay here! We must smuggle you back out, my foolish angel, and hope no one but the porter ever learns of your visit.'

'I don't care a fig for my reputation, and I don't want to go. I want to stay here, with you, tonight. Oh, make love to me again, all night, Davie! Let me feel down to my bones how right we are together, how right we will always be!'

'Do you trust that, now?'

She shook her head a little, tears glimmering on her lashes. 'I don't know. Maybe. All I do know is you make me happy, and for however long it lasts, I love you and I don't want to live without you.'

'It will be for ever, my darling. I'll send you to Maggie's—in the morning,' he added before she could protest, 'I'm not saint enough to turn you away tonight—and get a special licence, so we may be married immediately. But first, I'll do this. Wait here.'

'Couldn't you show me in the bedchamber?' she asked, giving him a pout.

'Once we get there, I intend for your attention to be totally occupied by other things,' he promised.

She grinned. 'I like the sound of that. Very well, get whatever it is you wish—but quickly.'

Davie hastened into his chamber, to a small box he kept on the table beside his bed. Carefully lifting out the ten-year-old article within, he carried it out to the sitting room.

'Hold out your hand.'

When, still looking mystified, Faith complied, Davie tied around her finger a small length of twine, soft and fragile now with age. 'Remember the night, just before you left for London, when I tied that on your finger, promising I would be your friend for ever?'

'You kept it all these years?' she marvelled.

'In words, I promised friendship, but in my heart, I vowed to love you for ever. I didn't think I'd ever be able to do anything about it, but I kept this as a memento to that love—and the chance that some day, it might come true. If I could keep this all those years with so little hope, how can you doubt that I'll love you even more passionately when you're my wife? I'll give you another ring, with gold and diamonds and whatever you wish, but nothing else could demonstrate how long and faithfully I've loved you. Or underscore my promise to love you to the future and back. But let's make it official.'

Going down on one knee, he took the hand with the twine ring and said, 'Will you marry me, Faith Wellingford Evers? To have and to hold from this day forth, for ever?'

She leaned down to kiss him. 'I will. And I'm ready to begin that marriage of minds and bodies right this minute.'

'Whatever you desire, my love.' With that, he snuffed out the candle, picked her up, and carried her to his chamber.

* * * * *

If you enjoyed this story,
make sure you check out
the first book in Julia Justiss's
HADLEY'S HELLIONS *mini-series*
FORBIDDEN NIGHTS WITH THE VISCOUNT

Watch out for two more books
in this series, coming soon!

And don't miss these two stories, also linked to
STOLEN ENCOUNTERS WITH
THE DUCHESS

THE WEDDING GAMBLE
FROM WAIF TO GENTLEMAN'S WIFE

MILLS & BOON®
Large Print – January 2017

ROMANCE

HISTORICAL

MEDICAL

1216 GEN STD LP

MILLS & BOON®
Hardback – February 2017

ROMANCE

The Last Di Sione Claims His Prize	Maisey Yates
Bought to Wear the Billionaire's Ring	Cathy Williams
The Desert King's Blackmailed Bride	Lynne Graham
Bride by Royal Decree	Caitlin Crews
The Consequence of His Vengeance	Jennie Lucas
The Sheikh's Secret Son	Maggie Cox
Acquired by Her Greek Boss	Chantelle Shaw
Vows They Can't Escape	Heidi Rice
The Sheikh's Convenient Princess	Liz Fielding
The Unforgettable Spanish Tycoon	Christy McKellen
The Billionaire of Coral Bay	Nikki Logan
Her First-Date Honeymoon	Katrina Cudmore
Their Meant-to-Be Baby	Caroline Anderson
A Mummy for His Baby	Molly Evans
Rafael's One Night Bombshell	Tina Beckett
A Forever Family for the Army Doc	Meredith Webber
The Nurse and the Single Dad	Dianne Drake
The Heir's Unexpected Baby	Jules Bennett
From Enemies to Expecting	Kat Cantrell

MILLS & BOON®
Large Print – February 2017

ROMANCE

The Return of the Di Sione Wife	Caitlin Crews
Baby of His Revenge	Jennie Lucas
The Spaniard's Pregnant Bride	Maisey Yates
A Cinderella for the Greek	Julia James
Married for the Tycoon's Empire	Abby Green
Indebted to Moreno	Kate Walker
A Deal with Alejandro	Maya Blake
A Mistletoe Kiss with the Boss	Susan Meier
A Countess for Christmas	Christy McKellen
Her Festive Baby Bombshell	Jennifer Faye
The Unexpected Holiday Gift	Sophie Pembroke

HISTORICAL

Awakening the Shy Miss	Bronwyn Scott
Governess to the Sheikh	Laura Martin
An Uncommon Duke	Laurie Benson
Mistaken for a Lady	Carol Townend
Kidnapped by the Highland Rogue	Terri Brisbin

MEDICAL

Seduced by the Sheikh Surgeon	Carol Marinelli
Challenging the Doctor Sheikh	Amalie Berlin
The Doctor She Always Dreamed Of	Wendy S. Marcus
The Nurse's Newborn Gift	Wendy S. Marcus
Tempting Nashville's Celebrity Doc	Amy Ruttan
Dr White's Baby Wish	Sue MacKay

MILLS & BOON®

Why shop at millsandboon.co.uk?

Each year, thousands of romance readers find their perfect read at millsandboon.co.uk. That's because we're passionate about bringing you the very best romantic fiction. Here are some of the advantages of shopping at www.millsandboon.co.uk:

* **Get new books first**—you'll be able to buy your favourite books one month before they hit the shops

* **Get exclusive discounts**—you'll also be able to buy our specially created monthly collections, with up to 50% off the RRP

* **Find your favourite authors**—latest news, interviews and new releases for all your favourite authors and series on our website, plus ideas for what to try next

* **Join in**—once you've bought your favourite books, don't forget to register with us to rate, review and join in the discussions

Visit **www.millsandboon.co.uk**
for all this and more today!